I0574248

APOCALYPSE MOI

MICHAEL WARREN LUCAS

Tilted
Windmill
Press

Copyright Information

Apocalypse Moi

© 2023 by Michael Warren Lucas. All rights reserved, including the right of reproduction, in whole or in part in any form. Published in 2023 by Tilted Windmill Press.

Cover image © grandfailure | depositphotos.com - https://depositphotos.com/158164698/stock-photo-silhouettes-of-woman-on-burning.html

Copy Editor: Amanda Robinson

Book design by Tilted Windmill Press.

Paperback ISBN: 978-1-64235-076-0

Hardcover ISBN: 978-1-64235-077-7

Drums with Delusions of Godhood ©2019, previously published in *Boundary Shock Quarterly: Apocalypse Descending*

Waking Up Yesterday ©2014, previously published by Tilted Windmill Press,

Forced to Talk, Like, With Your Mouth ©2016, previously published by Tilted Windmill Press

Moonlight's Apples ©2016, previously published by Tilted Windmill Press

Easing Final Fears ©2020, previously published in *Boundary Shock Quarterly: Alien Dreams*

Wifi and Romex ©2015, previously published by Tilted Windmill Press

Shoot Through the Heart ©2018, previously published in *Boundary Shock: Tuesday After Next*

Calling Control © 2014, previously published by Tilted Windmill Press

Easy, Step-By-Step Preparation ©2019, previously published in *An Interpretation of Moles*

Yesterday's Girl and *Forbidden Taste*, previously unpublished

This book is a work of fiction. Names, characters, places, and incidents either are products of the author's imagination or used fictionally. Any resemblance to actual events or locales or persons, living or dead, is entirely coincidental. This book is licensed for your personal enjoyment only.

Tilted Windmill Press

https://www.tiltedwindmillpress.com

Acknowledgements

When assembling a collection from over a decade of work, my greatest fear is forgetting to thank someone. It's tempting to thank only the people who still hang around me, or the folks who made the biggest noise in my life, or even the folks who are still alive. Those who have moved on are perhaps the most important to thank, though. Never forget those who helped you. Let's give this a try, then.

Laura Bickle, Blaze Ward, Glen T. Brock, Brigid Collins, Ron Collins, Rob Cornell, Leah R Cutter, T. Thorn Coyle, Dayle Dermatis, Colin Harvey, CJ Jones, Richard Jones, Bonnie Koenig, Alex Kourvo, Matthew Kroll, Mark Leslie Lefebvre, Stefon Mears, Kate MacLeod, Juliet Nordeen, Josh Peterson, Sharon Reamer, Amanda Robinson, Robert Rowntree, Kristine Kathryn Rusch, Dean Wesley Smith, Lucy A. Snyder, and Clarence Young: thank you. If your name should be on this list but isn't, please understand that my brain is an apocalyptic wasteland and when someone mentions your name, I immediately think of the crater named after you.

I am also grateful to the 92 Kickstarter backers who supported this book. While I would have dragged it into public anyway, their aid removed most of the pain. Not all the pain. It's not art if it doesn't sting. But they took away the pain related to cash, which is the most any creator can hope for.

Despite my best efforts to discourage them, my Patronizers support my work every month. I keep reminding that signing up at patronizeMWL.com is a terrible deal and that receiving unwarranted financial support makes me vastly uncomfortable, but apparently they consider "making me uncomfortable" a bonus. Kate Ebneter, Stefan Johnson, Jeff Marraccini, and Phil Vuchetich supported both the electronic and print versions of this book. John Hixson, Craig Maloney, Florian Obser, Maximilian Kühne, Ray Percival, sungo, and Peter Wemm supported the ebook. My thanks to you all.

This book is for Liz, always and forever.

Drums with Delusion of Godhood

1

Detroit Choreomania Response Squad #22's converted garage had high ceilings, a-top-of-the-line fridge and microwave, surprisingly comfortable twin beds, and the worst folding chairs Frances Young's ass had ever had the misfortune to occupy. By the last day of her duty week, her ass had assumed the same uncomfortable contours as the chair. All her sweaty workouts to repel early-thirties civilian flab from her glutes left her tailbone vulnerable.

But after hours of euchre with the worst partner in her life, she finally had a great hand. Both red jacks, and the other three short-suited high diamonds. So long as her idiot partner Evan didn't tell the dealer to pick up the cut, they'd win this game.

Poker might be vicious, but euchre got downright bitter. That's why she loved it. The rhythm of plays. The snap of cards hitting the table. Bluffing with a pause. She'd call euchre an art, if art wasn't so deadly.

And if Evan was as bad at cutting throats as playing cards, she'd rather go it alone either way.

She didn't even want to shift her weight. Her squad mates, the opponents of the moment, might think she was nervous. The military gene splice might have boosted her stamina and immune response, but she wished they'd armored her ass while they were at it!

Frances feigned boredom by gazing across the converted four-car garage. The squad's extended cab electric pickup looked tiny beneath the high steel ceiling, even with its roof-mounted lights and the monster four-speaker klaxon looming out of the stubby cargo bed. Feeble rays of September afternoon sunlight squeezing through the skylight highlighted a rectangle high on the puke-yellow cinderblock wall.

No television. The last thing they needed was for a CRS to get earwormed.

This job sucked.

Damn her stupid sense of duty.

Frances had joined up to escape the trailer park, sure, but the Army had taught her about duty. Maybe not duty to country, that was bullshit, but she'd come home to do right by her family and her neighborhood.

She sure hadn't signed up to play euchre.

The trailer park was gone, destroyed by insufficient soundproofing.

And euchre especially sucked with someone like Evan as your partner. The ARS rules said he had to be at least eighteen, but she wouldn't have laid money on one day over. He had the kind of pasty soft features that had been deprived of a desperately needed lifetime of punches. His brown eyes kept flicking from his hand to the cut card, the queen of spades.

What did he think, it would magically change between glances?

Pass, you dumbass.

Hank sat unconcerned, holding his cards almost face-down on the table. The gristly old Hispanic had made his living playing poker until the Grammys had killed thirty million people, and he looked the same no matter if a jack or a nine got turned up. Frances would have guessed he had a gene splice for on-demand impassiveness, but all he had was something for salivary gland cancer and the oh-so-common osteoarthritis patch.

If Evan told Hank to pick up the cut, the kid better be ready to carry the whole damn trick himself.

Sukey said, "Either you got it or you don't." The combination of a cheap weight control gene splice and the shortage of its supporting hormone pills made her face rail-thin.

Pass. Pass. Pass.

Evan grimaced in torment. His lips twisted. Parted.

"Pass."

Sukey instantly said, "Pass."

Frances' sudden elation made her smile vulpine. "Diamonds. And I'm going it alo—"

The horrific two-tone siren crushed her words.

Frustration made Frances want to scream.

Instead, she flung her cards face-down on the table and scooted herself back from the table, snatching her earbuds.

Siren or no, Hank had a great big shit-eating grin and Sukey was outright laughing. Frances' snarl probably made them laugh even harder.

Evan looked shocked, though. Frances had seen that look too many times back in the Army. She'd probably once had it herself, the oh-shit-this-is-real wide eyes and loose jaw. She wanted to tell him to snap out of it, but the siren drowned all sound.

She couldn't even tell him to move or he'd get them killed.

Instead, she jammed her snug earbuds in one ear and then the other. The electronics instantly replaced the piercing siren with a blessedly numb silence. The horrid siren became an annoying buzz in her teeth. Snugging the mic around her neck and verifying that it was right up against her throat, she hit the radio button. "Frances Young, comms check."

Lucy Rapida's calm "Young, comms check" through the earbud eased a sliver of Frances' tension. Not everyone pressed into duty at Dispatch was competent for the job, but Lucy had done some sort of signals analysis before everything went bad and knew her shit.

"Sukey Werther, comms check." A throat mic squeezed all the character out of a voice. How the hell did the woman manage to sound so nasal?

No time to wonder. Evan was having trouble fastening his mic, and Hank was already climbing in the pickup's driver's seat and punching the button to raise the garage door. By the time Frances got around the table to Evan, the kid had managed to get his mic buckled and started his comms check.

What had he been spliced for? Gene splices had been so cheap at the end, he'd probably gotten one for Dungeons and Dragons supremacy.

"All comms correct," Lucy said. "Silencing alarm. Sergeant Young, your squad."

Frances almost didn't grimace at the misused rank, instead squeezing her head into the riot helmet and buckling the stab vest. She needed every scrap of authority to keep the squad moving.

Lucy said, "Bard reported at Jefferson and Cadillac. A flutist, with victims."

2

Frances' noise-canceling earbuds blocked out the Klaxon of Doom in the truck bed, but its growl warbled through the truck's chassis and through the passenger seat and straight into her spine and ribs. Anyone within half a mile would know to lock the doors and cotton up.

At three-thirty in the afternoon, Jefferson Avenue was almost empty. The gasoline had run out a month ago, but a handful of electrics scooted out of the truck's path. Frances bent to glance in the side mirror. The cars didn't pull back into motion in their wake.

Good. Maybe they were dumb enough to leave their homes, but they weren't dumb enough to follow.

No—a one-passenger Tesla they'd shot past glided back into motion. Frances grimaced, but then the pocket car swung into a U-turn and headed back downtown.

Better. If your job was really critical, stay there. Sleep in the break room.

Between snobbish apartment towers flashing past on the right, Frances glimpsed slices of the peaceful ripples of the Detroit River. Rich downtowners paid too much for a little scrap of space overlooking the water, then sealed themselves away where they couldn't see it or touch it.

It had been too long since she'd walked Belle Isle.

The left side, with its restaurants and bodegas and side streets leading off into residential areas felt a lot more homey.

The apartment towers surrendered to the tall iron spikes of the fence surrounding the water park.

"Two blocks," Lucy said in her earbud.

Frances pulled her phone, touched a button, and tucked it away again. "Soundtracks on, everyone."

A comfortingly familiar low drone, distant crowd noise intermittently breaking through, filled Frances' skull. Sound dampening wasn't perfect, and even a few stray notes from the bard might trigger a gene-splice bug. The screaming, throbbing, and incessant hammering of her mother's favorite album, Front Line Assembly's *Live Wired*, would block out anything short of nuclear percussion.

The first track started way too slow, though. Two blocks wouldn't get her up to those weird pre-show soundclips, let alone the actual music. Frances skipped a track, immediately bouncing to guitars with delusions of drumhood backed by drums with delusions of godhood.

Better.

"Shit." The earbuds automatically lowered but didn't silence the music, dropping Hank's voice into the chorus and restoring the barrage when he stopped.

The bard was easy enough to see. A skinny black guy almost dancing down the road, elbows raised to hold the flute to his lips, followed by a whole flock of victims.

If it hadn't been for the victims, Frances would have told Hank to floor it and flatten the bard. About two dozen people trailed behind the bard, faces fixated on the flute as if their eyes were wired in place.

Maybe half of them wore green scrubs.

Frances walked this stretch every time she reported for duty. The Roostertail Urgent Care sat a few hundred yards further up Jefferson.

The fucking bard had gone inside.

Earwormed the staff.

The victims might recover. It had happened, especially when they weren't frenzied.

And they'd already lost so many doctors. Nurses. Medical people from phlebotomists to housekeepers. The hospitals had been full of patients, and too many of them had been watching the awards show when a pop star engineered to instinctively draw people to her music had accidentally discovered whatever gene-splice flaw made regular people vulnerable and artists into randomized time bombs.

Medical staff aside—three children between toddler and teen. Two white-haired men, one bald guy so wrinkled he looked half shar-pei. A teenage boy with the flu or allergies or something, snot streaming down his chin.

A handyman, hammers and wrenches hanging from his belt. She'd been trying to find someone to expand her home-brew setup for months.

A pregnant woman. Dammit. If you earwormed Mom, did you get the baby too? They all deserved a chance.

Hank brought the truck to a surprisingly smooth stop.

"Acoustics are consistent with a single instrument," Lucy said in her earbuds. "No accompaniment."

Small blessings—last month's folk guitarist had been bad enough, but she wouldn't have even *seen* the damned spoon player if she hadn't known to look for him. Who even played the spoons anymore?

Nobody who wanted to live. That's who.

But when something triggered the gene-splice flaw, they *had* to play.

"Sukey," Frances said. "You're on northbound traffic, get flares down. Hank, you take the truck around and flare the southbound." She had an impulse to grit her teeth, and fought it down. "Evan. With me."

Frances hopped out of the cab and slammed the door before anyone could respond. Something else she learned in the Army; always lead by leading.

But the Army had taught her to use her all her senses in contested territory. Her pounding soundtrack made the smooth pavement utterly alien. The grassy lawn of the water park beside her looked peaceful and pristine, even behind the implacable ten-foot iron spikes of the fence isolating it. The air right off the river still smelled green with just a hint of autumn. Puffy white clouds hung in an incongruously blue sky while Bill Leeb screamed about suffering.

The bard took a step towards Frances, a step back, a step to the side.

Sukey trotted away, already extracting flares from her mesh bag. Any cars that came this way would hopefully see the lights before the bard could penetrate whatever defensive sounds the driver had chosen.

Frances turned to Evan. The kid had closed his mouth, but sweat trickled down under his helmet. "This is it, mister," Frances said. "Cut that bard's throat."

Evan froze. "I—I thought I was backing you up?"

"You're new. If you can't do it, I need to know now."

Evan glanced at the bard and swallowed. Hard. She could even smell his fear. "Don't we use a gun?"

A week with her first drill instructor, and the kid would cut his momma's throat on command. Yelling at him now wouldn't do anything. And the squad needed a fourth.

"Look," Frances spoke quickly, so that the kid's earplugs wouldn't slip annoying slices of music between her words. "We don't know when more ammo's coming, so use a knife when you can. And bards are like measles. They're innocent, it's not their fault they kill people, but they do and we have to get rid of them. They can't be helped, they can't be cured. You had a reason for joining up, right?"

Evan nodded and opened his mouth.

"No," Frances said, "don't tell me for chrissakes, I just need to know you had a reason. Either that reason's strong enough for you to serve and protect your neighborhood, or it isn't. If the victims were frenzied I'd take Hank in and do it myself but they're not, this is the easiest bard you're ever gonna find, and if you can't do it I'll send you home with a pat on the head and a lollipop, but if you're gonna do it then grab your knife and get on it."

The kid just stared at her.

Five. Four. Three—

The decision crossed Evan's face. He drew a shaky breath, gave a little nod, and drew his knife.

Frances gave her own nod. "I'll watch your back."

She'd spoken the truth.

Problem was, measles didn't look at you all confused while you murdered them.

The bard didn't change his capering as they approached. His fingers danced across the flute, half-lidded eyes rapturous as he twisted and swayed with his music. For just two beats his step synchronized with Frances' soundtrack, and his feet struck the earth with the thunder of drums. The sight tightened her guts, as if the bard's compulsion had penetrated and joined her soundtrack, but his feet came down way too late for the next beat and she eased.

Decision made, Evan marched without hesitation. He carried the knife properly, guard by his pinky and cutting edge away from his wrist. If he could carry that attitude all the way through, and get through tonight's crying jag, he might do okay. Frances followed five feet behind, eyes flickering around the quiescent, fascinated crowd, her own knife in hand.

Stainless steel was badly named. Evan would have to clean his tonight.

Evan was only a few feet from the bard when Lucy shouted "Signal change! The tune, it's—"

The victims frenzied.

3

One moment, the two dozen victims were nearly quiescent.

The next, they erupted like competitors in the Mosh Pit World Championship. Bodies slammed into each other. A five-year-old leaped at one of the geezers, crashing into the old man's knees and knocking him to the ground. The man bounced back up, blood welling from his forehead, and charged a teenager who was flailing at the pregnant woman, who ecstatically shouted and kicked at everyone nearby.

The bard stood untouched amidst a rapidly expanding cloud of gleeful mayhem.

Frances tasted coppery adrenaline as her guts plunged. She opened her mouth to shout at Evan to get back, but a twenty-something man in green scrubs had already dashed at him.

Evan snapped his hands up in an instinctive defensive posture. Exactly the wrong way to use a knife.

Frances choked out "Frenzy!" in the throat mic and dashed forward.

The doc or whatever crashed into Evan and knocked him back.

Forget testing Evan. The frenzy wouldn't even slow until the bard died.

And the bastard flutist was maybe ten feet away.

Frances raised her own knife, screamed with the soundtrack pounding in her skull, and charged.

Lucy said something about bad signals and Sukey shouted something about screaming.

An older woman raced to intercept Frances, too spry for her white hair and plump figure, calf-length flowery dress billowing around her, heedless of Frances' raised blade. Frances didn't want to hurt a victim, didn't have time to engage, but when the woman raised her hands at the last second Frances tried to bounce out of the way, but the victim was too damn agile—shouldn't someone that old and heavy have bad knees or something by now—she crashed into Frances hard enough to send the two of them staggering.

The woman's expensive-smelling lemon-and-basil perfume filled Frances' nose.

A blow—fist? elbow?—rattled her padded helmet against her skull.

Frances' unarmed combat instructor had made them practice pivoting unarmed attackers away, but the woman ricocheted away on her own.

The victims danced all around her now, bewildering whirling colors and twisted faces and thrashing limbs. Frances desperately scanned the crowd, trying to pick out the bard from the chaos and ignore the woman spinning one of the kids around by their hair and a plumber pummeling on the iron fence with his hammer and wrench and the scrub-clad man on the ground laughing as one of his coworkers kicked him again and again in the gut, all while Frances' soundtrack shouted over and over about a last dream.

She'd unpack it all later.

In her own bad dreams.

There! By the fence! Shuffling sideways, still bound downtown, rapt with his weaving and bobbing flute.

Most of the bards she'd dealt with had seemed oblivious of their surroundings. They'd played without concern for anyone but their audience's rapt response.

This one had set off this frenzy to protect himself.

Frances wouldn't have even a flash of guilt putting him down.

And with his back to the fence, he had no place to run.

Frances charged.

Time stretched. The familiar album seemed to pick up extra notes in her ears, extra throbbing, extra hammering drums that echoed in her bones.

A child staggered into her path, scalp bleeding where masses of hair had been ripped out by the roots. Laughing.

And too close to avoid.

Lucy said something, but Frances was too busy steamrollering the kid to listen. Frances raised the knife.

The bard met her eyes.

For half a second, she read a message in that gaze.

A mix between *hear me love me* and *end this end this.*

She crashed into him, slamming him hard into the iron fence.

He didn't stop playing.

One thrust buried the blade in his throat.

Blinding blood gushed over Frances' face.

But the bard, pinned between her and the iron fence, sagged.

She felt the flute leave his hands, then his body leave his feet.

Bard down.

Even if he somehow lived with a knife in his throat, he couldn't play.

It didn't matter if someone needed killing, if they were using a gun or a knife or a flute; murder in self-defense left burning ice in Frances' heart that no amount of overwhelming rhythm or rotgut whiskey could ease. She let the drums fill her, mingling with her heart, and grabbed hold of the fence with one hand while wiping her eyes with the other. "Bard down. Bard down."

Too many rhythms, all mixed together, tangled in the frozen fire of her heart.

Frances didn't have time to waste. Someone was going to crash into her any second. She had to get her heart under control, in more ways than one, see if the victims would wind down or murder each other.

See if any good would come of killing a man who, a year or ten ago, had just wanted to be a better musician.

She opened her eyes just in time to see a teenage girl charging at her. Frances bounced a step forward, enough distance so she wouldn't get crushed against the fence, and met the girl with a spin and a push of her own.

Lucy shouted in her headset. "Bard not down! Bard not down!"

Frances' heart somehow beat faster. The flutist was down, though. Blood still surged, but weakly, around the buried blade of her knife. The flute had rolled away, somewhere.

"Percussion!" Lucy shouted. "I'm picking up large-scale percussion. Can't... identify instrument."

Frances spun around. How had she missed a drum kit, a bass drum—

The handyman.

His hammer and that big wrench danced across the fence's iron bars.

Suppose you knew metal. And you knew drums.

Those extra drumbeats in her soundtrack. The ones she'd thought were her own sheer excitement.

How much resonance could you get out of a mile of fence?

Enough to echo in her bones.

Her soundtrack, the real soundtrack, screamed about resisting commands.

But that complex rhythm echoed something inside her.

She'd *leaned* on that fence.

Conducting that madness into her.

Frances swallowed the rush of fear. Maybe she'd been earwormed. Maybe in another breath her own gene splice bug would take over and she'd start thrashing and kicking and screaming.

Her knife was still buried in the first bard's neck.

Whatever time she had left—

A scream of blended defiance and rage ripped out of Frances' gut and out her throat. She lurched into motion, body-checking a clawing snarling old lady out of her way, willing her feet to keep hammering the pavement. Even if the earworm took hold, even if this bastard bard had already poisoned her, the last thing she'd do was slam him away from the fence, give Evan or Sukey a chance to stick the knife—

Totally focused on the way his wrench and hammer danced across the fence, the handyman-turned-bard didn't even turn his head.

Frances crashed into his flank.

The sinuous, obsessive rhythm shattered.

The wrench flew overhead and vanished.

Frances' feet tangled with the new bard's. Tools dangling from his belt dug into her thighs and coffee-breath gasped into her face. Then she had a foot hooked in place to sweep his leg, and rode him straight to the pavement.

She didn't hear when his skull hit asphalt. But she felt it.

No knife. No gun.

Frances wrenched the hammer from his grip.

4

Frances focused on her breathing. She could tell her heart to slow all she wanted, but it only listened to her body. Breath leads the body, she told herself. Slow the breath, fill and empty the lungs, and the rest will follow.

It would be so much easier without the pervading stink of blood or the stickiness on her face, but still:

Breathe.

Breathe with the music. Each breath one beat longer than the last. Ignore the stink in her nose and the way the pavement dug into her kneecaps, and feed her lungs.

Frances kept her chin raised. She wasn't sure she had the strength to rise, and the warmth of the handyman's torso beneath her was a constant reminder that she didn't really want to look at what remained.

The earworm victims had already stopped their frenzy. They hadn't quite reverted to passive fixation, either. More than one face had soft tears. Expressions twitched with confusion and fear and, most promising of all, anger.

Frances didn't know if they'd recover. But getting pissed off at being earwormed was a good sign.

The six bodies sprawled on the ground were a bad sign. The flutist, in a pool of blood. Two older people, dead from stroke or coronary or some other variant of 'not strong enough for a frenzy.' Two people in green scrubs.

How many medical people could they lose and hold civilization together?

And the wreck of the handyman.

She really needed to get off the handyman.

There, past the blood-soaked children (forget docs, how many *kids* could they lose?) who were starting to bawl—Evan.

The new guy knelt on the pavement. Hugging himself. Even from this distance, his flushed tear-covered cheeks were obvious.

Frances didn't have the energy to rise. Motivation would have to do. She wrenched herself up without lowering her gaze, and staggered over to Evan.

Evan held his knife in a white-knuckled fist, but as far away from himself as possible, as if repelled by it but afraid to let it go. Blood streaked the stainless steel blade.

One tired step. Another.

"Evan…" Frances sank down beside him.

Evan shook his head.

Frances carefully pried the knife out of his fist, dropping it on the hot asphalt. "Evan. Look at me."

Where she hadn't dared look down, Evan obviously didn't dare look up.

Her mind flashed back to a baking-hot barren road, where a freshly deployed younger Frances had emptied her guts into an even more barren desert. Not even the taste of puke had drowned out the stink of blood. Unexpected sympathy surged. "You gotta choose."

"I killed her," Evan whispered.

"People died." Frances jerked a thumb at a tall woman in green scrubs who rubbed her face as if trying to wash something invisible away. "But others might recover."

Evan twitched so fiercely Frances could almost see his stomach knot.

"We have to." The words burned Frances' soul. "Either we stop the bards, or everybody dies."

Evan only shook his head.

"Euchre or bards, it doesn't matter." Frances could still taste that long-ago vomit. "Decide if you're gonna take charge of the hand or not."

Evan closed his eyes and shuddered.

Frances wanted to grab Evan's shoulders and pull him into a hug. But she couldn't. Murderous reality allowed no comfort.

Evan slowly opened his eyes.

Picked up his knife.

And wiped the bloody blade across a dead doctor's pants.

Frances told herself they'd won. The victims' faces were even gaining animation. But the blood smeared on her face felt like an extra burden.

"When we get back," Frances said, "I'll show you how to clean that."

Evan swallowed. "Thanks."

Lucy said, "No bards within audio range. Bards down. Soundtrack down."

The guitars and drums faded from her ears, leaving her with the numb silence of the sound-canceling earbuds.

Somewhere in the bottom of her mind, though, drums continued. A sinuous, haunting, insistent rhythm beat out on iron and bone.

Frances swallowed a surge of fear.

She'd be all right. She wasn't earwormed. She'd be fine.

She needed a shower. Put her uniform in the washer. She'd feel better.

Then back to snapping cards against the table.

Waking Up Yesterday

The bed felt soft and warm. Deep.

That was *wrong*.

I didn't smell anything. That was wrong, too.

A soft cyclic grind repeated endlessly, like a motor with a loose belt. Running water, then a valve squeaking as someone turned it off.

And I didn't hurt. I'd put in two hours at the dojo last night. I should have aches, stiffness, the gentle fatigue of well-worked muscles, all the symptoms of the middle-aged amateur martial artist. That stiffness just wasn't there. But neither was the arthritis in my hands or feet. My back didn't merely not hurt, it felt lithe and rested and ready to assault the day.

But my teeth hurt.

Impossible. I'd fixed my teeth. Twenty caps, sixteen root canals, long hours gripping the arms of the dentist chair. I could drip acid on my teeth and not feel anything. But deep inside the gums, they ached.

And the warm bed… jiggled. A waterbed.

I hadn't slept on a waterbed for a quarter of a century.

I opened my eyes. A blurry shape circled against the whiteness overhead.

My vision was 20-20. I had my eyes fixed, too. I couldn't have blurry vision.

All the things I hadn't had growing up. All the things I'd fled.

Everything looked blurry. But I knew the shape of the room. I knew the pressure around my gut and the weight hanging around my limbs.

And I knew the whirring shape.

The ceiling fan. In my childhood bedroom. Groaning helplessly against each rotation.

I sat up, moving too quickly in the waterbed, spinning my head around. The plywood shelves around the room, bulging with secondhand paperbacks, library cast-offs, and little weird odds and ends that I'd found around the farm town. My own body, once again flabby and overweight, stretching the secondhand pajamas my mom always bought.

I reached up. Greasy hair slid between my fingers. I still didn't smell anything, but Mom had smoked four packs a day and drank a dozen beers by noon. Dad smoked almost as much while chewing Vicodin against his blown back. The constant thick smoke had overloaded my nose. I hadn't really known how anything smelled until I was nineteen. Including me. That's when I finally got girls to talk to me.

My penis throbbed painfully against the synthetic pajamas. Shit. Mister Happy hadn't been that stupidly perky since I didn't know when. My right hand instinctively reached to grab him through the cloth, but I diverted the hand up to my chest instead. Fine hair covered smooth taut skin.

What had happened? How old was I? Nineteen? Eighteen? What the hell? Could I even *drive*? Was I in *school*? *High* school? My heart slammed against my ribs and sweat made my pajamas even more sticky.

The grimy linen curtain over the window rustled. Manure, diesel, and spring compost on cool air overcame my cigarette-stunned sinuses.

No, no, no. I rolled to my side. The little table was right where it was for all those years of childhood. I squinted painfully, identifying each shape. More used paperbacks. A cassette player. The tiny lamp with a cheap paper shade. The shade had fallen off one night, landed on the bulb. I hadn't noticed until the plastic laminate began smoking.

Glasses. *The* glasses. Cheap plastic frames. Actual glass lenses that weighed about ten pounds. I'd insisted on glass, because plastic scratched and I didn't think I could keep anything safe. I fumbled the clammy things onto my nose. My nose pinched and burned as the plastic touched—a pimple? I vaguely remembered always having a pimple on the bridge of my nose. When had that gone away?

How old was I?

I forced myself to take a deep breath. Another. How could I go to sleep at night forty-six and wake up a teenager? The same damn teenager I'd been? Was I supposed to fight my way free again? Break out of a drunk family and make something of myself. Again?

Doing the work didn't bother me. I'd sweated off the pounds once, I knew how to do it. But the guilt still burned in my gut. I'd tried to work with my family. Tried to improve myself, and in the end had walked away from Dad, Mom, siblings, everyone. At twenty-five I'd given up on them. Then Mom died before we ever made up, then Keith. My sister Dora took care of Dad until he died, then moved somewhere out west. We hadn't spoken in years. Thinking about it now sent woodworms of worry gnawing through my gut.

I worked my tongue in my mouth, feeling rough irregular teeth. Dora had gotten the braces. Dad only got so much disability money, and "a girl's gotta have good teeth to catch a husband." My cavities hadn't dug into the nerve yet, at least.

My heart hammered inside my chest. I was hyperventilating. My neck and jaw shook with tension. Dizzy. Fear. No—total dread. *Stop it. Slow down.*

I peered around through dusty spotty lenses. The books were all used, so the copyright dates wouldn't tell me anything. The desk? No homework there, just parts of an old computer that one of Dad's friends had given me. That old beast had what, enough memory to hold half a program? Was that the one with audio cassettes instead of a hard drive? No, there was a disk drive with a glass of water on it. I'd had to cool the drive with ice every night as I puttered with it. If I'd known my future was in writing software, I would have paid more attention to it.

The *Star Trek* calendar on the back of the door. Mom bought me one every year until the blowup. I got out of bed and waddled over, loathing the excess weight smothering me, looked beneath Spock holding his tricorder, and subtracted one year from another.

Eighteen. About to start a worthless anthropology degree, because it was interesting and because I had no clue what to do with myself other than be anyone else and, when that didn't work, drown my sorrows in carbohydrates.

I leaned against the window frame. Splinters from the unfinished wood dug into my palms as I stared out at the fields surrounding the house. My family inherited most of the land and leased it to a farming conglomerate. Rural Michigan sunshine. Fresh air. Fresh-plowed furrows fuzzed with green. Tractors grumbled beyond the treeline. Fifteen miles beyond those trees lurked the town of Lapeer, with dusty feed stores and repair shops that stank of grease and smoke and the public schools I'd endured. Weren't they doing engineered corn back then? No, it was still cross-breeding, nobody had done gene transplants yet. I thought. What else was missing? Cellphones. Internet. Online shopping. If I wanted something, I'd have to actually haunt a store.

Maybe I should invent genetic engineering. Or ecommerce.

This was not happening, dammit. I slapped my cheek. Yesterday I'd gone to the client. Made peace between the warring factions of Accounting and Shipping. Sweated at the dojo. Back to my expensive lifeless apartment. No family. I didn't dare marry—and kids, hell *no*. I had no idea how to treat a family. Only how not to do it.

Another deep breath. Martial arts teaches you to center yourself. Maybe my body had never trained, but my mind was still in there. I forced myself to breathe against the torrent of vitality and panic flooding me. How had I gotten through my twenties without exploding?

If I couldn't find my way back—if I had to live this out again—I'd change one thing.

Nothing to regret. I'd clean up my life more quickly, without amputating my family.

The dresser was full of too-small clothes. Random junk I'd dragged home nearly thirty years before filled the closet. Childhood toys I didn't play with anymore, but

I didn't get rid of because they were what I had. I found my clean clothes in a heap on the floor, right next to the heap of dirty clothes. Most of them were on the snug side, but I found a newish pair of baggy jeans and a blue shirt with broad horizontal stripes, socks and underwear without too many holes. Battered tennis shoes and a leather belt. Nothing I'd normally wear, but they wouldn't actively humiliate me. I gathered everything up, opened the bedroom door, and almost bodyslammed my brother.

Keith was two years older than me. He got Dad's metabolism, so he was nail-thin even though he ate crap like the rest of us and drank like Mom. But he'd figured out how to get along in the world before me.

I felt a rush of adrenaline. Sympathy flooded through me at his red hair and those bright blue eyes. Impossibly alive. *You die in eight years. Drive a car into a telephone pole at a hundred plus, you and your girl, drunk off your ass. Murder-suicide by driver's license.*

Right now, in his old jeans and new Skinny Puppy T-shirt, he oozed miraculous vitality.

"Watch it, fuckwad," Keith said, cocky smile sprawled across his face.

Adolescent hormones flooded me.

Maybe my mind was forty-six years old. Keith was a distant memory. I remembered the occasional screaming match. But his words ripped scabs off my memory, and I remembered just how angry Keith's constant jibes had made me.

We'd fought growing up, of course. That's what brothers do, you go into the backyard and slug it out behind the garage where nobody can see, then tell Mom you got scuffed falling down the compost heap. He was always bigger, stronger, faster.

What they call muscle memory is really in your brain. You practice something long enough, and your brain does it automatically. My pudgy fingers curled from the tips to the pads, then rolled into my palm. My thumb locked tight against and across the knuckles. My hips twisted, weight shifted, and my reverse punch cracked into Keith's solar plexus.

The punch was weak. I had no muscle tone. But I had technique, my will and my whole body's motion focused into the width of my top two knuckles. Pain ricocheted up my arm. The knuckles weren't used to the impact, and the familiar clench strained my unfamiliar hand as I recocked.

Keith rocked backwards, a gasp of air escaping his mouth. He hit the opposite wall, arms outspread, eyes bugging from his face. That was new.

Dammit! I hadn't wanted to punch him. I told the kids at the dojo about self-control all the time, the importance of acting rather than reacting. Hormones and youth had overcome a decade of training.

But I'd escalated things. If I backed down now, he'd attack. He'd put his first man in the hospital sometime around now.

I stared at Keith. "I didn't realize you were there."

Keith gaped soundlessly. His hands flailed up to his chest.

"The air's knocked out of you." *Kick him*, my hindbrain screamed. *Don't let him recover.* "Relax. You'll breathe in a minute." I slouched past him, shoulder brushing the hallway's nicotine-stained drywall, deliberately turning my back. *I'm in charge now.*

One step.

Another.

The wooden floor creaked behind me.

I spun on my front foot, weight wobbling as I turned myself around.

Keith's haymaker swept through the space where my head had been. Overextended, he stumbled. His fist cracked into the drywall with a dull thump and a dry puff of gypsum, punching a hole.

"Dammit!" he shouted.

"Keith!"

Mom. I froze in instant recognition of a voice twenty years gone. Keith gritted his teeth and jerked his hand out of the wall.

"What you boys doing up there?"

I said, "Keith just tripped." My voice didn't quiver despite the boiling cauldron of hope and fear and love and anger in my head.

"Keep it down, you two."

I turned my attention back to Keith. "I don't want to fight you. But I won't put up with your bullshit anymore."

Keith's eyes blazed and he shook his bruised hand. "You need to remember who's in charge here."

I made myself breathe. "You are completely in charge. Of you. I'm in charge of me." The hand I'd punched him with only tingled. I might be porky again, but my eighteen-year-old self recovered like a Porsche rounding a curve.

I saw his weight shift to his front foot before he even moved. Sidestepped his charge. A hand clamped onto my shoulder. I pointed my toes and swung my leg back, my teeth clenched as the stretching tendons of my inner thigh screeched in outrage. Keith shifted his thighs to protect his groin, but I'd already launched my knee straight into his gut. Air exploded out of him. He buckled.

My body and buried memories screamed at me to kick him again. Pummel him. Make it stop. Forever.

My knee shrieked in outrage at the impact.

Instead I said, "When you want to talk, I'm here. But we're not living like this anymore." I left Keith curled around his pain and limped away, favoring my knee.

I wanted not to believe. But you can't be in a fight, can't have aching knuckles and a tender knee, and not accept. I was eighteen again, starting over.

Ancient dirt stained the bathroom door's white enamel, but the eye-and-hook lock worked as well as it ever had. Merely pissing in a toilet that filthy made me feel soiled. Black mold ringed the bathtub and filled the channels supporting the glass doors. I'd have to clean the tub. I was probably the maid now. But I'd deal with that later. Maybe I could convince Keith to help me keep the place up. It'd be good for him. He wasn't dumb. Once I started dropping weight, once I cleaned up, he'd start to come around. Dad's thick blue dandruff shampoo filled my hand and seethed in my hair.

I'd forgotten Keith's hostility. He coped by becoming angry, by pushing people around until they did what he wanted, by becoming the biggest thug in the room. Seeing him again burnished ancient memories, spiked them sharp into my life.

But maybe I could change my family.

Maybe Keith wouldn't die. If we could build a relationship based on respect, maybe I could keep him out of the bars. Be an example. The lung cancer was probably already nibbling at Mom, but if she went to the doctor now they'd find it. Or maybe I could get her to quit. And Dad. I'd always wondered if he'd really hurt his back that badly, or if he'd just gotten too comfortable with the pills until they ate his liver.

As a freelance software developer I worked with all kinds of difficult people. You have to demonstrate your understanding of their problem, a sincere desire to help, and your own competence. The combination gets you a seat at the table. How much worse could my own family be, I wondered as I dried myself with the stiff towel and pulled myself into the alien jeans.

And I needed to sweep the floor in here. Nobody'd done it in weeks. Then mop. With bleach. Strong bleach. The whole house needed a coat of paint. I'd learned how to do basic home repairs in the last twenty years. I had more energy than I'd ever known, and the endless time of youth. I remembered long evenings in my bedroom working three-thousand-piece puzzles and rereading TV show novelizations. I could do anything with those hours!

I studied my face in the spotted medicine cabinet mirror over the stained sink. Round. Soft. But my hairline started a couple inches above my blue eyes. Acne to die from, but my morning beard was rich and brown. No gray anywhere.

Five toothbrushes, all the heads worn down and frayed. I had no idea which was mine. It'd be simpler to get a new one.

I pulled the shirt over my head, straining to squeeze my skull through the neck. Changing my life wouldn't be that easy—it would be harder than anything I'd ever done. But no regrets, this time.

Clean, dressed, and with polished glasses, I unlocked the door. Keith wasn't in the hall outside the bathroom. The doors on either side were closed. The hole Keith punched in the drywall formed a dark pit between his bedroom door and mine, but smaller cracks and gaps formed dark constellations all the way down. At the far end of the hall, ancient cobwebs thickened by dust filled the top of the stairwell. Neglected water stains rippled and haloed the drywall overhead.

I had a lot of work to do. I hitched the pants more comfortably around my waist and started down.

Fading memory had scrubbed a lot of the main floor over the years. I had no recollection of the faded circus poster thumbtacked to the living room wall. I'd thrown out a couch far better than the threadbare yellowed corduroy thing up against the far wall. I remembered the large-screen television that Mom had bought with the tax refund when I was in junior high, but not how it bulged into the room like a tumor thanks to the three-foot-thick picture tube and ridiculously huge wooden cabinet. It showed a youthful woman turning a wall of boxes to expose letters as a studio audience cheered at maximum volume. And at the other end of the room was Grandma's castoff Formica kitchen set surrounded by metal-legged chairs with randomly missing feet that stabbed and scarred the dusty tile flooring the kitchen.

Mom and Dad sat at the table, staring at the television. "G," Mom said, her voice throaty as she exhaled a veil of smoke, and my soul stuttered at the sight. I'd remembered her exactly, down to the dirty blond hair and the baggy sweatsuit over rolled flab. "Call G."

Dad lifted a forkful of some starchy mess from the heap on his plate. His skull shone through his pale skin. "R." His voice was gruffer than Mom's. The fork wavered before his mouth as his unfocused eyes wandered around the television.

Keith sat beside them. His eyes tried to threaten me, but when I calmly didn't react he turned his attention to the plate of food in front of him.

Tuna noodle casserole. I hadn't eaten anything even vaguely like that in years. I wouldn't eat starch, I told myself. I can do that starting now. Don't even need a broom or a paintbrush.

"There's no B," announced the television.

"G, you dumbass!" Mom shouted. "I said G."

I studied the kitchen counter with revulsion. Someone had wiped the front of the microwave, but hadn't scraped out the grime from between the mechanical pushbutton controls. The stove hadn't been cleaned, nor had the front of the fridge. With a bit of trepidation I opened the refrigerator door.

"Pills," Dad said. "While you're up."

I blinked, turning back to the table. Mom and Keith stared at the television, but Dad looked straight at me, elbow on the table and hand supporting his heavy head.

Did I want to fight Dad on this right now? Could I shift everyone at once?

I glanced around the cluttered kitchen. I didn't even know where his pills were.

Dad's eyes narrowed.

"G!"

The television said "I'm guessing. 'On the Yellow Brick Road.'" Victory music swelled.

Dad rotated his hand in a hurry-up gesture, not taking his eyes off me.

Dammit. Pills. Where had he kept his pills? I cast my eyes around the kitchen. The mason jar full of debilitated spoons and spatulas. An old cereal box snuggled against a sadly used dish towel. Dirty dishes heaped like junkyard cars. Cereal boxes atop the fridge.

I opened a cupboard. Plastic glasses, shatterproof plates, all poorly hand-washed. Hadn't those been on the other side of the sink? Had I been knocked *side-ways* in time? Even as I thought that, I knew that it wasn't anything of the sort. I hadn't recalled the kitchen in any detail in years—heck, I'd left those memories scattered like gravel under my wheels.

Did I have wheels now? No, just the family truck, a rusty rattling death trap started with a screwdriver instead of a key. I'd had to bum and hitch to college. Who had given me a ride? Larry? No, I hadn't met Larry until my second year.

Who did I hang around with? Anyone? Most of my high school friends had gone to college, and the few who remained were miles from here. Jim had taken his first year off, I thought. He was probably at home, down in town.

What else had I forgotten?

I crossed the grimy sink and flung another cupboard open. More boxes and cans, soup, old baking mix—and a wicker basket with translucent brown plastic bottles with typed labels. I reached into the basket and pulled out one. Vicodin. I had the queasy feeling that if I dug further down, I'd find more narcotics than I ever wanted to know about.

Dad held out his hand.

Was I really going to hand my dad the drugs he was addicted to?

I'd done it before. I remember being twelve and being sent to fetch a pill and a beer. It wasn't anything unusual, it was just one of my chores.

The other game began. "G!" Mom said. "There's almost always a G in a place."

The bottle shook in my hand.

"You look kind of sick," Keith said. I heard the note of false solicitude underneath his words. "You feeling okay?"

"I'm fine," I said. I took two steps and dropped the pill bottle on the crudely gouged Formica of the table. Dad grabbed it before it could roll away, popped the top, swallowed a pill, and recapped the bottle in one practiced movement.

"Si' down and eat," Mom said, eyes still on the television. "Tuna. You love it."

If I had a mouthful, I probably would love it. I could feel the craving in my stomach. Worse, though... Dropped into this setting, the role the family had assigned for me dragged at my heart. My oldest memories ached for my place in this room. Craved it. I couldn't remember which drawer the forks were in, but a vivid memory of sitting in the second chair from the end slapped the back of my head. I could feel the lumpy ripped vinyl underneath me, with the hard knot on the left side digging into my buttocks. The metal bars chilling my back. The unspoken resentment at asking someone to pass the potatoes only to have Dad grab the bowl, take the last scoop, and hand me the empty dish. The years I'd scraped my way through school, my decades in software development, all that receded in my mind. Had I really gone to sleep twenty-eight years from now? Or was all that just a deluded nighttime dream?

Giving Dad the pill bottle had been a mistake. Sitting down to a breakfast of last night's leftovers would drive me neck-deep into what I'd been. I'd find myself in my bedroom late at night, methodically testing jigsaw pieces against each other and wondering what I could have been if I'd only tried.

Uncomfortable is comfortable if you don't try.

Mom said "Wha' do you mean there's no G?"

I walked back to the refrigerator and grabbed the smeared chrome handle. The front held bowls with ill-fitting plates over the tops in a sad effort to keep them fresh. I didn't want to see what grew behind them. But the plastic fruit and vegetable drawers were beneath the bottom shelf. I pulled open the left drawer and extracted two fairly new apples. Apples alone weren't a meal, but it would get me through the morning.

I couldn't be unique. Had this happened to others? There were always people who seemed to be ahead of everyone else. Had Steve Jobs gotten a second chance? Warren Buffett? Einstein? Maybe I could change the world, make it a better place for everyone.

The faucet gurgled and choked when I turned on the cold water. I wanted to dry them off, but not with anything on that counter, so I blew the worst of the water off them and turned back to the table.

Mom and Keith were staring at me.

Keith's lips tilted up at the ends, and his eyes bounced between me and Mom. His free hand arrhythmically drummed the tabletop, precariously close to his half-full plastic tumbler. His quick breaths flapped his button-down shirt against his bony chest. He was ready to move, to leap at me, to pay me back for the insult that far exceeded the injury I'd given him.

Mom's gaze was just as sharp as Keith's. Her lips were pressed in a tight line, and her jowls quivered with suppressed tension. I remembered the vein that pulsed in her forehead just before she exploded and drove us from the house. Her flannel bathrobe, worn to patches of translucency, was belted tightly against her bulging gut. She sucked her cigarette so hard that the tip brightened and sank the remaining half-inch down to the filter in a single breath. I'd pissed her off, somehow.

The fruit, dammit! We never washed fruit when I grew up. I don't know if anyone did nowadays. We just ate it, chemicals and all. The pesticide load in my veins was probably all that kept the germs in this hole from eating me alive.

Mom took the stub out of her mouth and jabbed it into an overflowing heap of butts on the saucer beside her empty plate. "You don' wan' tuna?" she said.

"I don't feel like it today."

The uncapped feet of Dad's chair scraped the tile as he pushed it back to stand. "Town."

"Gimme some spice drops," Mom said. "Cigs. And grab a piece of meat for dinner." She didn't have to mention beer. Dad only drove to town to get beer.

The empties, heaped beside the back door in garish gold and black, reminded me that one of my jobs had been to take the cans out to the pit. There wasn't a deposit yet. One day, towards the end of my life here, I'd gotten the bright idea to dig out the corroded empties to take them to the scrap metal dealer. I'd worked all day, made less than ten bucks. I remember glaring at the change and small bills in my hand, furious that my hours of work hadn't paid off.

But I'd started working. That had been the point where I decided I could do better. That I would climb out of this hole.

Dad walked unsteadily towards the door. The Vicodin hadn't kicked in already, had it? Was I going to let him get behind the wheel stoned?

"You don' wan' tuna." Mom said again, in the exact same tone of voice.

Dad closed the door behind him.

"I just don't feel like it this morning."

"Fine." She shook another Marlboro out of the pack, put it between her lips, flipped the antique lighter open, and sucked the flame into the tobacco. "You ask me to make enough for leftovers, now you don' wan' 'em. That's fine."

Keith's lips twitched upwards again, watching me watch Mom.

I felt the need to apologize as a physical pressure against my throat. To take my place, to sit in my chair and eat the meal my mother had prepared for me with her own two hands. Because she loved me.

I didn't need this. Not now. "I'll eat it later, Mom. Promise." The words tripped easily out of my mouth. I'd really promised trouble later. I wouldn't eat a slab of that glutinous ruin if I had any way around it. Growing up I'd always said things like that to avoid trouble, to avoid hurting anyone's feelings, to just avoid, period. "I just feel like getting moving this morning."

"Tha's fine." She turned away from me to stare at the television, dismissing me from her presence.

"Where's Dora?" I asked.

Mom dropped her fork. "Have you jus' lost it?"

Shit. Dora had run away more than once. She always returned in a few days, usually in the back of a police car, hangdog but unrepentant. She let herself be dragged back rather than starve or turn prostitute. She had the drive, but not the knowledge. Mom wouldn't tolerate talk about Dora while she was gone.

"I told ya," Keith said. "He ain't acting right today."

You have no idea, kid. "I just feel like moving. Full of energy. That's all."

The pickup roared just outside the kitchen window. Gravel pinged the side of the house, then Dad was away.

"And just where d'ya think you're going?" Mom said.

"Just going to walk around." I sank my teeth into the apple. The dull ache in my teeth flared into a half-dozen needles of pain. My eyes watered and I silently cursed myself. I needed to slice an apple before I could eat it.

"He don't remember," Keith said. "He made a big deal about that job at Kelsey's, and now he don't remember."

I felt my eyes widen. *Kelsey's?*

"Nah," Mom said. "He remembers. He's playin' the fool. That's why he's talkin' all college. He don' wan' no uppity job."

Kelsey's.

I couldn't remember how many jobs I'd held back then, but I wouldn't forget the blown interview at Kelsey's. I'd woken up early. Showered. Shaved with a precious new safety blade. Worn my best shirt and pants. I remembered fumbling with the buttons going down my front. I'd skipped breakfast, ran outside, and bumped into Keith.

He shoved me back. I wound up on my back in the muddy patch behind the pickup.

Kelsey's had been special. It wasn't a job doing farm work. It had been at the little grocery store. Miss Kelsey needed someone who could do math, who could stock shelves and count cases of beer as they came off the delivery truck. It would have been a step up—a small step up, but still a step.

I'd gotten Dad to delay his beer run, washed the mud off, gotten into my second-best clothes, and urged Dad to hurry all the way into town.

Miss Kelsey shook her head as I came into her tightly crammed store. When I apologized for being late she said, "It's like this. You've got what it takes to make it. You could be good, if you wanted to be. But someone who's late to the job interview, they're gonna be late to work. And I can't have someone who's late to work all the time." That's when I decided to never be late again.

I felt my face flush behind the apple.

Keith bellowed laughter. Mom turned to the television to silently watch a sports car commercial.

Sparks connected in my brain.

I hadn't bumped into Keith by accident. Either time.

Twenty-eight years ago, he'd waited for me outside. He made sure I'd trip into that mud. How had that mud gotten there, anyway? I didn't remember there usually being a puddle out there.

I'd woken to the sound of running water.

The bastard had made the mud just for me.

This morning, I'd spent too much time in my bedroom.

Keith had come looking for me.

He wouldn't let me break my place in the family.

I knew I'd told Mom and Dad. I knew I'd babbled about the Kelsey's job the night before, because I'd had to go home and tell them I hadn't gotten it. Mom had smiled, and said that it was okay.

But this morning, Dad left. He knew I needed a ride. I'd told him. And he left.

Mom could have said something.

But nobody had said anything until Dad left. In the only vehicle.

I'd tried to change my life.

My family had dragged me back into my place in theirs.

It wasn't just the way I ate, or the fact that I couldn't smell for shit through all the tar and nicotine. The first time, Keith had sabotaged me. But this time, my whole family had silently conspired against me without saying a word.

If I tried to paint a wall, someone would kick over the can. Not only would I have to clean it up, any time someone noticed the prickles of paint that had sunk into the gouges in the hardwood floor they'd remind me I was a klutz. If I cleaned the bathroom, someone would trash it again.

You can only improve if you want to. And it's a lot easier to sit in the old chair and eat leftover tuna casserole.

All these years I'd cursed myself for arbitrarily severing my family ties, and I'd forgotten why I'd done it. They're called *ties* for a reason. Sometimes they tie you down.

Dora had figured it out years before me. She didn't know where to go except *away*, and didn't know what to do when she got there, but she'd figured it out.

I pulled my teeth out of the apple without taking the bite. Without a word, I walked back into my bedroom. Shut the door behind me. The heap of clean clothes on the floor went onto the bed, where I quickly folded them all. Some of them would clearly have stretch to get on me, but the weight would come off soon.

The closet. I flung cardboard boxes aside, looking for the puke-brown Old Whaler tobacco tin. I found it in a crate of busted-up action figures. Forty-three dollars and change into my pocket.

From the top closet shelf, I pulled my old Boy Scout haversack. The clean clothes stacked neatly in the bag.

Searching dresser drawers, I skimmed through all the debris I'd thought precious yesterday and didn't care about today. Twelve-bladed pocketknife with scissors and screwdriver and leather punch, in my pocket. I had to slice apples somehow. Old flashlight with dead batteries, Scouting awards, broken radios and circuit boards and parts of plastic models I'd broken years earlier, all trash. Skip the canteen and the tightly-fitted camp cooking kit, but take the box of matches and the thin cotton rope. I had a lot better idea what to take this time.

A new toothbrush, still in the flimsy cardboard box—in the pack.

Shoes. I'd seen a tangle of shoes in the closet. The hiking boots still fit me, and were a better choice than threadbare sneakers. The sneakers were lighter and more comfortable, but the weight of the boots didn't concern me. Dry unblistered feet did.

Spring could be cold and wet up here. Jacket. Rain poncho.

The apples went into the top of the bag before I tied it shut.

And I'd have to sleep. I snatched my musty sleeping bag and lashed it beneath the knapsack. I hadn't used a backpack in decades, but my hands automatically let out the straps and pulled everything over my shoulder. A hip belt would have helped distribute the load, but that was okay.

Mom and Dad's room. The bottom drawer of the paper-flooded desk. My birth certificate and Social Security card folded nicely into my wallet.

This time, maybe I'd marry. I might even find the guts to have children. I couldn't do worse.

I returned to the living room. The game show had ended. Mom lay on the couch watching a talk show host who had died fifteen years ago, while Keith shoved another helping of tuna noodle casserole in the microwave. Neither looked at me.

I walked to the television and hit the power button. The house probably hadn't been that quiet in days.

Mom said, "Wha' the hell you doing?"

Keith stared at me, brows furrowed and head cocked.

"Mom," I said, staring into her face, memorizing every line, every detail. "Stop the damn smoking. Lung. Cancer. Will. Kill. You."

Mom coughed in shock, eyes bugging from her face. The cigarette fell from her lips.

I turned to my brother. Keith's mouth hung open. "Keith. You're going to drive into a tree, drunk. You'll kill yourself and your date. Quit it."

"You don' talk to us that way" Mom said.

"I don't talk to you at all." The one thing that worked right around here was the screen door, swinging easily open. "Tell Dad to knock off the pills. They're trashing his liver. It's an ugly way to die."

The door bounced shut behind me.

I hooked my thumbs under the shoulder straps and set off to find my sister.

No regrets.

Forced to Talk, Like, With Your Mouth

I couldn't imagine why Donner had chosen this… this *place* for us to work.

All us freelance IT people work remotely. That's what the Internet is for. We take the work we can find, when we can get it—a few hours here, a couple there. We share jobs like Uber shares rides. But if Donner was going to pay to drag a bunch of rock star programmers and sysadmins and database folks to one place so we could do some intensive work on a new project, he should've picked someplace cool. Rented a big condo near the Valley, or Vegas. Or went to a big luxury hotel with a whirlpool and a sauna and a decent sushi place next door or some Indian. Someplace civilized. Someplace where a young single guy with a Mustang, like me, could've maybe found some women looking for a hookup, gotten a decent drink.

It's not like we all worked for Donner full-time or anything. Yeah, a week's full-time-plus work would pay my bills that month. Giving one client a whole week is a risk, you gotta tell all your other clients that you're tied up for that week, plus travel time. They'll find someone else to fill the spot, sure, but there's a chance they'll like the new guy better, that he'll do it faster better and cheaper. Donner was paying bonus, though. Said he'd cover everything, and give me a chance to do the most challenging work of my life. How am I supposed to turn that down?

If I'd've known what it would take just to get there, I might've said no.

It started by flying to Portland, Oregon—pretty cool place, I know. But then I had to pick up my rental, this thing with almost enough room for my suitcase and a Chihuahua, and drive through this insipid valley full of wineries and these weird farms that looked like they only grew grass and stubby twisty trees. Looked nice, sure, but the only way through was this two-lane freeway choked with traffic. Like, 101 in the Valley Monday morning choked. For an hour, maybe two.

Then there's the mountain road. A rock wall on one side, a plunge to certain death on the other, these thick heavy trees everywhere that block out the sun. Two lane road again, except the spots where the mountain gave them a little room and they added a second lane to one side or the other and everyone drives like a meth-mouth trying to get around the granny doing the speed limit minus ten before the passing lane evaporates. That's another hour or two, depending on how many grannies you hit.

There's a second way through the mountains. It's a dirt road. The GPS refuses to take you there, won't even admit it exists, but Donner mentioned you could turn off at the Historic Covered Bridge sign and go that way. Dave tried that, and he walked into the hotel drenched in sweat and pale as a vampire.

Ah, yes.

The "hotel."

Take Booth City, an Oregon coastal town, all this beautiful water and waves and seven miles of gorgeous fine-sand beaches that run all the way back to these looming, crumbling clay cliffs. Up on top of the cliff, fancy restaurants all up and down the road through town. (Note the singular—*road*.) And it's full of hotels. When Portland gets hot, the whole place drains into Booth City. From May through August, the town has a population of a hundred and fifty thousand.

In November, when the skies churn gray and the wind screams off the Pacific and the waves have got their angry drunk on? Seven thousand.

The hotels are desperate for business. You could get a room in a five-star with a pool and a sauna, plus breakfast—real breakfast, not that terrible instant scrambled egg and stale chocolateoid donut crap—for maybe a hundred bucks a night. Four stars, no sauna, maybe fifty bucks.

The place Donner picked, the Flotsam, didn't have a pool. Or a sauna. It did have random junk from the 1940s and 1950s everywhere, though. Half of it fake. An old rusty sign that said *Street girls bringing sailors must pay in advance* right by the front door. Like *that* ever happened. These faded advertisements for Sea King Tuna and Kobol Cola. Signed black and white pictures of people nobody remembered, carefully framed roadside art by—by nobodies. Posters for boring old flicks like *Boris Karloff IS The Mummy* and *Frankenstein*. The doors had the cheesy locks that probably half the hackers I knew could pick in a coma. The guy who checked me in, a living advertisement for gastric bypass surgery, had this great big cheerful smile all the time like the trepanning drill went too deep.

The place didn't smell bad. Not exactly. They'd scrubbed the bathrooms and all the old fixtures, and they'd washed the sheets on the spring mattresses, but all that stuff was old. Like, sheets with ten threads per inch. And I didn't know they even made mattresses with springs anymore. Who would buy one when you can get memory foam? All those used hardback books in every room, the kind you buy by the banana box, and the weather so damp you could stick out a straw and take a good deep drink right from the air.

So I get there, ready to log on and work, and what happens?

The Wi-Fi is crap.

I got a shower. The shower stall's all tile, a little wider than my shoulders, and the nozzle's the same height as my shoulder. The Flotsam had their own soap, some local artisan stuff, so that was okay. They only had pear and apple, though, and I smell better with citrus. I should've probably been glad they had soap out there at all.

Donner has us all meet in this big space upstairs. It's not really a room, just a wide spot in the hall. It's not like you can close the doors to shut everyone out. But we've got the whole Flotsam, so nobody's going to bother us. There's two mismatched chairs, then a bunch of different Goodwill-reject couches crammed in everywhere with maybe a dozen, fifteen people I don't know. Someone, probably more than one, needs deodorant, and a couple people have way too much cologne. I find a spot at the end of this poofy couchish thing, next to this big blonde chick wearing a tank top and lots and lots of black-and-white tattoos. She doesn't look at me, just shifts a little so we don't touch and keeps working on her laptop. It's one of the new Toshibas, with the 4K screen and the quadrophonic sound and probably enough memory to run a dozen virtual machines. Nice specs, but that horrible Toshiba keyboard sticks, and the keys are just a little too small for my hands. The hardware can out-play a home cinema, but it looks like she scrapped Windows and put in some sort of Unix desktop with a plain background and three side-by-side text-only terminals, so she can't be all bad.

I sit, and the couch tries to swallow me.

The chick snorts, but quietly. I yank myself out of the hole and up on the edge of the couch. It's covered in this weird spiky cloth—touch it one way and it's real smooth, but go the other way and it scratches you. Where do they find this stuff?

The table in front of us is topped in tiny pointy seashells. A bunch of them broke a long time ago, leaving all these scratchy pointy tips.

I built my laptop. It's a 17-incher with a pile of ECC RAM and four top-of-the-line processors, it'll outperform anything on the market. A friend made the case for me, very thin solid brass with clockwork hinges and engraved enameled keys with real springs. More steampunk than Wells and weighs about half a ton. That table would've scratched the hell out of it so I balance it on my knees, boot, and try to get enough Wi-Fi to get my email.

We work in silence for ten minutes before this little pale guy with short-cropped black hair walks in. "Hello, everyone!"

The first person who talked since I came in.

I look up. It's polite.

It takes a moment for it to click. This is Donner. He looked bigger on Skype. In person he seems kind of frail for someone in his thirties.

About half the team keeps typing, waiting for Donner to say something important.

"Save your work, people." Donner spreads his hands. "The Internet is going down in five."

"What the fuck?" says the bony kid who'd claimed the leather chair.

"Four," Donner says. "I want your attention. Three."

A bunch of folks start typing more quickly, like they could finish their work before the Internet disappeared. I use tmux so I can't lose any work, but most people aren't that smart.

"Two. One."

Donner reaches up to a wireless router mounted right up by the ceiling. I hadn't noticed it among all the other crap nailed to the wall. You could hear everyone groan as he pulls the power cord.

"You can take notes," Donner says. "But I want you to pay attention for the next few minutes. And the next week, but the next few minutes really."

I open a text file, give it a title of the date in an easily sortable format, and wait. Clients get weird ideas. It's best to go along if you want to be paid. And after coming out here, I was damn well getting paid.

Donner lets the groans fade before speaking. "Welcome to the Flotsam Inn. I'm Colin Donner. You've all worked for me before, but most of us have never met. You've all worked together, even if you don't recognize each other. We built Cross-Cal and ChefShare together. Everyone here has top skills, none better."

His words seem to settle everyone. Hands are still on keyboards, but nobody's grimacing. If you want someone to pay attention, you say nice things about them.

It's sugar, I'm thinking. *Sugar to make the medicine go down.*

"But the projects we've done before have had some issues," Donner says. "And for this new project, which I'm calling Raindrop, I want everything to go down smooth."

Yep. Medicine.

"Let's start by going around the room. Give your Internet handle first, so we know who you are. Spell it if you have to. Then give your real name, so we know what to call you this week." Donner jabs a finger at the chubby guy. "You first, then circle around."

The guy's jaw works and he swallows something. "DSW, like the shoes. Dennis Willis."

The neckbeard geezer next to him says, "Grog. Handle, and real name. Grog Lillian."

We go around. The chick next to me is Shard, with the underscore, which is kind of cool. We've sysadminned a whole bunch of projects and she's always online. I give my handle and my name, and she glances my way and gives this little nod that says she remembers me too.

"This new project doesn't need running code right away." Donner waves his hands as he talks, almost knocking this 1960s ceramic mermaid off this little shelf. "Every time we hack together a tool, we slap together a web interface and nail a back end to it. Then we spend the rest of our lives patching around it. This time, we're doing it right." He drops his hands. "We are here to architect a back end. We all know it's going to need a database, but I don't want to come back later and find out that the table design can't handle adding a third, or a fourth, or a twentieth server. The web server architecture is to be designed from the ground up to be expandable and scalable. And use unified protocols. We are *not* going to mix SOAP and XML-RPC and, God help me, SunOS RPC, like *someone* did to me on ChefShare." His glare plants on Grog the neckbeard, who honestly seems to not give a shit.

Donner's face gets all serious, and he looks around, deliberately looking everyone in the eye. This one dude, Skyjack, doesn't look up when Donner gets to him, just keeps typing. Donner keeps looking. Finally the next guy over, I think it was Noodles, nudges him, and Skyjack looks up to see Donner and everyone staring. He turns this funny color and takes his hands off his keyboard.

"Some design decisions up front," Donner says. "You will abide by these. We are not mixing operating systems or distributions. We are not mixing protocols. We are not mixing programming languages. You all know all of the tools we're using, or you can pick them up quick enough. You'll get the specifics in a few minutes, but I'm giving the basics now."

He starts on this list of protocols and languages. Each word gets a groan from someone: The Ruby fans don't like Python, the Linux guys don't like SkyBSD, and nobody likes OpenNebula except those nutjobs down at NASA. And Donner, I guess. I sysadmin anything, but I'm really a SkyBSD guy, so I'm good, though I gotta say the Apache web server Donner wants gives me hives.

"Now," Donner says. "I know you people. You want to start work. Create a prototype quick and get something out. The Wi-Fi here is terrible, and the cell coverage is worse. You'll be lucky to get a bar of 3G. This means you have to think before you work. DBAs, you stay here. Sysadmins, you get the dining room. Client-side guys, the lobby. You lot in particular, remember, *cross-platform*. Each team will find a project description and specifications, on paper. They stay on paper. No uploading."

I flinch. I can't help it. How are you supposed to perform a keyword search against a *paper* document?

Donner spreads his hands. "Go over the specs. Use the whiteboards. Play with some ideas. Networking crew, you need some specs from the other teams to do much, but there's a roadhouse a quarter mile down the hill. Walk down. Get a beer. There's no Wi-Fi there either, so talk to each other. Get to know each other. Be back in two hours, go up into the sunroom. Raindrop's gonna take us a long time."

Donner's sight circles the room and he says, "We're going out for Chinese for dinner at seven PM. Breakfast is at nine AM, in the restaurant downstairs."

This, was gonna suck.

"And by the way," Donner says. "No electronics at dinner. At any meal."

If Donner didn't pay so well, I would of blown the project, Booth City, and the whole damn state of Oregon. And never come back.

So I'm down in the dining room with Shard and Tanqer and Bilebog. The dining room's like the rest of the place. The walls are stained and varnished wood panels, with these little decorative strips running up and down every four feet to mask the joins, like the builder didn't even hear of drywall. Every surface has 1950s junk hung on it or sitting on it or dangling from the ceiling. You can smell the kitchen, cinnamon and sugar and coffee and probably a wood-fired stove. There's a few booths around the sides, and a few tables with one or two chairs each. Everything's glossy wood, nothing matches. These people must of gone into every estate sale in Oregon, bought one thing from each, polished it up with that lemon stuff, and stuck it in here. The middle of the room has this great big table with mismatched paisley cloth napkins and grab bag cutlery. Maybe a dozen different wood chairs that look about as comfy as rocks. Maybe we don't need recliners, but hadn't they ever heard of cushions? Or even IKEA? Then there's this four-by-eight whiteboard straight out of Silicon Valley, sitting on its wheels like Curiosity ready to rock all over Mars.

The second we walk in, though, it's the view that slaps us. The back wall is all old double-hung windows with mullions, and the whole thing rattles in the wind. We're on top of a cliff here, and get a great view of the Pacific. The ocean's pissed off today, these great big waves thrashing around so much that they don't even stay together long enough to get to shore, but crash and smash into each other way out there. You can hear the noise all the way up here. A gust of even harsher wind spatters drops of water on the slumping glass windowpanes.

Do the waves splash all the way up here? Or is that just *more* rain?

Tanqer stops staring first. He knows virtual memory like nobody. Turns out he's a big guy with this beard you could hide a weasel in, which looks really weird on his Mexican face.

There's a corner booth by the window, with long, curved, cracked red vinyl seat and two of those horrible chairs. Four three-inch D-ring binders on it, each with a page printed *RAINDROP – Systems Administration* in forty-point type slid into the clear plastic front. The booth's tight enough that the table dents Tanqer's gut, but he slides all the way around to put his back to the corner and pulls a stack over to him.

Paper. What the hell?

I check my phone. Still no Wi-Fi, and I'm getting zero bars of cell reception, so we might as well get started, then. I slide in the other way and take a stack. Bilebog and Shard both grab chairs, and we start turning pages. The design is fine, but how Donner's given it to us is just sadistic. The font is too big and the printing's too wide to read easy. It's like trying to read papers back in high school, or one of those novels my mom is always trying to get published. Water spatters the window behind me, and this chill draft tickles my neck. It's like being a pioneer or something.

I'm just getting my brain wrapped around the architecture requirements when Bilebog says, "This is bullshit." Bilebog's a storage guru but he's got this scary overbite and kind of funny eyes, and he's so skinny his bones stick out, and he wears this tight wick-away shirt so everything shows. I can't even look at Bilebog without thinking *hillbilly*, which isn't cool but, you know, he just totally looks it. He reads faster than me, or maybe he's just skimmed, because he's about halfway through the doc already. "I could do the storage for this in a second on Amazon."

"Amazon's a Linux shop," Tanqer says. I know he types really fast, but his voice is slow and has this Georgia drawl, so he's like a bearded Mexican good old boy. Who would of guessed? On the Internet nobody knows you're a dog, except the NSA, who knows you're really a megalomaniacal hamster piloting a dog machine built out of Habitrail and kibble. "You can't run SkyBSD storage on Amazon." Tanqer's right hand is fumbling around the windowsill beside him, touching all these little knickknacks, while he's looking at us like he doesn't even know what his hand is doing.

"That's what I mean." Bilebog flips back a page. "We're doing all this work to make SkyBSD do what Linux already does."

I am so damn tired of operating system wars that whenever I hear one start I want to stab someone, but this table doesn't even have a spoon handy. Everybody has their favorite Linux, or BSD, or Plan 9, or whatever, and some sysadmins even like Windows or, Kali help us, Apple. "Look," I said. "That's what the client wants, so that's what we do."

"I provide services," Bilebog says. "I provide storage."

"Then you provide it," Shard says. Her voice kind of grates, like it's saying *you will not ignore me*. "The job says no Linux. He wants the SkyBSD TCP stack, dynamic ASLR, and bare metal storage. That's what we use. You're the expert. So do it. Or can't you pull it off?" That's Shard, always going straight for the balls.

Bilebog's skinny jaw drops and his eyes bulge. "Hell yeah I can do this."

"Then how?"

"Fiber channel, Hammer on a GEOM—"

I sit back and listen, trying not to fiddle with my phone. I do some storage, but mostly I configure services. I mean, I can make a web server instance puke up pages faster than anything, but I let other people handle the bottom layer. Bilebog and Shard start going back and forth, cutting each other off, spitting back and forth on different software storage architectures and how to lay out disk racks and which type of drive controllers they need for a project like this. It's fascinating stuff—I mean, I do some storage, but they're a bunch of levels above me, and I'm learning a lot just sitting here and listening to the argument. Bilebog's face is getting redder and redder, like he can't believe that Shard dares challenge his mastery, his forefinger stabbing the table every time he uses a technical term like he's driving the word into the wood. And he's using a *lot* of technical terms, like he thinks they'll impress anyone here. Shard's sitting back, all relaxed and kind of mellow, nodding at some of what Bilebog's saying but cutting him off now and then to throw out a question or tell him a better way do it.

"The CAM system doesn't work that way," Bilebog says.

"Sure it does," Shard says. "Look it up, it's in the manual."

"I *would* look it up," Bilebog snaps, "but we don't have net."

I can't help checking my phone, and it's gone right to the little X that means we don't have bupkis.

Shard gives this thin smile like she's been hiding the winning Magic card and has finally lured Bilebog into place to crush him with it. "I'm running SkyBSD on my laptop. With the manual. And the source. Let's look."

Tanqer opens his mouth. He's been sitting quiet this whole time, looking lost in his own private world, probably one with Wi-Fi and where his jeans and polo shirt and fleece jacket fit right in. He's picked up this little china statue from the windowsill. I couldn't tell what it was, what with the faded paint and the way Tanqer's rolling it around in his hand like Grandma with her worry beads, but maybe it's sort of two diseased Cocker Spaniels humping. He's one of nature's fiddlers, has to have something in his hand all the time, and he'll probably pick it up and stick it in his jacket pocket to fiddle with later. Tanqer's Southern voice seems to slow everything down around us, conversational sticky syrup or something.

Tanqer says, "If the storage path works like Bilebog says, there'd be horrible buffer cache back pressure." Bilebog looks like someone's just surprised him by shoving the plasticized puffer fish hanging from the ceiling overhead up his butt, but Tanqer goes on with, "The whole system would just go down under load. I don't know if Shard's right, but I'm gonna have to say it. Bilebog, it can't work that way."

It's quiet. Thunder rumbles somewhere far off, and a gust of rain hammers the window. You do not argue with Tanqer on the buffer cache—I mean, you just don't, you're more likely to argue with Steve Jobs about the iPhone and get an answer back even with him dead. Shard's looking all smug and leans back in her chair. The tank top shows off her tattoo, all these fine black lines going back and forth, and I'm trying to figure out what they are and how far down they go without looking like I'm staring at her (great) boobs when she says, "Thank you, Tanqer."

Bilebog's lips make silent words, half words, like his brain just can't even, and he's glaring lasers at Shard. The bones under that skintight blue wick-away shirt have this twitch, and I get this image of something inside his chest clawing to get out. I'm waiting for him to scream or punch her or something, but then his jaw cranks sideways and he spits out "Fine. We do it your way." He looks out the window. I hear him mutter "Women shouldn't do computers, anyway."

Shard flushes, and for just a second there's this terrible rage in her face. I've seen her temper online, she's a vodka bottle filled with gasoline and Bilebog's just jammed a rag down her neck and lit it, but her face smooths out and she doesn't say anything, like she's swallowed it and it's going to blow.

This uncomfortable crap is why meatspace sucks.

"We better get something down before dinner," I say. "I'll grab the whiteboard." And we get a bunch of stuff sketched out before the bus arrives to take us all to dinner.

Dinner was shockingly good, tender chicken and fresh seafood and melt-in-your-mouth pork, veggies I haven't seen outside of Chinatown and sauces I know better than to ask about, everything seasoned straight out of Beijing, served on big platters with a ridiculous amount of decoration, all these fine red lines baked into the china. Seriously, some of the best I've had. It's served by this Chinese family that barely speaks English, everyone from the stubborn sulky high school girls up to gleeful Grandpa bringing bamboo trays out of the kitchen, and all of us sitting around this big long table that ran the length of this little shoebox restaurant with the rain pounding down around it. I listen to a couple of database guys talking query optimization, and when they slow down I ask one of them about squeezing a little more performance out of synchronous queries. Plus there's this weird Chinese beer, little gold-labeled bottles with all that weird tiny print on each and no English at all. Two each, but the network guy sitting next to me, Hamz, he's a teetotaler and I scam one of his for grabbing him an extra case of no-cal Red Bull when I go to the grocery store tomorrow.

Shard and Bilebog sat at opposite ends of the table, not looking at each other.

We get back to the Flotsam all tired and full and perfumed with so much Chinese dried red peppers that it's gonna leak out our skin for the next three days, and then damp from the quick run from the bus to the door. Tanqer has the room next to me, but we don't waste time talking. There's an hour of shitty Wi-Fi before Warden Donner throws the switch and it's lights out on the cell block. I give quick lousy answers to emails from other clients, and see Bilebog and Shard on our usual Internet chat channel, everyone bitching about Donner's little game. When Donner cuts our lifeline, I fall asleep listening to the rain and the wind and the occasional "whuff" of air through the inch-high gap under the door of my room. The building creaks and thuds and groans with the wind, sometimes like there's some of those wooden-shoed Hollandaise people dancing around on the roof.

My alarm's set for seven, so I'll have lots of time to shower and dress and whatever before the nine o'clock breakfast, although I don't know what "whatever" is supposed to be if I can't check my web feed. Donner said that Mister Happy at the front desk is the best cook he's ever known and that we should come ravenous, but he said that after we ate dinner last night, so what the hell. I'd probably just grab a yogurt and a piece of seasonal local fruit from the buffet, same as always.

Instead of getting woken up in dawn's early rain by my phone buzzing Katy Perry's "Hot & Cold," someone hammers on my door at bite-me-o'clock like they're nailing their list of demands to the church door. I grunge my eyes open and pull on my pale blue sweat suit with the less bad bleach spots, trying to make my ears sort out what the bastard's shouting. It takes me a moment to get the rusty gears in my brain turning enough to recognize the words, "Police! Come on out!" What the hell is this, some kind of raid? I know some of the people on this team use, they're pretty open about it on chat, but come on! It's a hotel; you can't tell me that in Oregon they wake up every room for anything less than a full-on imminent meth lab explosion in room 420.

Uniformed cops herd everyone into the dining room, which looks a little different at four AM, let me tell you. The windows kind of reflect the dining room because of the four different chandeliers hanging cockeyed from the ceiling, but that reflection's on top of this deep liquid black that seems to press in on the rippling glass, like we're at the bottom of the Marianas and the faintest crack will bring tons of water in on us. Then I see a crack in one of the windows, and it gives me this little extra chill.

"What's going on?" a guy in furry sweatpants and a replica Throbbing Gristle tour shirt asks. I think he's QJK but I didn't talk with him at all during dinner so I'm not really sure, you know how it is when you get a whole bunch of faces at once. I just shrugged.

The others in the team don't look right, either. Tanqer is wearing only these cotton PJ bottoms that just aren't enough for the chill seeping through this room, and beneath that hairy beard he's got this hairy chest that's already starting to go a little gray, all over abs that really could use a few hours at the gym. His face is slack, and I know the didn't-sleep-at-all look. Grog has these camo PJs, and Skyjack, honest and for true, is wearing double-extra-large Little Mermaid pajamas that look hand-made, not looking anyone in the eye and his face bright as a tomato. Shard actually got yesterday's jeans and a T-shirt back on, but she's shifting her bare feet back and forth. So am I, though—these floorboards are chilly and clammy and the varnish gets sticky with all the humidity in everything. My mouth tastes like I'd been drinking drain cleaner, which I might've—I've got no idea what was really in that Chinese beer.

Plus there's cops. They don't look sleepy. There's a couple by the windows: one in the doorway to the kitchen, one in front of the bathrooms, two at the door to the lobby. We didn't have enough Wi-Fi to do shit last night, we didn't go out, what has the cops in a tizzy?

Then Donner comes into the lobby, with this tall bulky guy in a brown tweed suit I wouldn't give to Salvation Army and a blue tie that looks like it came from the Old Sal discount bin. Donner looks worse than any of us, black circles under his eyes like someone cracked him in each and beard stubble you could use to sand the varnish off the floor. He's also wearing yesterday's clothes, with a great big Chinese gravy stain running down the middle.

"People," Donner shouts. We're not saying much, but everyone looks at him. Once he's sure he has our attention he says, "I, I…" He takes a deep breath and rubs his eyes. "I have to say…" Donner shakes his head slowly, eyes empty, and looks over at the cheap suit.

"I'm Detective Manny Bandowski," he says, making me wonder if the cop college teaches that big booming voice. "Mister Mark Clinton was found dead early this morning."

I look over at QJK, and he's got this funny look like he doesn't understand what the cop said, which is fine because I don't really get it either.

Donner raises a hand and chokes out, "Bilebog. Someone murdered Bilebog. Cracked his head with something."

"Murdered?" I say, but nobody hears me, because everybody around me is saying the same thing, or something like the same thing, or just giving a good old sincere WTF, and the wood paneling around us just echoes it back even with all the nostalgia crap nailed to the walls. I can and can't believe it—you say all the time that you're gonna kill a guy, it's all over the chats, but nobody really does. You can't. You don't know what they look like, or where they live, or if they're even a guy. They could be a hamster doing the dog thing, or even rarer, be a chick. Bilebog was an ass, yeah, but he's no more a troll than half the other people in this room, and if we started killing off all the trolls the whole world would have to go back to teletype and stone tablets. It's a shock, like when you discover what happens when you're a teenager and you first wash your dong real fast, there's this whole world that just opens up and explodes in your face and makes a sticky mess and nothing will ever be properly clean again.

The detective gives this whistle that just cuts through all the words, he's like Band Saw Bandowski, and everyone just shuts right up. Maybe they can teach the voice, but either you've got the two-finger Whistle From Hell thing or you don't. "We need to talk to each and every one of you," Bandowski says. "We don't have room down at the station to process twenty-eight of you, so here's what's going to happen. You're going to sit in here. Or lie down, whatever. No talking to each other. My men around the room, they're going to take talking seriously. Our detectives will come get each and every one of you. We've got a couple teams, so it won't take as long as you might think. Once we've talked, you can go back to your room."

Well, crap.

My brain is full of all these jumbled thoughts—no, I'm not even really thinking, I'm full of these weird feelings that I don't have a name for. Confusion's big there, but I keep thinking about Shard and Bilebog and that livid look on her face when Bilebog was an asshole. I really want to go online now, hook into a chat group where nobody's doing anything important and just spill it all out, change the names and dump it on strangers and try to put some kind of sense to it, but I didn't even bring my phone and there's no Wi-Fi. It's not like I can even try to talk to someone, the way those cops are eyeing us like hungry dogs waiting for the command before lunging for the meat.

I sit on a ladderback chair by the big table for a few minutes, but the hard wood hurts my butt and my eyes ache and I can't meet any of the curious looks everyone's throwing everyone, and the smell of lemon furniture polish and BO is kind of turning my stomach in knots. Maybe the smell isn't the only reason, but it sure isn't helping. So I look up at the cop in front of the bathroom, who gives me this cold eye back, and I scoot the chair back and ask him if I can take a piss. Even my bladder's kind of frozen up, but it gives me a chance to splash icy cold chlorine-scented tap water on my face and try to clear my brain. It gets the scudge out of my eyes, but the brain still limps along. So I give up, go back into the kitchen, lay with my head on my sweatshirted arm on the clammy sticky floor under one of the looming black windows, and try close my eyes, trying to ignore when some police officer calls a name even though each shout makes me start.

I'm totally shocked when, maybe five minutes later, someone calls my name. It's this old bag of bones detective with cigarette-stained wrinkly skin, standing in the doorway. I blink in surprise, not sure if I'd heard correctly, and he raises his voice to call me again. When I stand up everyone's looking at me like I'm some alien critter.

It's not just me, I know, they're all looking at anyone who gets called, but it's not fun to be the bug in the microscope. Nobody wants to meet my eye, not even Tanqer, but he puts his hand on his chin like it's casual and puts his index finger across his lips. All Tanqer needs to add is a breath and pursed lips to get *shhh*, but he doesn't make a sound. Shard's sitting in a chair, arms crossed, her head tilted back to rest on the top of the chair back, exposing her neck, her blonde hair hanging down behind the chair.

They take me to this bedroom that nobody's using, set up just like all the other rooms, but this one done in a circus motif, with paintings of like trained elephants and feral clowns, which I really don't ever need but especially not before sunrise, and Bag of Bones turns on a recorder and gives my name and introduces himself as Detective Goddard and the clean-cut dude wearing half a bottle of Costco Special cologne as Detective Fish.

"Like the rocket guy?" I say.

"Precisely like the rocket guy," Goddard says, nodding. "Tell me how you knew Mister Clinton?"

"Bilebog, yeah." I rub my jaw and work my tongue, like loosening up will untangle the snakes writhing inside my brain. "Known him online for years, but we, like, just met in meatspace today."

"You were both on the…" Fish flips a page in pleather-sheathed notebook. "The systems administration team. Designing this Raindrop thing."

"Right," I say. "Right." The cerebellum snakes just won't stop churning. I'd thought that the furniture polish out in the dining room was messing with my stomach, but Fish's Special Spicy cologne is worse, or maybe it's just me.

Goddard looks straight at me, like he can see right into my head and get my serial number off the inside back of my skull. "Do you know of anyone who had anything against Bilebog?"

Goddard using Bilebog's proper handle is kind of a relief, like suddenly we're talking about the same person. "Lots of people online," I say. The snakes in my head seem to connect with the churning in my gut, and it all comes out. The technical discussion between Bilebog and Shard, with Tanqer cutting Bilebog's legs out from under him, and Bilebog getting pissed and being an ass, and that look on Shard's face. I don't want to tell them about the look on Shard's face, or how she gets mad. I really don't. You lie to the cops about your weed stash, maybe they'll let you slide, but murder is this whole different thing, and murdering one of your own, you've got to take that serious even if you don't want to.

I like Shard better than Bilebog. A whole lot better. I mean, she's sharp and knows it all, and even without the (amazing) boobs it's not even a contest.

But with the cops listening to every word, with that psycho clown on the circus poster giving me the happy eye, I say what I'd seen. Fish writes it all down, even with that little digital recorder running, like they don't really trust the tech, which only shows that the cops aren't total idiots. I slow down a couple times, because I really don't want to say anything that puts the fix on Shard, but the truth is I'm spilling my guts and Goddard and Fish don't have to even play good cop/bad cop, they just have to ease the path for me a little when I get tangled up or run down. They tell me I'm doing the right thing, and offer to get me some water. Finally, they use this little electronic thing to take my fingerprint virginity.

When Fish tells me to go, when they finish wringing me out and squeezing me dry and telling me to go back to my room for a bit and get some rest but not leave town, when I'm trudging up the stairs to my room, I hear Goddard calling for Denise Grant.

I bet that's Shard's street name.

So I get back to my room, not really seeing the crap paintings and figurines and whatnot. It's eight in the morning, so I get a neck-high shower with the pear soap and put on some clothes that don't stink of sweat and cigarette cops and yesterday's Chinese dinner. There's no Internet, and I don't feel like going through the design spec binder sitting on the little glass-topped table by the man-eating lounge chair. So I stack a couple pillows against the headboard, grab my laptop, and sprawl on the bed in my stocking feet to play some serious Freecell. I don't know how many games I've won when someone knocks on my door.

It's Tanqer. There's nothing as fiery as an angry Mexican, and even his beard seems poofed out, like the weasel living in it had its mad on too. He'd stopped by his room to pull on his black fleece jacket, and he's got his hands stuffed in the pockets like he's trying to warm them. He straight-arms my door the rest of the way open and stomps in, then with exaggerated care closes the door behind him. His Georgia accent doesn't keep him from talking fast when he says, "Did you tell the cops about Shard and Bilebog?"

"I had to," I say.

"I told you to keep your mouth shut!"

"What, you want me to lie to the cops?"

"Bilebog was a complete ass," Tanqer says. "None of us would have tried to kill him, but if he pushed it, shit happens. Shard shouldn't go down for that."

"Look," I say, "there's evidence and things. Fingerprints, DNA. They need more than just my word to press charges. But they'd find out."

"How were they going to find out?"

"What, you lied to them?"

"It's not a lie, I just didn't say everything I saw."

"So a lie of omission," I say.

"It was just a little slam. She wouldn't have done anything."

"I didn't want to say, but what was I going to do?"

"Keep your mouth shut." Tanqer is getting more and more angry. His hands are out of his pockets now, and he's got something in his right hand that he's turning over and over again, one of evolution's fiddlers. But he's waving his arms around as he does it, and he's a little too close to me, like we were down in Mexico or something.

I take a step back. "You can't go killing people, Tanqer."

"Who said I killed anyone?"

"I didn't say anyone killed anyone. I said they argued."

"You fucking asshole."

"What?"

"You sold Shard out."

"Like hell I did."

"Shard sure didn't tell them. I didn't say a thing until that Detective Goddard pushed me on it. Because he already fucking knew. Because you told him." Tanqer stops waving his hands to shake his fist at me.

His fist is this tight knot, but he's got something sticking out between his thumb and forefinger. The little scrap he's been playing with. It's part of the head of a mutant Cocker Spaniel, just a curved slice with the eye and an ear and old, faded paint.

But not everything on the chip is faded. I see bits of brighter brown.

There's a smeary thumbprint in something like old ketchup.

Or dried blood.

I stare at the scrap, then at Tanqer's outraged face, then at the scrap again.

Tanqer sees me look at his hand. His anger collapses, and with this horrified look he stuffs his hand and the broken scrap back into the pocket of his fleece.

His expression tells me everything. "It was you."

Tanqer doesn't say anything.

"Why did you do it?" I say. "He didn't do anything to you."

Tanqer's thick beard starts to quiver.

"Tanqer, man. What happened?"

"I went on up to his room," Tanqer says. "Told him how women belong in computing just as much as we menfolk do. He gets all riled up and takes a poke at me. I had that little angel figurine in my paw, you know, just rolling it over, but when I hit him back..." His shoulders droop. "I hit him back, and it breaks, and the side of his head just caved right in. So I picked up the chunks, threw them over the cliff, and ran back to my room."

I'm shaking my head here. "It's not like you meant it, dude. You didn't go up there to kill him."

"Someone had to tell Bilebog to chill." Tanqer's pocket is shuddering as he's fighting the urge to take his hand out and twiddle something around. "Women can tell a guy he's a jerk, but he won't listen. You gotta have another man tell him. That's all."

"So we tell them that."

He steps back. "I'm not telling nobody nothing!"

"You can't let Shard go to prison for this, man."

"She's not going to prison."

"Why do you think they have her off somewhere?" I snap.

"They don't have evidence."

"They'll find evidence."

"It isn't there." His face is pale and tight.

"Don't you watch TV? Means, motive, and opportunity."

"Nobody saw her there."

"Have you even *looked* at the door locks?" I'm having trouble not shouting. "You could pick them with a Q-tip!"

"They won't find the means, then. The weapon."

"Do you really think you picked everything up? Every little piece?"

"It didn't break that much."

"So they don't find anything." The hotel room felt oppressive, like the stained and varnished pine paneling was closing in on me. The floor-to-ceiling strips that covered the joins suddenly looked like these widely spaced bars. I'm all sweaty again, and sticky, and the humid air feels like I'm breathing underwater. "How many little thingummies in this place could be the weapon? Huh?"

"They'll sort it out." Tanqer's got his eyes squeezed closed, his hands balled in his pockets.

"Maybe they will," I say softly. "But you know what? It's gonna take time. A long time. And Shard's going to have a really shitty time until then. Nobody'll hire her, for one. Wherever she lives? Whatever she's trying to do? It'll be gone. She'll never get it back."

"She's smart. She'll manage."

"She's tough, yeah. But she'll lose her rep. She'll have to start over, from the bottom. And nobody will ever really trust her again."

"She's a girl. She'll be fine."

I just sit there quiet, looking at his face, all tense like he was on the rack, and say, "Tanqer. You stood up for her because it was the right thing to do. And now, listen to yourself. It's okay to let her lose it all, because she's a woman?"

This weird quiver runs up and down Tanqer. Like his brain sort of triggered every muscle he had, but without any real instructions.

I keep my voice quiet, like we were waiting for Santa and I'd just seen soot kicked down the chimney. "You willing to live with that? You really okay with being like Bilebog?"

Tanqer seems petrified.

Then the tension runs out of him. His eyes open and do this rag-doll sag. "Shit."

I nod. "It was an accident." There's something I should do here, I know, but I can't figure out what, so after a couple twitches I reach out and pat his shoulder. "You tried to do the right thing. You were right, man. Someone had to tell him he was an ass."

I hold my hand towards the door.

Tanqer undoes the door.

"Come on," I say. "I'll keep you company."

We catch Detective Fish coming out of the employee bathroom behind the check-in desk, and I tell him that we need to talk to him, but when Tanqer opens his mouth Fish takes his arm, polite-like, and says we should have this conversation in the back, properly. Goddard sends me away after a few, so I go back to my room until the cops call everyone out again and let us clear out.

Everyone but Shard.

They'd already sent her to the station.

I'm hanging out on the hotel's front porch. There's this old wood rocking chair, hickory or something, but it's real old. Someone thought it was a good idea to put a female mannequin in the chair, dressed in an old World War Two sailor's outfit. And they've got this bicycle chained up to a scrub tree right by the porch, supposed to be for visitor use, but the tree's grown through the wire-coated chain and the seat's fallen off so you'd probably get rectal tetanus if you tried to ride the thing. The whole dirt parking lot is surrounded by giant rhododendrons, all dripping wet from the storm, and the air's so wet the humidity and clamminess has seeped through my clothes and made me feel all squishy again. I've been hanging out there a few hours, ever since the wind blew the storm away and left us with this bright blue sky and a cold wet chill over everything. I don't have my laptop. Shard is totally going to kick my ass for bringing up the fight, for getting her dragged in and grilled and who knows what. She can smack me around all she wants, I'll heal, but that laptop is cased in polished brass and nobody but nobody's going to scratch it up, not even if I got them busted. This car pulls up to the front, it's like five years old and beat to crap and back, with all this rust. Nobody with any self-respect would drive a heap like that, so it must be a cop car. Or a bad lawyer.

The back door opens.

Shard gets out. She's got her chin up, and this triumphant look on her face. She slams the door and takes a step, then sees me sitting on the steps and just stops.

I look back at her.

She stares at me.

Someone's got to get this ass-whipping rolling, so I say, "Hi." They say that's how you start.

"Hello," she says.

The air is soaked. It's more humid than anything out here, and my mouth is bone dry.

"So," I say. "Yeah."

She looks at me.

"I told the police about the fight," I say. "I told them how Bilebog was an asshole and how you looked like you wanted to kick his crotch so hard that when he scratched his chin his nose would grow."

Shard just nods. "And?"

"And what?"

"Who else would have told the cops? I didn't. Sounds like Tanqer didn't."

"So…" I steel myself. "I'm sorry."

"For what?"

"For telling them."

She gives me this look like I'm a kindergartener who's just eaten the paste. Again. "What else would you have told them?"

"I didn't want to say anything, but it happened."

"Yeah, it happened. But what were you going to do, lie to the cops?"

I hadn't realized the snakes in my gut hadn't gone away, they'd just tied themselves into this giant knot, but suddenly the knot dissolves and the snakes just kind of slither away, taking all this crazy tension with them. "You're not mad?"

"Way that Fish guy put it, you were the one who got Tanqer to fess up."

"I hadn't thought of it that way."

She rolls her eyes. "Obviously."

She looks at me in silence for a moment, daring me to speak.

"So," I say. "Um, the Internet here is still crap. And I bet you're hungry. Raindrop's kind of shut down today, but you want to go find some food? Someplace with less crappy net?"

Shard gives a little nod. "No, I don't think so."

I'm crushed. Maybe Shard doesn't blame me, but she sure doesn't forgive me.

"I think," she says. "I think I'd rather stay here. We've got to fill in for Tanqer *and* Bilebog now. And if we can't squeeze some extra dosh out of Donner for pulling him out of being shorthanded, not to mention all this murder bullshit, I'll trade in my laptop for a Vic 20."

The weight lifts off of me. "Vic 20s are pretty cool machines, actually."

Shard comes up the steps to the porch. I take a step back and open one of the double doors for her, but she grabs the other door handle and pulls it open. "Yeah, they are. One question for you, though," she says as we walk into the world's most cluttered hotel.

"Sure."

"What the hell is this Raindrop thing supposed to do when it's finished?"

I shrug. "Damned if I know."

Moonlight's Apples

1

Follow a two-lane road to the bottom of Ontario, out in that no-man's land southwest of Toronto, and you'd eventually hit the Privateer Beachfront Bar and Hotel. The walls were solid red brick and nineteenth-century planks, the furniture cheap and flimsy, the beer cold, and the pan-fried perch and fresh cut potatoes the best in the world.

I just hoped it was delicious enough.

I parked my brand-new deluxe full-size Ford pickup on the sandy lot, facing north, and left the windows cracked a couple inches. My ride has all the trimmings—I know what they say, that the big trucks are for guys compensating for something. I didn't have anything to compensate for, lots of ladies will tell you that, thank you. But if people were gonna measure me by my truck, then I was gonna have the biggest, baddest, most loaded set of chrome-plated balls in Canada.

This would have been a great day to bike down here, with the August sunshine and the cool breeze right off Lake Erie and everything green and growing. Maybe the Ducati for a change, or even break out the classic Harley.

But I didn't trust myself to handle a bike. I barely trusted myself to drive the truck.

Walking from the truck to the fenced-in patio, without leaning on anything, almost did me in. My pounding brain rolled loosely inside my head as I trudged across the loose sand, and the hollow sucking pit of my stomach swayed with every step.

If I was smart I would have brought a cane, but I've never leaned on anything or anyone. Not my parents. Not my friends. And sure not some damn chunk of wood.

My pants swung uncomfortably, chafing at my waist. I'd tied them with a length of rope, because my belt couldn't tighten far enough. I'd fought to lose a hundred and thirty pounds in ten years, and in the last twenty-six days I'd dropped another thirty.

More than thirty. I hadn't dared step on a scale in a week.

God-damned raspberries.

And double-God-damned Moonlight on Oak Leaves.

I made it to the split rail fence surrounding the Privateer's brick patio, casually planting my butt against a rail like I was just chilling. My breath rattled in my chest. The lake breeze caught my sweat-soaked Front Line Assembly T-shirt, billowing it out.

A month ago, that shirt had been snug. It was the biggest shirt they had at the January show, though, so I'd bought it.

Chuck's bar had a good crowd today. Beachgoers slathered with sunscreen filled the flimsy plastic chairs, chatting and drinking Molson and just catching the sun. The steady lake breeze, strong enough to windsurf, muffled conversations but not the occasional spike of laughter. A brat at the closest table whined that the fries still had potato skin on them, and the chicken nuggets weren't like McDonalds. Just *barely* far enough away that I couldn't slap his kiddie teeth out. At the back of the sandy parking lot, ten or twelve weekend bikers in clean leathers stood around their gleaming Hondas, posing like they'd know what to do with a fist. I wanted to go over and show them how a real biker handled himself, but barely had the oomph to keep my feet under me. The smells of deep-fried potatoes, fried hamburger, fried *everything* knotted my stomach and made my head pound even harder.

My girl Pammy, one of the year-round waitresses, noticed me there as she waited for the bartender to finish up a tray. She got this puzzled look, the *I know you but I can't place you* gaze. Can't blame her—I've changed a lot in the last month. But the confusion cleared in a second, and she gave me a stunning smile before pulling the radio off her apron and saying something.

Chuck came sweeping out of the glass back door thirty seconds later. He saw me, and surprised worry slapped him to a stop. He recovered in a second, though, and came straight at me, gliding through the milling horde of customers like he was skating for the Olympics. "Dale? My man! Good to see you, it's been a while! Was starting to think you'd gone pro musician or something."

"Not likely," I said. "My music's still mine."

Chuck let his worry show and offered his hand. "How you been? You aren't looking so good."

I took Chuck's hand. Fortunately, my butt was planted nicely against the fence. Otherwise, I might have reflexively clutched him for strength. "Been sick."

"No shit. Anything I can do?"

"I hope so," I said.

"Listen, we're full up, but you hang on, I'll get you a seat at the bar."

"I don't mind waiting," I said, waving at the queue of families and college kids that curved around the front of the Privateer's brick façade.

"You don't get the line." Chuck insists my money's no good here. I had loaned him the cash to buy the place, and wouldn't take a penny interest. But that's what you do for old friends when you strike gold.

"Seriously, though," I said, "I think I need a to-go."

"It's no problem."

It's a real *big problem.* "Really." I lowered my voice. "I've been sick, and things don't always, y'know, go right. But a straight order of your perch just might get me back on my wheels."

Chuck grinned. "Sure. Two minutes."

That meant someone else, a paying customer, would wait for their lunch. I usually wouldn't stand for that, but with the sun stabbing down like a shiv and my mouth dry as dust I didn't argue. Instead, I nodded and closed my eyes against the light.

I'd swallowed every drop of bitter water I could force between my lips, but the heat still baked my shriveled brain inside my skull. The rabid hunger had passed weeks ago, leaving a hollow burning pit in my gut.

I needed food.

Nothing stayed down.

No, that wasn't honest.

I couldn't make myself *swallow* anything.

Wild raspberries. Red and black, supernovas of thick sweet juice on my tongue. Burning their way down my gullet. The memory made me shake like the first time a girl had put my hands on the buttons of her blouse.

Dammit. Don't think about raspberries!

I had given up sugar. I'd surrendered breads, pasta, pancakes, even those incredible thin pancakes at that bed and breakfast down the road from my place, all in the name of dropping weight. Not an easy task, when every gas station and grocery store and hardware shop shoves sugar at you.

You can quit smoking. You can quit heroin, or gambling, but you can't cold-turkey food.

But if I could beat spumoni, I could beat those raspberries.

Raspberries.

How did I have enough water left in me to drool?

And that's not normal sweat. It's like paste. I'll never get the stink out of this shirt.

Chuck returned before I could get my breathing back under control. "Here you go, m'man," he said, slipping a heavy Styrofoam box into my hands. "Double perch, double slaw, hold the fresh cuts."

I sucked in a breath. "That's too much."

"It's leftovers, man."

"Your stuff's no good leftover." The perch is great heated up, just not a patch on fresh.

Chuck held my shoulder a moment too long. "You seen a doctor?"

"Yeah," I lied. "They can't help me."

He studied my face. "You got the number here. You need anything, you call, okay?"

"You got a business to run, dude. I'm fine."

"I got a business, yeah." He waved a hand at the teeming crowd around him. "That means I got thirty people working for me. I can send Pammy up to your place and have twenty-eight left over. Twenty-four. Something like that."

I couldn't help grinning. Chuck had bombed math all through grade school, and I'd reminded him ever since he'd bought the Privateer. "Sixteen."

"Besides," he said, lowering his voice. "You got me that pissed-off shark disguised as a Toronto lawyer last winter, when Pinkerton started playing the zoning board."

"Hey, you're the one who paid him."

"Yeah, but every lawyer *says* he's tough. *Your* dude made old man Pinkerton bawl like a bitch, right in front of the board and God and everybody. I don't care what the fight is, I got your back."

Something trembled behind my eyes. I refused to break down and cry. That would convince Chuck I was dying of cancer, when really I was starving to death. I made myself say, "You hold 'em, I'll hit 'em."

"See you soon, right?"

"Damn straight."

Some subtle noise from the back of the patio caught Chuck's attention. "I gotta get this," he said.

"Later." Chuck had this weird ability to know when a fight was about to start. He took crap from me, but not from customers—especially if it might mean breaking his furniture.

Detouring past the patio bar, I stuffed two twenties into the tip jar and walked with exaggerated caution back to my full-chrome pickup.

I'd parked facing north to leave the driver's leather seat shaded. With the lake breeze pouring through the windows, the cabin barely felt like an oven at all. I set the box of perch on the seat beside me, pulled the belt around my bony hips, and sat for a moment, breathing, trying to get the whirl in my skull to stop.

Starvation made everything feel distant. All I needed to do was eat, and all this would go away.

And I had the best food in the world right here in my lap.

2

My pickup wasn't going to get any cooler, even with all four windows cranked all the way open. My cornbread-fried perch wasn't going to get any crispier.

I picked up the glass Mason jar from the passenger seat floor, half-full of water from the family well. I'd grown up with this water. Everywhere I'd traveled in the world, the water hadn't tasted quite right. This was proper water.

I took a swig.

Metallic. Chalky. So bitter, my tongue rebelled.

I made myself swallow.

Once my tongue could slide smoothly over my palate and the water had cleared some of the fog from my brain, I lifted the cardboard carryout box and flipped it open.

Chuck made the best pan-fried perch in Canada. A little bit of cornmeal, a little bit of lard, a little bit of sizzle, and *pow!* Pure deliciousness, on a plate. Even in winter he had fresh fish, brought in from the coast or the American South. His tender perch came apart with the merest brush of your teeth. The little plastic tubs of off-white tartar sauce, thick with spices and chopped pickles, seemed both unnecessary and vital. The perch delighted without them—and yet, when you dabbed them with sauce, the perch became a totally different delight.

Yeah, fried. But Chuck's perch was the last culinary indulgence I'd left for myself. Plus, that fantastic cabbage-and-carrot slaw with the vinegar dressing was so healthy and satisfying that it pretty much counteracted the fat, right?

He did great fresh cuts too, with just a touch of paprika and garlic. But I hadn't done potatoes in years.

These perch were the reason why I backed his restaurant. Chuck's good at all the other bar food, but once you tasted the perch you'd return for more.

I'd call it addictive. But now I knew what addictive food is.

I sat for a moment, plastic fork in fist, remembering how the filets tasted, their sheer sensual pleasure. I'd sat on the Privateer's back patio countless evenings, mostly in the off season, hanging with Chuck and drinking rich European beer and eating perch, shooting the breeze and watching the sun dip into Lake Erie. My back and shoulders trembled with tension that I tried to will away. Finally, when I couldn't stand it any longer, I stabbed a filet and jammed it between my unwilling lips.

The perch crackled with grease and coarse-grained cornmeal.

The fish? An unnaturally hot lump of dead flesh.

I tongued the filet to the side of my mouth and brought my teeth together, crumbling the perch into separate slivers.

It's not rotting, I told myself. *This fish was swimming this morning!* It was the same perch as always, the same fantastic perch Chuck had made a fortune on for nine years now.

But the stenches of grease and cornmeal and dead fish clotted in my nose.

Swallow, you fuckwit. Swallow!

My jaw shook. My throat clenched.

Beneath my protruding ribs, my shriveled stomach knotted in revulsion.

I doubled over and spat the sodden mouthful into the box lid. My mouth felt like someone had dropped a deuce in it, and I scrabbled for the jar of water, swilling mouthfuls between my teeth and spitting them out the window onto the newly waxed Buick sedan parked next to me so they could dribble down to the sand.

Ever since I'd plucked those berries off the thorny vines, on a path that hadn't been there an hour before and had never appeared there since, nothing else had been good enough.

That left Moonlight on Oak Leaves and her obscene offer.

No.

I was a dead man.

3

I'd left home when my dad tried to push me into farming, like him. I took up motorcycling to tell the world to stop pushing me around, didn't break my neck with all the stupid tricks I tried, and made my name stunt riding. People got a kick out of seeing a fat kid try to kill himself doing flips on a motorcycle. Dale Devon became "Dale Dervish," and the stunts I'd done for fun became a job.

That job was okay. You have to make a living somehow. Might as well get paid, paid lots.

But I'm a friendly guy. Some kids asked me how to get started as a stunt driver. I told them to get out there and try. To do the things they wanted to do, whatever they were. Word got around, and more people asked me how to be successful. When I didn't have time for everyone, people offered to pay me to talk. I liked doing that, too—telling people to stop watching TV and go do things worth doing. I've got a knack for calling people lazy, shiftless bastards and making them like it. What started as a few beers with a couple smart kids exploded into this motivational speaking thing.

The whole point of everything I said was, get off your ass and do something.

And people sat on their asses and talked about how right I was.

The more I raised my speaking fees, trying to tell people to go to hell, the more they offered me.

Last winter, the reality TV bastards called my agent to pitch "Dale Dervish Dares." I'm up for jumping out of airplanes and white-water rafting and swimming with Great White sharks—sounds like a total blast, really—but suddenly it wasn't going to be me doing it.

I'd be a *product*.

I told my agent it was a short jump from there to the action figure.

Mister Agent said, "Funny you should mention that…"

I canceled every appearance, liquidated my business, and came home.

Rode a little. Played guitar a lot. Hung with Chuck and other old friends who'd never left.

And last month, I found the raspberries.

4

After my perch disaster, I went straight home. I dry-swallowed a tasteless multivitamin gel cap, forced down more bitter water, grabbed my guitar and headed into the woods.

My folks left me fifty acres of smooth Ontario farmland, plus another hundred irregular acres of primordial old growth forest lining plunging glacial ravines and exposed cliff faces. I rented out the farmland, slept in the nineteenth-century house, and spent a lot of time in the woods.

Walking slowly, my exhausted brain drifting, I didn't realize where I was going until I stood at the lip of the gully. I'd found the raspberries down there.

Not exactly down there—the path didn't exist anymore.

I'd looked.

Many times.

Bringing the guitar back to the gully felt right, though. I didn't have the strength to come up with a justification. Instead, I worked my painful way down the steep gully walls, clutching whip-thin trees and planting my feet against tumbled branches for safety. The battered guitar case moved with me, a couple feet at a time, until I set the scarred faux leather case on a low slab of glacial rock and undid the latches.

The guitar, an inexpensive acoustic Yamaha, was special. Not because I inherited it, although I had. It hadn't belonged to anyone famous. It didn't have a name. The case was way too big, and I'd filled in the excess spaces with outworn flannel shirts.

It was special because I loved playing it. I wasn't any good, but that didn't matter. Every time I played, five or six or seven days a week, I improved. I'd never played for anyone except my parents, and that only because Mom taught me.

I didn't play guitar to beat anyone. I plucked for myself, and merely touching the strings was winning. My music didn't belong to anyone else. Nobody was ever going to pay me to get on stage, or do guitar stunts, or do motivational guitaring. I loved playing well enough to accept playing badly.

In a world that wants to buy everything of mine, my music was never for sale.

The thick old trees overhead filtered the sunlight into dapples. A breeze rustled the branches, but couldn't penetrate down into the gully. A thin trickle of water coursed down the point of the gully, forming the tiny inches of the stream that started here. I'd followed the stream once, as a kid. It wove through the woods, joined with other streams, and finally met up with Renfrow Creek, a tributary of the Thames.

The massive flow of water that divided London, Ontario started right here, in a clay gully lined with scrub bushes and layered years of decaying leaves, untouched by any feet except mine for decades. In a forest full of special places, this piece of land had always felt still and sacred.

Sitting cross-legged on a clammy shallow rock, my feet above the water, my right hand formed A major. My left thumb caressed the gleaming strings. Scarred knuckles flexed.

The mistuned chord was the loudest sound in the gully.

Hollowness filled my skull. My muscles begged for sustenance. But I adjusted the keys until my baby sounded right and launched into a Valdambrini piece, trying to sink everything I had left into the music.

Maybe it was the echoing clarity starvation brought into my brain, but the song seemed more clear to me than ever. My soul didn't have any thoughts left to shove between me and the old-fashioned gut strings. Complex plucked chords shivered up the gully walls and out into the maple boughs, for the audience of squirrels and hawks.

At the end, I rearranged my fingers to begin the next piece when someone said, "Very nice, Dale," in a voice as smooth as a razor through silk.

I jerked in surprise.

Moonlight on Oak Leaves was a pale-skinned woman. Not pale as in Caucasian, but so pale that she looked almost like chilled alabaster. Her eyes were hot black above a gentle nose and a tiny mouth the color of ripe—*raspberries*, dammit. She wore draping silk in blood scarlet and the green of a jack pine. The cloth brushed the ground, somehow not tearing in the brambles and not collecting dirt.

The first time I'd seen her, by the raspberry bush, the unearthly brush of her fingers on my forearm had sent me bolting back to the gully.

My enervated back hurt, but I made myself stand. I turned my back on her to nestle the guitar safely in its case.

She was still there when I turned around.

Behind her, I saw the missing path.

Part of the gully wall had vanished, forming a new canyon with a well-trod foot path weaving between chunks of grey-brown clay. The first time I'd seen that path, following it forty feet had taken me into a part of the forest I'd never seen.

A part of the forest that wasn't *anywhere* near the forest.

My gut clenched again, this time with hunger. Something in me screamed that if I ran up that path, I'd find tomato bushes with thick, heavy fruit, gleaming, ripe and ready to be devoured. Fruit trees, pregnant with cherries and pears and pomegranates, never mind the season.

I made myself face Moonlight on Oak Leaves. "What are you doing here?"

She spread her hands. "You opened the path, my handsome manling. You put forth your music and called me."

I reached back to yank shut the lid on the guitar case. "My mistake. I'll remember not to do that."

"There's no need to rush away," she said in lightly affronted tone. "I see that your world treats you harshly. Here, there is no threat."

I shook my head. "The only threat is you."

"Have I threatened you?"

"I've done some reading. You're an elf. Fairy. Something like that."

Her voice grew thicker. "I am *from* Faerie. Not *a*. From."

"Whatever." I waved that away. "The old stories say that if you eat fairy food, you can never go home."

She laughed. "Foolish mortal tales."

"No, we can go home again. We just can't live here."

"And yet, you came. You ate."

"Yeah," I said heavily. "I played here. I went to this—this weird trail. I tasted those raspberries."

"You did not *taste*," she laughed. "You *devoured*."

"All right, fine! I ate one, and that was it." These woods were full of wild berries, nuts, mushrooms if you knew where to look and what to look for. I'd sampled their wealth for twenty years, only plucking a few here and there. But at that first tangle of raspberry vines, with those huge luscious fruit, one taste and I'd plunged my hands among the thorns like a starving man, grabbing everything I could and shoving it into my mouth, bits of leaves and stems and all, heedless of the bloody scratches on my hands.

She nodded. "You ate. You bled into our soil." Her voice became firm. "You are inexorably bound to us. That's why I've come, to ask again."

"You want me to give up everything and be your pet musician," I spat.

"Not at all, sweetling! We would give you wealth and fame. Our lands have not had a mortal musician in these many years. You would be *cherished*."

Over the last few weeks my hunger had faded to a distant ache, like a whole-body toothache. Now it charged back, a crushing fist of desire clenching my guts. I tried to remain upright, but a sudden swirl of weakness made me grab a rock for support. My blood hammered in my neck and my knees shook.

"It hurts to see you so," Moonlight on Oak Leaves said. "Please. Accept my offer. Do not torment yourself so, I beseech you! Come to us. Let me help you. All you have to do is play for us. Play that music that stirs your heart."

I made myself breathe deeply, forcing my diaphragm to stretch for each lung-ful of air. My head cleared enough for me to turn my back to the rock, leaning my buttocks and back against the cool stone. "I'm not giving everything up," I said.

"Of course not," she said. "Mortals need their own kind. You could come visit your little friends, and even sleep in your nest if you could bear it."

Everything hurt. Starved muscle and weakened tendons screamed for food.

But I'd already seen how this worked. Sleep one night in a Fairyland bed, and I wouldn't be able to tolerate my top-of-the-line memory foam mattress. Wear one Faerie shirt, and my own clothes would become unbearably coarse.

Moonlight on Oak Leaves said she wanted the one thing I'd never given any-one. Instead, they'd get everything I was.

I took one last deep breath and said, "When I'd eaten all the berries, you were there."

She stood inhumanly still.

"I might have just wandered in, but you knew I was there. You waited," I pant-ed. "Waited until I was hooked. So you could make your damned offer."

"You had to know we spoke the truth. Anyone can promise delights beyond mortal ken. I proved the truth of my bargain before even offering."

"You proved you would screw me over," I said. "No deal."

She shook her head sadly. "You are going to your death. I hope you will change your mind while you still breathe."

I shook my head.

"Your pain tears at me," Moonlight on Oak Leaves said.

"Then let me go."

"I cannot, manling." Sorrow suffused her pale face. "You chose to eat of Faerie. You choose to offer your blood to our land. I cannot send back what you freely gave. Still… next to your instrument, you will find something for you."

The rock's chill had begun to sink into my back, giving me a shiver despite the summer's mugginess. "I don't want anything from you but freedom."

"It is not a gift," she said. "We cannot offer gifts. It's a payment, for your music today."

I made myself straighten and glanced over my shoulder.

Next to the closed guitar case sat an apple the size of a grapefruit. Its red skin shone with a richness that I'd only seen on rubies, and the faint green patch on one side did nothing to sap its perfection. The thick wooden stem looked almost muscular—it would have to be strong to hold such a fruit to its tree.

Without even touching it I knew how it would feel. Cracking sharply between my teeth. The fresh juice slicking my mouth and lips. Fingers sticking together as I nibbled it down to the core. Spitting the seeds. My memory brought up the best of every apple I'd ever tasted and forged a perfect apple for my imagination.

Worse, I could smell it. Its aroma suddenly filled the gully, all crisp and sweet, crawling up my nose and down my throat to hook my stomach.

I think I whimpered.

Moonlight on Oak Leaves said, "Three times you can open the path with your music. Three times may you refuse. Refuse me once more and you shall surely, ignominiously, starve. And my sweet, you deserve so much better." Her voice became husky. "And so much better I *will* give to you."

I whirled back to face her, but she'd disappeared.

The path was gone.

Her words had broken the apple's spell, however.

With shaking fingers I fumbled open the guitar case and extracted scraps of flannel padding until I had an apple-sized gap near where the neck met the body. Using a worn flannel shirt as a glove, I gingerly lifted the apple into its cradle and clipped the lid shut.

I wanted that apple. I ached to eat it.

But if I ate it, I'd be even more hooked than I was now.

5

The family home dated from the 19th century, but that didn't mean we had kerosene lamps and a wood stove. I'd grown up with Formica counters and a mostly reliable fridge and pipes that gurgled and thrashed all winter long. When I'd made my first fortune stunt biking, I'd sent Mom a wad to redo the kitchen. Now I had rich blue granite countertops with scattered sparkling crystal, dark oak cabinets with fancy glass knobs everywhere, a refrigerator big enough to hide a body and a garbage disposal that could eat one. The setting sun cast sharply angled rays through lace curtains fluttered by the shifting evening breeze. The lath-and-plaster walls were painted a bright glossy white that resisted stains, repelling even the persistent grease above the huge gas range where I had once perpetrated my own spattery cooking.

I set the guitar case on my great-grandfather's table and used oven mitts to extract the apple and set it on the counter. A sweet, cidery aroma infiltrated the room, making me remember cool autumns and childhood hay rides and rich homemade cocoa.

This was August. The only place cool around here was the mold-plagued basement beneath the kitchen floor.

Climbing up out of the gully had left me exhausted. I'd needed to sit on a stump and pant for air, trying to clear my head. A few hundred yards at a time, stopping for rest when my enervated balance turned my steps into weaving spirals, I'd struggled back home. Now I poured myself a glass of cold tap water and sat in an antique ladderback chair, making myself choke down bitter, metallic sips.

The water wasn't really bitter. Or metallic. I'd grown up drinking from this well. I'd had it tested last year, and while it was a little rusty there wasn't nearly enough to give it this kind of taste. Those fey raspberries had yanked my standards so high nothing could touch them.

Except the apple, lurking on the counter.

Moonlight on Oak Leaves didn't look like a serpent.

My gut clamored at me to grab the apple and chomp into it. Something told me that this lone fruit had everything that my body craved. The first bite would ease the pain in my burning throat and sinuses. The second would soothe its way down my throat. The third would unclamp my stomach, spreading healing balm across shrunken tissues.

I hadn't swallowed anything but water in twenty-six days. This one massive apple was probably more than my stomach could hold.

But I'd probably suck it down to the core, ripping every bit of life out of it.

And it would get me more hooked.

I knew more than one guy on the bike circuit who'd gotten hooked on heroin, or weed, or crack, or pills. The smartest one of those, old Jerry Rabb, told me how the first hit was great, but it was the second hit that did him in. Once was an experiment, or trying to fit in, or a whim. When you decided to go back for your second hit, though—that was when you sold your soul to the drug. You knew what it meant, where it was headed, and still, you set your feet on that path and walked to Hell.

I was not going to go that way.

Once was ignorance.

Twice would be a decision.

Ontario summers are hot and muggy, though. If I just left the apple on the counter, it would go bad.

I sipped the water, staring at the apple. All the reading I'd done on the Internet said that faeries didn't exist. Some people claimed to have seen them, like they'd seen Bigfoot or Nessie or healthy lasagna. Their stories didn't match up, though, and only a few coincidental bits seemed to fit Moonlight on Oak Leaves.

I had to think. Somehow.

On the blue sparkling granite counter, the apple gleamed. A huff of muggy breeze brought me the smell of juice, and I suddenly had to swallow my own saliva.

I raised the glass to my lips and froze.

I'd faced this problem before.

Drinking barrels of cola a day had rotted my teeth, so I'd switched away from it—first to iced tea, and then to water.

As a beverage, water kind of sucks.

So I'd added a slice of lemon to give it just a little flavor.

My hands shook. I carefully set the glass down on the table.

Could it work?

My heart hammered in my chest like I'd blown a tire coming down off a high jump, and fresh sweat glued my T-shirt to my armpits and back. The exhausted vertigo that constantly threatened to overwhelm me seemed to poise itself for attack as I climbed to my feet and walked deliberately to the counter.

The bamboo cutting board was right in the cupboard where I had left it. I set it next to the apple.

As thoughtfully as a surgeon preparing for an appendectomy, I refilled my glass of water and placed it a couple feet from the cutting board.

My left hand went back into the oven mitt. I gingerly held the apple to the board.

Mom had left behind three knife blocks. I grabbed one of the ultra-sharp steel knives.

Some people put half a lemon in their water, but I'd learned that a shaved slice worked just as well.

I only needed a small cut.

I turned the apple, looking for a place I could easily cut a sliver free.

On the shoulder. Near the stem.

I gripped the apple through the heavy quilted glove and balanced the knife above the fruit.

Sweat trickled into my eyes.

Apple aroma filled my nose.

My stomach clenched.

I held my breath and—*slashed*.

The knife went through the fruit like the apple wasn't even there. A slice of apple no larger than a quarter slipped free of the apple and glided down to the cutting board.

The apple's smell intensified, driving hooks into my nose. I didn't have time to spare for the sudden trail of drool trickling from one side of my mouth. The warm, white, exposed flesh enticed me in a way nothing had since I was a child, making my heartbeat unsteady and my knees uncertain.

Then the exposed apple flesh faded. White became brown in the space of a breath, then collapsed into bubbling black putrescence.

The apple, too.

The rot began sizzling along the apple, creeping along the ruby red skin with a stench like last week's roadkill deer.

My gut screamed to bite the apple, to devour what I could before that decay spread too far and I lost the whole thing. I couldn't do that. I *wouldn't* do that. I wouldn't eat it all, engulf it like a desperate animal.

Why? What had I done that—

The knife.

Steel.

All the stories said fairies didn't like steel.

Dropping the steel knife, I reached for the third block to pull out one of the ceramic blades. Without any forethought, I aimed the knife a fraction of an inch beyond the edge of the growing rot and plunged the edge into the gleaming apple.

With a couple more hurried, desperate slashes, I amputated the rot before losing more than an eighth or so of the apple to the bubbling putrescence.

It wasn't a perfect apple any more. Thick yellow-brown juice ran along the knife's ceramic edge and trickled down to the cutting board. Lumps of deliquescing, steel-poisoned apple made putrid lumps on the counter, and gooey black tar marred the rejected metal blade. I had to stand for a moment with my hands pressed to the counter, trying to catch my breath and calm my pulse.

I'd lost a chunk of fruit. But I had more than enough to try.

With the ceramic blade I sliced a sliver of rich white apple, backed with a strip of red skin. The fantastic smell overwhelmed the rot, once again inciting protests in my gut.

I *wanted* that apple.

Instead, I held the sliver on the knife blade, swung it to the glass, and plunged everything into the water. For good measure I swirled the knife around, trying to get the juice off the blade. Pulling the knife from the water, I wiped it on the edge of the glass to keep every drop of precious apple within.

No matter how desperate I got, I insisted, I would not lick the knife blade.

With shaking hands, I raised the glass to my lips.

The water still had that bitter metallic flavor, but it carried something else.

Just a hint of something else.

But a hint was enough.

I drained the glass in eight long swallows, carefully leaving the apple sliver stuck to the side.

Soothing, cool water sank into my guts, and stayed there. A calming sensation spread from my stomach, creeping out into my limbs. The dehydrated daze circling my head receded for the first time in weeks.

Refilling the glass, I glared at the apple.

Shaved apple, sliced apple, apple juice—how thin could I spread this?

I'd beaten sugar.

I'd beat this, too.

Too much food too quickly would rip me apart. Some homemade applesauce for my neglected, crippled stomach. With four regular apples. A good hit of fresh-ground cinnamon. And one tiny sliver of very special apple.

As I cooked, I planned.

6

Two days later I parked a red wooden wagon up at the edge of the gully and clambered down, lugging my guitar after me. I still ached, and my every movement made weakened muscles burn, but my soul felt clearer than it had in weeks.

The sky had a few clouds today, promising scattered rain, but at the bottom of the gully the thick branches and leaves fifty or a hundred feet overhead muted even the August glare into a diffuse glow. Tan and yellow and gray rocks, the exposed bones of the world ripped bare by glaciers ten thousand years ago, showed through brown clay flesh. The rivulet trickled quietly, off towards the city, the sea, the Earth.

My damn Earth. Not some fairy fake.

I uncased my guitar and settled onto a comfortable rock to play. While I prefer the baroque period, I'd looked up a few chords and licks before leaving the house. I had no idea if Survivor's *Eye of the Tiger* would reopen the path to Fairyland but again, it felt like the right piece for the moment. The rhythmic chords shimmered up the gully walls and into the centuries of trees overhead.

Where the path had appeared stubbornly remained gully wall. I glanced at my hands to check a particularly complex chord, though, and when I looked back the path had appeared.

Moonlight on Oak Leaves strode down the path towards me, as unearthly and beautiful and inhuman as the last two times I'd seen her. Today she wore glimmering white, not silk but some other expensive-looking fabric that billowed around her without the faintest breeze to stir it. It seemed an extension of her gleaming skin, flesh and fabric impossibly flowing together.

I nodded at her and kept playing.

By the time that last chord followed the rippling stream out of sight, Moonlight on Oak Leaves stood on the gully floor, smiling at me.

"Hey," I said.

She smiled. "Today finds you in a finer fettle, young mortal. I'm glad you've availed yourself of your treat."

"It wasn't a treat," I said. "It was payment. You told me so yourself."

"Indeed it was." Her eyes glittered like alexandrite. "I gather you have contemplated my offer."

"Indeed I have," I drawled, rising to my feet. My back ached and my quads burned, but less than they had last time I'd come down here. I nestled my guitar safely back in its makeshift nest, clipped the case shut, and turned to her. "Growing up, I always thought this place was magical. Down here, this little gully... you could feel it."

I tried to sound confident, despite the sudden twist in my heart.

I'd thought this through.

I'd made a decision.

The logic made sense, but logic can be a way to go wrong quickly.

Had I seen only what I wanted to see? Had I rejected an important rumor amidst all the Internet's babble?

It wasn't too late to back out now.

But I wasn't going to be her pet.

"I loved this place," I said.

"Places are worth loving," she said. "Places can never betray you." One hand turned palm-up towards me, as smoothly as fine-geared clockwork.

"What kind of places do you love?"

"You might have the opportunity to find out."

"You're not going to add that to your offer?"

"Why?" Her smiling red lips, a glimpse of brilliant white teeth between them, made my heart beat even more quickly. "You have not chosen to starve to death."

"You're right," I said. "But you seem—*polite*. So you'll bear with me a moment while I explain a couple things."

"What makes you think I won't simply… turn away?" She looked back at the path. "It is graceless, trying to prolong the moments until you announce what we both know you shall choose, what you must choose."

"Must?"

"You do not play your lute like a man who has chosen his own death."

"Fair enough. I've made a choice." I put a foot on a low rock and leaned forward. "I made a fully informed choice. And you know what I learned?"

"That mortal life is precious," she said. "And you treasure yours."

"Oh, I knew that! I knew that the first time I jumped a motorcycle over a ditch, didn't break my neck, and didn't get caught." I smiled. "I learned that not many other people have wound up where I am now. Not since Internet message boards, at least."

Puzzlement creased her brow.

"It's where we can learn things."

"I have seen your mortal libraries," she said, voice high with condescension. "Your *newspapers*. And encyclopaedia. So many pretty facts, all dressed up in their finery and paraded like wisdom."

"Newspapers." I snorted. "You don't know even know what the Internet is, though." I felt my eyes harden into a glare. "Because iron—and steel—really is poison to you."

"Politeness has boundaries," she snarled through clenched teeth. The gully suddenly seemed darker, as if the invisible sun beyond the boughs had passed behind a cloud. "If you think mortal iron can harm me, I will disabuse you of that upon your request. But do not think that I shall return again."

"I wouldn't dream of harming a lady," I said. "Not even a creepy fairy lady like you."

The faint breeze picked up a sudden chill note.

I ignored her sudden snarl. "See, if you had much contact with the outside world, with the real world, you'd have some awareness of how we talk today. I can talk to almost everyone in the world. Everyone who speaks English, at least. And I can read what they say. And if this sort of thing was common—if people kept getting sucked in by your schemes, by your bait—then someone, somewhere would have said something about it. You sure aren't going to even *touch* a tablet. So I'm it."

"I already told you," she said. "We have not had a mortal musician in many, many a year."

"But you would if you could. You haven't—so you *can't*."

I waited a beat, but she said nothing.

"Places like this." I raised my hands at the trees, the glacier-carved rock, the flecks of distant blue sky beyond the bounty of leaves. "These are rare today. And that path behind you is well-used."

"This is a lovely place," said Moonlight on Oak Leaves.

"It is. But I'm not your musician."

I dropped my voice, making it flat and hard.

"I'm your *landlord*."

Moonlight on Oak Leaves' mouth opened a touch. She paused half a heartbeat. "Ridiculous."

"A ridiculous notion indeed," I said, emulating her voice. "I've read that you can't lie, so maybe it really is ridiculous to you. Maybe it's ridiculous that you've been brought this low. But that's where we are. You said I could say no three times? Well, you get to say no once, and then we're done."

"You have nothing to offer."

I held out my hands. "Do you know what a motorcycle is? It's iron, and steel, and grease. I'm a master biker. And where we're standing would be a great training ground. Dale Dervish's Driving School."

Shock flashed across her face, almost too fast to see.

"We'll have to cut down the trees, of course." I waved my hand to illustrate. "This gully, I'll need to pave with asphalt. You don't know asphalt? It's like tar and concrete. There won't be anything left alive for half a mile. And I have a whole bunch of surveyor stakes in a cart up on top of the hill. I'm ready to start today."

"Do not ask me to believe that you would choose to starve yourself!"

"I have forty pounds of pork roast simmering in a very special apple sauce. Eight good old-fashioned stoneware slow cookers, lined up on the counter. I kicked fucking *sugar*. I can taper myself off of your crap."

Moonlight on Oak Leaves turned as still as a statue. "You cannot. It is not possible."

"What I do know," I said, "is that I would rather die trying to break free than give in to you. My music, my life—it's *mine*. And before you get any ideas, my buddy Chuck is my executor. If I die, he'll have this place filled with concrete in a week and the trees sold off in a month. He's got the GPS coordinates—a map, that is, and everything."

For the first time I'd seen, uncertainty flickered on her face. She licked her lips. "What is your offer?"

"Food's part of it," I said. "But that's asking the wrong question. What can *you* offer *me*?"

I'd started with motorcycles to push back against my dad. I'd started with the speaking bit to yell at people. But here, finally, was someone worth fighting.

I didn't know how many poor bastards they'd sucked in. But with a bit of work and some home canning, maybe some freeze-drying, I would be the last.

I'd make sure of that.

I did know that I was going to call them fairies.

And they were going to like it.

Easing Final Fears

Clouds of sunrise-stained smoke billowed over the field of trampled mud and laced the air with the flat tang of explosives and the bitterness of soiled blood. The haze seemed to drift under its own power. There had to be a breeze, but the clumsy synthetic senses in this ridiculous land-bound body insisted the air was still.

A rifle ball whistled past my ear.

Sudden terror made me squeeze even further down, but my bare feet slipped in the greasy mud and I plunged to my knees, spattering filth over my stolen primitive coveralls. My hands splashed into the muck a beat later, a talon-span from a broken mud-covered rock.

I have a natural aversion to mud. Preening it out of feathers takes forever.

But these deranged humans thickened mud with their own blood, their own *meat*. I wouldn't be here long enough to need to clean this freakish smooth body, but the unavoidable thought of having to preen this filth twisted my unnatural bowels.

Humans felt nausea? That'd be the most minor contribution to knowledge in the Volt's history.

A cannonball burst somewhere not too far off, the blast rupturing the air and drowning out mammalian cries and the clang of metal. My body's heart beat so quickly it almost buzzed.

My every instinct screeched to trigger retrieval.

Abandon this body. Surrender any hope of verifying my theories.

But the Volt needed me here.

Discovering humanity had overturned all Volt scholarship. If one predator species could somehow become sapient, defying all knowledge and reason, another could. Most of the Volt claimed that a predator species couldn't survive long enough to develop space flight, but they were the same voices who had insisted that a predator couldn't evolve sapience.

The next predator might not be so primitive.

If the Volt met a space-faring predator, we had to understand them.

My lungs rejected the toxic air, shuddering and convulsing, the hacking driving my forehead perilously close to the mud.

The rifle balls were only slightly more deadly than the smoke they shed.

A puff of breeze brought a window of cleaner air, letting me wheeze enough to clear my chest even as it brought another gutful of corpse-stink. I desperately wished I'd been able to skip respiration, but humans reacted badly if a person's body didn't breathe.

When an intelligence that's somehow evolved from an opportunistic predator reacts badly, the best place to be is "on a different planet."

I'd carefully assembled this shell to mimic human behavior. He breathed. His skin greased itself with exertion. I'd even restricted myself to narrow human optics and hearing. The last researcher to attempt a mental capture had a human-looking shell, but he'd broadened his vision up to normal spectrum. Telemetry showed that researcher noticing something a human couldn't see. The humans had noticed him noticing.

They'd reacted badly.

The one concession I'd made to my own senses was smell. Humans knew that some of their kind had better olfactory senses than others, and that grotesque skull had lots of space, so I'd included a full chemical array.

I deeply regretted that choice.

Even if I got away from the reeks of gunpowder and cannons and dying men, my body stank with that complex slime of wastes and salts they called *sweat*.

Staying on my knees, hands in the mud, I tried to clear my lungs while the good air lasted. I focused my gaze on the muddy rock next to me, rather than peer through the smoke into the frenzy.

I'd made a horrific mistake.

I'd designed the most indestructible shell I could, given the limitations of human genetics and their over-padded bodies. My thoughts were constantly distributed between this body and my own in the research pod in orbit. If this body was murdered, my mind would retreat to my natural body.

I'd recall my success. My failure. The mind-scarring horror of a cannon-load of chain shredding this body. Such memories had dragged other Volt to hideous, lingering true deaths.

My body might be designed to endure a predator frenzy—but my mind wasn't.

No civilized mind could be.

Within this smoke, throughout the surrounding countryside, humans fought and died for the right to beat and murder other humans.

Maybe I should retreat.

A retreat would cost me everything, but I would be alive.

Most Volt had given up on understanding humans. They didn't threaten us, so we could let them destroy themselves. If they somehow learned how to set talon on another world, we could seed their planet with tailored oophagous bacteria and let them compassionately die off.

Some of us, mostly those who thought that herd animals should be killed as they began to suffer from age, thought we should end them now. Every human mind we'd captured displayed nothing but predator fear and rage.

The Volt supported this expedition simply to silence my squawks. I kept insisting that fear and rage would drive a creature to make a weapon—but not to *learn* how to forge. Fear led to dropping rocks, not to melting them. Our understanding of the predator mind was shallow, despite the dozens of mental captures my predecessors had taken.

Centuries of mental captures across dozens of intelligent species had shown us that when an individual knowingly faced death, when they had a breath to contemplate their own imminent extinction, its mind focused on its greatest truths. If I could capture a human mind at the moment of death, I could show that their spirits had something other than mere terror and hunger.

I could learn what drove them.

Somewhere out in infinite space, a second predator would achieve sapience. The Volt needed to understand such minds.

A few more breaths, and my lungs were clear.

That shape in the mud—it wasn't a rock. It was a human foot, knocked off a body by one of their nightmare killing tools. An awful waste.

How could anyone even hope for proper intelligence to evolve here?

Through the smoke, off to my left, a human screeched.

My body echoed my annoyance by twisting up one side of its mouth and tightening its teeth together. Interesting.

The scream kept going.

I took a deep breath of clear air while I could get it, rose to a crouch, and staggered over the erratic ground towards the shriek.

A hill coalesced from the haze, as tall as a couple of humans, covered with grazed-short grass. An oak tree perched at its summit, the white flesh of its fresh-split trunk steaming and scorched, the bobbling of the two halves only now settling. A young human had fallen near the tree. He held one of those weirdly flexible hands over the opposite shoulder, as if his feeble digits could stop the blood flowing from the shredded meat that had once been him.

The literature all agreed that wounded humans were extra dangerous. But this was the first I'd seen that might fit my needs.

My shell was supposed to insulate my mind from the shell's instincts. Somehow, though, the rapid pulse and quicker breathing energized my already healthy fear.

I could signal for retrieval now. I'd made my attempt. I'd visited the Predator Planet. I'd stood among humans. I'd even seen one.

But if I did that, the paradox of predatory intelligence would remain.

The Volt needed that paradox's wings broken. Some other researcher would have to try again. Or the Volt would ignore the risk of sapient predators until it was too late.

Bending at the waist to keep myself as short as possible, I made myself totter through the mud and up onto the slope of grass where the maimed human lay.

His gaze caught me, and he dulled the screams to quick panting. Pack behavior—*I'm hurt, find me before the others do!*

I took another step closer, and my shell's digestive bladder cramped. Mild acids surged up the food channel. The uniquely awful sensation made me lurch, requiring me to stop and put my hands on my knees until the spasm passed.

In my tests, that bladder hadn't cramped except when starved.

My tests had not been strenuous enough.

The human watched me with a killer's concentration. His breath hadn't slowed, but he'd stilled his muscles. All he needed was foliage to conceal himself and he'd be lurking in ambush.

The cramp didn't really pass, but it eased enough that I could stagger forward, out of the squelching mud and onto a slightly dryer slope of badly trampled greenery. My shell quivered with its own enzymes by the time I reached the man, sinking to my knees on his wounded side.

I had practiced their pack protocol many times, but confronted with an actual bleeding, dying human my instincts screamed for me to flee. Live predators were to be avoided, intelligent or not. I made the mouth open and breathed the sounds that made this pack's words. "I am John."

"Bill," the man hissed between clenched teeth.

My shell's respiration accelerated, making the heart beat even more quickly. The enzymatic reaction amplified my natural instinct to flee. Instead I raised my empty hands, the standard method this pack used to indicate a not-hunting state. "Let me see your wound."

The human stared at me for a breath, eyes so wide open that without the anchoring muscles they would pop free, then dropped his head back into the damp grass. With obvious reluctance, he dragged his hand from the wound.

Beneath the blood it looked like a rifle ball injury, straight from our catalog but smaller. Humans had modified their weapons for this frenzy. I shouldn't have been surprised. They did the same at every frenzy, making them more and more lethal. A hopeful trend—these monstrosities would almost certainly destroy themselves before endangering us.

Moving very slowly so as not to startle the human, I laid a hand on his blue uniform shirt, right next to the wound. My sensors triggered automatically.

The rifle ball had punched through muscle and skin to lodge between his bones, releasing blood before cauterizing the injury. He wouldn't bleed to death. The ball hadn't broken any bones. While his glands were already triggering responses to the foreign bacteria dragged with the ball, his body lacked the antibodies or strength to prevent their breeding.

I took my hand off his chest.

The human raised his head again. "How's it look?"

"Not useful." I said.

His face seemed to shrink. The eyebrows pointed inward and his lips tightened. Strange.

I rose back into that uncomfortable standing crouch, making my shell's spinal muscles ache. "You will not die of your injury."

He dropped his head. "Thank you, Almighty."

"You will die of infection resulting from the injury."

The human's head twitched back up and he said a few of this pack's semantically null words.

"You will not die soon enough for me," I said. As protocol demanded, I said, "Goodbye and God bless you" before turning away.

More semantically null words, delivered quickly and with force.

The wind had shifted in those few minutes, clearing some of the gunpowder clouds. From this little hillock I could see the humans massacring each other, maybe two minutes' run distant. The two packs had dissolved into one giant monstrous clash of flashing metal and skin, with shouts and screams from the humans and their slaved beasts alike.

My digestion pouch cramped at the sight.

At least the cannon had fallen silent, those horrific things useless against such a churn.

To either side of the massacre smaller packs ran towards me, as if to evade the main slaughter. I suspected they were "flanking," not fleeing the nightmare.

Or: the existing frenzy lacked space for them, so they intended to expand it.

The muddy coveralls marked me as being not of either pack. I'd thought they would protect me. Studying the churning, screaming horde, I couldn't help wondering: were they attacking the other side? Or were they merely killing anything not of their pack? I needed to get closer. Find a human dying of his injuries. Capture his mind right before it dissolved. We'd finally gain insight into what made human intelligence so destructive, so eager for murder.

My wholesome instincts revolted at this overwhelming frenzy, demanding I quit. Return home. I'd experienced slaughter telemetry sent by earlier researchers, but the records couldn't appall me as horrifically as my visceral presence in this churning, stinking field of wasted death.

The growing wind carried the stink of the struggle away from me, bringing in its place the fresh scent of trees. Somehow, that smell made the shell's innards tighten even more painfully.

I'd seen predators fight before. But never thousands of them at once.

Something crashed into one of my legs.

I plunged forward, face hitting the grass, my body's cartilaginous beak flashing pain signals straight up through my skull. The smallest finger of the dominant hand shrieked with shocking pain—a snapped bone?

Researchers had failed because of not including pain responses in their shells. With my shell rolling down the slight hill and my whole hand paralyzed from one small broken digit, I wished I'd followed their example. Human pain is far sharper than it needs to be—it doesn't merely warn, it incapacitates.

What good is a reflex that signals danger by paralyzing?

I flopped over twice before coming to a stop on my back in the mud at the bottom of the hill.

A few strides above me, the injured human I'd spoken with struggled to his feet.

My horror grew. I'd been so stunned by waste and ruin that I'd forgotten the most important rule of human infiltration:

Never turn your back.

The injured one was lurching down at me.

One arm hung limp from his maimed shoulder. His feet had trouble on the hillside, and the pink in his face had faded to white with the loss of the blood soaking his shirt. Weirdly flat predator teeth exposed, he shouted more of those meaningless words that promised violence.

The throb in my hand seemed to swell but grow more diffuse. I wrenched it free from the mud with only a small gasp. I could move, if I had to.

The human used his working arm to pull a dull black rectangular metal shaft from a pouch on his belt. No, not a shaft—a cutter. Humans didn't have proper beaks, so they had to make their own.

A *knife*. That was the word.

This knife was as long as his hand, made of a dark metal except for the gleaming sharp edge.

I drew my knees up and kicked, trying to push myself away.

My bare feet slipped through cold, nasty mud.

The only thing you can do with a predator is escape.

Lying on my back in the slippery mud, I could only thrash.

This shell I'd lavished such care on? Memories of dying in it would cripple or kill me.

All the details I'd gotten right? Useless.

Predators kill. It's what they do.

Somehow, I'd alarmed this one.

I hoped my telemetry would keep transmitting until my end.

The human's foot slipped. With a pained cry he toppled, tumbling down the hill.

I pushed against the ground again. One heel found a rock or a root, letting me scoot a few vital inches.

The human bounced off the grass, onto my legs, and right up onto my gut.

The impact deflated me, pushing the air out with a whole different kind of pain. Not quite paralyzing. I'd thought my own stink was appalling, but this human had the same stench several times over. I had sweated since sunrise; he had stewed in his own grease for days.

But he'd barely rocked to a stop when he screamed again. He tried to grab at his maimed shoulder with the other hand, but he wasn't willing to release the knife or shift his weight off me.

My heart hammered unpleasantly, and the human's mass kept me from pulling in the air my body demanded. The pain signals from the broken digit didn't stop, but somehow tuned themselves lower, clearing my mind.

Away.

I put my palms onto the human and heaved, trying to work those tiny shoulder muscles into shoving myself out from beneath his bulk.

The human gave a different shriek and raised his working arm.

The dark metal knife-beak glittered in the morning sun.

I reached both hands up and grabbed his forearm, desperate to hold that knife at a distance.

The human trumpeted his hunting cry and thrashed on me, grinding me into the muck. The bones supporting my chest creaked with his mass.

My locked-straight arms burned with the effort of holding his knife. I tried to kick myself free, but his mass pinned me.

He twisted again, trying to spin the arm, and sent us rolling to the side.

Mud splashed into my eye and into that stupid soft beak, but suddenly my torso could expand. My gaping mouth sucked in muck and air to fill the hollowness. Wet dirt at the back of my mouth made me cough and gasp even harder, but I kept my hands around his wrists and my elbows locked.

That horrible fake-beak-knife splashed through the mud above our heads.

The human's face, inches from my clear eye, gleamed white. He'd kept his own insanely twitching face free of the mud. An explosive breath sent drops of clear fluid spattering into my cheeks.

How was I supposed to deal with this?

Humans were killers. My people, we ate after killers died. When a predator attacked us, we flew away. I'd spent much of my life practicing in human bodies. Knowing how to walk and run and breathe and speak wasn't enough, not nearly enough to face a ravenous human ruled by predatory instincts.

Looking so close into his raving face, though, I understood the Volt.

Humans weren't intelligent. Not really.

They'd figured out how to use tools, sure.

And they communicated with one another.

Maybe one day, the descendants of the maniac trying to stab me would develop nuclear fission and wipe themselves out.

The reason nobody had found an intelligent predatory race? They exterminated themselves.

I'd been wrong. There was nothing else.

Deep comprehension was too late to save my mind from memories of death.

My telemetry might save future researchers, though.

The human bent at the waist, throwing a leg up into the air, then crashing it down at me.

A whole new agony burst out where my legs met my torso, rippling up the body's central nerve cord. Muscles seized, squeezing the air out of me again.

I'd debated skipping those stupidly sensitive reproductive organs. Their absence had killed one of my predecessors, though.

I wanted to bend myself double, to curl around that fresh pain. Wheezing with effort, I kept my arms straight as my knees involuntarily pulled up.

The human wheeled his arm around, somehow using my locked arm as a brace to raise himself above me. His predatory madness gave him a strength I couldn't hope to equal. Only the dire wound in his shoulder had kept me alive this long, my mouth and eye full of cold mud and my chest rattling for air.

The worst bit? My body was going to churn into the filth.

A cannon burst or human-slaved hunting beasts would break it into pieces. Just like that lost foot.

This world's highest species would never have a chance at my flesh.

The human loomed above me, knife in hand.

I held the arm as far away as I could.

He bounced on my ribs. Fresh pain echoed through me.

My elbows loosened.

His arm swooped in, his teeth even more exposed, the whites of his eyes popping red, bacteria-rich mud saturating his wounded shoulder.

My gaze wouldn't leave the knife even as my thoughts screamed into the telemetry.

These human monsters were unapproachable.

We would never capture a sapient predator mind.

But they were smart enough to exterminate themselves. They couldn't stop themselves.

Teach them fission. End this farce.

The human put his weight behind his one good arm. His knife plunged at my body.

Unable even to breathe, I gave one final, reflexive heave against the arm, trying to shove it away, trying to push myself away, trying to not die here and rot wasted in the muck.

The human toppled onto me.

Spasmed.

Seized.

I saw nothing but one mad, staring, twitching eye. His tightly fisted hand dug into my chest.

But somehow, the blade didn't.

I spat out mud and sucked down a breath. The human's bulk somehow felt softer, as if he had lost weight in the last few seconds.

I thrashed again. The human toppled off of me to lie face-up in the muck.

Wrenching myself to sit upright, for a second I could only sit there and gasp.

The man's good hand still held the knife. But my final thrashing had turned his wrist just enough to send it into his gut. A line of blood burbled from the corner of his mouth, barely disturbed by his jerky breath.

Revulsion filled me.

I'd killed.

I'd—somehow—murdered a predator.

I slumped in the freshly churned mud, stirred into fresh mounds and troughs by our struggle. Dirty water accumulated in the deepest gouges. The air stank of our sweat and old blood and the noxious fluids the knife had ripped from the human's bowels.

Sunlight warmed the mud on my face, stiffening my cheeks.

Somehow, I had survived a predator attack.

I knew my body well. I'd designed every joint, every muscle, every organ. And every part of it hurt from oxidizer deprivation and the predator's struggle.

My hand didn't want to move, but somehow I dragged it over to his head.

The human twitched at my touch. His hand still clutched the handle of the knife. His fingers moved as if he was trying to tug the makeshift beak free, but the tool didn't move.

This time, the sensors in my palm said the human was dying. Quickly.

But it knew it was dying.

We had no hope of understanding predators. But I'd explicitly come here to capture a mind in this state. It wouldn't support my obviously erroneous theories. Nothing could. But I could perform the work I'd come for. I could make abundantly clear why I changed my beliefs.

I triggered the capture array, and the predator's mind flowed into the mental cell I'd prepared for it.

Impossible words flickered through me, attached to ridiculously intertwined predator concepts. *Love. God. Family.* I didn't need to understand it all, merely pass it into the embedded recorder and let the telemetry take it from there, but I couldn't help watching the flow as my shell heaved for breath.

Duty. Love. Country.

Images flickered through the tangle. Human faces. Presumably ones he'd killed. *Family.*

Concentrating on the flowing mind kept my mind off my aching knees sunk in the sticky mud and the burn in my overworked muscles. My chin dripped repulsive fresh-stewed sweat onto the dying human's face.

The same faces again: a female adult and four fledglings.

Family. Fear.

So dying predators knew fear—but not fear for themselves? Interesting.

Love.

The human's body twitched around the knife. His heart stuttered and his lungs seized.

The mind would collapse soon. I only needed to hold his head until that moment. Ignore the distant screams and the rising reek of burnt gunpowder.

The man's thoughts had a center, I realized in a flash of excitement. Those faces—*they* were the center. Everything tied to them. All the fear, all those concepts, they tied straight into those faces.

The largest fledge looked somewhat like him.

They were his kin.

Shock flooded me. He was a predator *to keep other predators from his close kin.*

I focused on the idea. Telemetry should capture my thoughts, but I wanted to be certain this epiphany came through. We raised our young high above ground, where predators couldn't reach. What would it be like to *be* a predator, with a massive body trapped on the ground, and know all the way through your solid bones that anywhere you could raise your young, another predator could find them?

You'd hunt more fiercely. That fierceness they called *love*.

If you could reach a primitive understanding with other predators, you'd join together.

Humans hunted others before they could be hunted.

And now, as this human died, a wholly sensible but impotent fear for his fledges consumed him.

My earlier epiphany dissolved under this revelation.

I'd succeeded where nobody ever had. I had already transformed the Volt's understanding. Even if cannon chain shredded me this very second, future students would study my telemetry.

We *could* comprehend predators. Maybe, maybe even help them?

And if I made it home with mind intact? Respect. Mates. Privilege.

All I had to do was continue collecting until the mind dissolved.

The pupils of the human's eyes dilated. His chest stopped twitching.

His chest relaxed.

The mind grew fuzzy. He heard the screams and clashes of the distant frenzy, and knew it came for his fledges. The love-fear blossomed into primal terror.

A scientist should not interfere in an experiment, but I couldn't let anyone, not even a human, die in such anguish.

Keeping my hand on his head I leaned my face down by his ear. "Do not fear." I drew another breath of stinking mud. "Your fledges will not suffer. They will be eaten quickly."

Fresh fear flooded the human's mind.

Then he dissolved into death.

I sagged in exhausted triumph.

My collector reported that it had the mind whole and safe. I sealed it away. Maybe with enough study, I'd understand why he'd attacked me. And even amidst this monstrous slaughter, my effort to assuage the human's dread left a spark of warmth in my spirit.

Time to signal retrieval.

But the mud.

Cannon fire or no, I couldn't just leave this body for the mud.

Foolish, I know, but I used the arm without the broken finger to push myself onto my knees. I wasn't sure I could stand, so I hugged the injured limb to my chest and painfully crawled through two body lengths of mud to the edge of the grassy hill. Only once my feet were free of the mud did I collapse and roll onto my back.

With a final breath, I signaled for retrieval.

Overhead, explosive haze turned the blue sky to gray and rendered the sun a mere bright spot. The ground shook, but not as forcefully as my heart. The last thing this body saw was the shadows of vultures circling beyond the gunpowder haze, waiting their chance.

Wifi and Romex

1

Toby had come to think of the Pendleton Building's basement datacenter as a living thing. The three towering fifty-ton air handlers hummed constantly, their odorless breath flowing into every other row of cabinets at a precise at sixty-nine degrees and fifty percent humidity. The six-foot-tall customer equipment cabinets, each stuffed with dozens of computers, inhaled that cool air in through the mesh front and exhaled out the back, where the air handler returns swallowed it again.

Long trays suspended from the ceiling carried twists of yellow and blue and red cables from rack to rack, nerves between the machines that made the world work.

In the fenced-off area, power conditioners gobbled eight megawatts from the St Louis grid and polished it nice and smooth and steady before feeding the thousands of computers. Even the massive air handlers couldn't eliminate the faint flat ozone smell.

And at the front of the room loomed the Cage, walled off from painted floor to ceiling with an ultra-tough chain link fence. The door demanded a keycard and a code. Toby didn't have either, but sometimes he peered through the plastic-coated wire mesh at the optical switches and fiber and connectors that made the Pendleton Building's basement datacenter a "life-sustaining services facility."

When a hospital did remote surgery, the signal that transmitted the master surgeon's deft motions to a distant robot passed through the Cage. The stacked and racked specialized computers inside the Cage carried communications for police, fire, government—everything that made the world work.

The snooty lawyers and architects and engineers that had overpriced offices in the Pendleton Building sixty floors overhead thought that they ran the world, but Toby knew better.

Toby didn't run the world. As a lowly bottom-level network engineer, he was just one of the elite few who knew how the world worked.

At moments like this, running new network cable in the back of the concrete-lined datacenter at two o'clock on a Wednesday morning, Toby didn't feel like a chubby, spectacled, middle-aged dork whose only social life was the weekly board game night or the occasional sci-fi movie fest with similarly unattached friends from college. He didn't feel like an awkward dweeb who at thirty-four *still* couldn't work up the cojones to ask Kirsten the accountant out for coffee. She had that personalized signed picture of James Doohan on her cubicle wall and in winter wore a twelve-foot scarf striped in all the right earthy colors, how totally nerdy could you get, and she didn't have a ring, but Toby couldn't even give her the chance to tell him to go to hell.

Down in the datacenter, though, he felt like a doctor, a Special Forces soldier, someone who listened to the clatter and roar of the datacenter's body as it carried the information that saved people's lives. After years of practice, Toby's ears could dissect the noise to pick out the beep of a failing hard drive or the clatter of a dying fan. He knew every sound the datacenter could make.

That flat, dull "pow" didn't belong here.

Toby looked up from a heavy coil of category 7 cable. Had one of the wrist-thick master fuses blown? But he wasn't working power tonight, there wasn't a thunderstorm, how could it—

Then the scream.

Toby's heart seemed to stop beating. He'd never heard a scream like that, but some atavistic wiring in the back of his brain told him this scream wasn't anger, or joy. It wasn't even pain.

This scream was mortal horror.

Another flat *pow*.

The scream stopped mid-breath.

An angry voice took over, the growled words swallowed by the machine room's howl.

2

Heart in his throat, Toby gingerly started to put the wire crimper back on the tool cart, but stopped himself. The rickety cart rattled and squeaked every time anyone touched it.

The noise was useful, most of the time. You could usually track whoever was working down here by the sound.

Toby really, really didn't want anyone to know he was here.

That noise couldn't have been a gunshot.

Maybe someone had grabbed a high-voltage line. Blown one of the DC fuses.

A nasty voice whispered, *blown it twice?*

But nobody should be down here at this time of night. And while the building tenants all had keys to get at their equipment, they still had to call in to Operations before coming in. Toby would have gotten a message.

How would he know what a dying scream sounded like, anyway? It wasn't like all the action movies he'd seen used real death cries.

Toby set the wire crimpers on the cool concrete floor beside the cart. Trying to keep his steps silent, he stepped over the coil of network cable and crept to the end of the aisle to peer around the corner.

Three rows of cabinets stood at attention, then the Cage, then the reinforced double doors at the datacenter entrance, maybe fifty feet away.

A man stood right inside the door, shouting into a bulky handset radio like an old walky-talky. The man wore black cargo pants, a gray sweatshirt with the hood up, and dark glasses.

Even at this distance, Toby could see the gleaming dark pool of blood on the floor next to the man.

And the body laying in it.

Rule one: no liquids in the data center! Toby clamped his teeth against a hysterical giggle and made himself ease back before jamming his fist against his mouth. The air coursing down from the overhead vent chilled the sweat suddenly soaking his T-shirt at the small of his back.

A dead man.

Someone killed, right here in his datacenter.

And a killer—right here.

With Toby.

The grainy-eyed achy feeling from unscheduled overnight work dissolved, replaced with simmering fear.

Toby grabbed his phone from his belt. No signal. There was never any signal down here. The concrete-lined basement, with all the power lines and network cables, was practically a Faraday cage. And he hadn't bothered putting Skype on his phone.

The datacenter had a phone, a land line. On the wall.

Right outside the Cage.

He had keys to the main electrical closet, at the far end of this cabinet row. The door was steel. If he locked it from the inside, nobody could get in. They couldn't shoot through it either, not without video game guns.

They'd never even know he was there.

What could the killer do here, anyway? The equipment in the cabinets belonged to the customers upstairs. If a bunch of lawyers lost their files, so what? They had backups, or they should have backups. It'd serve them right if they didn't. Those jackasses never bothered giving their IT guys time to test the backups, maybe they'd learn a lesson.

The only important stuff in the basement was the Cage. And the Cage was impenetrable without a key card and the passcode. Even heavy-duty long-handled wire cutters couldn't cut through that reinforced mesh.

A gasoline engine roared, drowning out the air handlers.

The screech of grinding metal made Toby wince.

Big wire cutters wouldn't do, but a big enough saw sure would.

3

Toby swallowed the lump of hot fear burning his tonsils and peeked around the edge of the cabinets once again.

The killer stood with his feet widely braced, holding some kind of saw up against the wall of the Cage. A flurry of sparks spiraled back over the killer's hands as metal ground against metal.

A sudden *thunk* made Toby jump. The saw's squeal jumped in pitch and the cyclone of sparks faded. Almost instantly the pitch fell back and the sparks resumed their full flow.

Toby eased back into hiding and leaned against the cool mesh door of first cabinet. The killer had cut through one of the Cage's strands in, what, a minute? Less? The wires that made up the Cage were about two inches apart.

In minutes, the killer would be able to tear down some of the city's most vital communications.

The stink of the gasoline engine wrinkled Toby's nose. The air handlers had picked up the saw's exhaust and were already spreading it through the room. That wouldn't be good for the machines.

Forget the machines. The machines were not important, that freak just killed someone!

Toby grabbed his phone. He didn't have voice signal, but the datacenter Wi-Fi worked fine.

A swipe and two taps brought up his chat client. His coworkers were all offline, as were his friends—

Uncle Dale was online. Of course. Dale had been Toby's cool uncle, teaching him how to fix cars and shoot a pistol and rewire a printer. Then he'd tried horseback riding on his sixtieth birthday, and had cracked his back falling before he even got his butt in the saddle.

These days Dale stayed up half the night waiting for his pain meds to work, and all day to complain about how he hadn't slept from the pain. Dale could talk to anyone, for hours, about anything or, more usually, nothing. Toby loved the geezer, or loved the childhood Dale had given him, but nowadays could only handle him for about five minutes. He'd connected online with Dale only because he was family, but he'd set the chat client to always tell Dale "do not disturb."

Now he tapped Dale's picture and typed *UD you there?*

Tobester! How they hanging?

Toby typed *Help! Call the police. Pendleton building.*

Police? What's going on?

A man with a gun. Someone's dead.

There was a long pause. *You sure?*

Toby gritted his teeth. *Blood everywhere. Call 911. Please. Now.*

The chat client sat still for a long breath. Toby realized his hand clenching the phone was shaking.

He told it to stop.

The hand ignored him.

He finally seized his one hand with the other to try to still it.

It didn't work.

Dale didn't answer.

And didn't answer.

Toby's hands weren't the only part of him shaking. The tremor had spread to his shoulders. His knees wobbled on their own.

Dale wrote back: *On with them now.*

Toby's chest hurt. He'd been holding his breath. His hand skittered on the touchscreen and he sent *Tell them killdeer cutting mice sustenance cage.*

WTF?

Damn autocorrect. Moving slowly and deliberately, fighting the electrified nerves that made the overhead lights seem painfully bright and transformed the constant flow of cool air into an irritating chilly rasp on his face, Toby spelled out *Basement computer room. Life sustaining services cage.*

K.

Toby's whole body screamed for him to flee. To scurry into the power room and lock the door behind him. The wireless didn't work in there, though.

Once Uncle Dale told him that the cops were on their way, he'd barricade himself in the power room and stay there until some kind uniformed officer offered him a blanket and a donut.

The police station wasn't far. Five minutes, maybe?

Police ask can you get out?

Toby's hands suddenly didn't want to work at all. He eventually managed to type "tra," and the auto-complete thankfully offered up *trapped.*

A fresh fear struck him, and Toby quickly silenced the ringer. He'd never feel the buzz of an incoming message down here, with the subtle vibration of countless computers and the saw's bone-rattling grind, but he wasn't got to let some stupid mistake give him away.

I'm okay, Toby insisted to himself. *As long as that saw is going, he's not coming back here. I'm gonna be fine.*

The saw cut out.

4

Without the saw's jaw-clenching scream, the datacenter's normal roar felt like deep silence.

Sweat drenched Toby's cotton T-shirt and sent his light wire-frame glasses sliding down to the tip of his nose. He felt a terrible need to swallow, but his tongue felt so dry he feared it might crack. The air tasted of dust and ozone and exhaust and, maybe, just a little bit of sticky coppery blood.

"You're not answering your radio!" someone bellowed. People who worked in datacenters could converse in an almost normal voice. Visitors always spoke way too loud, overcoming the hurricane of the air handlers with force instead of skill.

"You know I can't hear shit over the saw," another voice shouted. The killer.

No, not *the* killer. Toby had to force his lungs to draw breath. It wasn't one killer. The new guy might not have murdered the man on the floor, but he hadn't said anything about it. There wasn't a *what have you done*, or even an *oh, drat, you killed him*.

The newcomer had trod in another human being's life blood and said nothing.

Two killers.

"Tannenbaum wants to know how long." The newcomer's voice was higher pitched. A woman?

"Twenty minutes."

"If this place is still running when the Robinson Building goes down—"

"I said twenty minutes. Plus however long you spend asking me questions."

Toby almost sagged in relief. Twenty minutes. The police could get here in five, hopefully.

But the Robinson Building? What did that have to do with anything?

A strange beep cut through the air handlers. An indistinguishable voice crackled. The walky-talky?

"Shit," the male killer said. "How'd the cops find out?"

Another crackle. "The basement?" the woman said. "But—"

Both fell silent.

"Listen, Chuck," the woman said in a voice a little too casual, a tiny bit too loud. "I'm going upstairs to check on the hostages. Let you work in peace. Call the second you're done, okay?"

I know that tone of voice, Toby thought. He made himself stand, demanding his shaking knees support him. The voice you use when you want people to hear what you say, not see what you do.

A lying voice.

Toby's phone buzzed at his belt. Toby ignored it to turn and flee.

The door at the far end of the row of cabinets called him. The electrical closet. Concrete walls. Chunky steel pipes set in the ceiling, conduits for the massive power cables snaking through the building. A steel door with a serious lock, as if all the megawatts funneled into the building at that point might conspire together to break for freedom.

The tool cart half-filled the aisle. Toby made himself slow enough to turn sideways, to slip past it without touching it and setting the rickety rattletrap thing into clattering motion.

When this was over, he was going to demand they get a new cart. Something plastic. With rubber wheels. Well-greased, stealthy rubber wheels.

Focused completely on not touching the noisy cart, Toby didn't notice the wire crimper he'd set on the floor until his foot thudded down on it.

Toby's foot slid. His ankle twisted.

Overbalanced.

He crashed sideways into a mesh-doored cabinet, ricocheted sideways, arms waving wildly for balance, everything spinning around him, other foot coming down so heavy that something inside it gave a snap that resonated through the foot and up his leg, a bizarrely painless tremor that promised later suffering.

His hands slammed into the cart.

With an ear-splitting clatter, the tool cart crashed into the opposite row of cabinets. A screwdriver and a couple of sockets tumbled free to smack against a cabinet and bounce off the floor.

Toby sprinted for the far end of the aisle. Something stabbed his right foot, the slipping foot, with each step—sprained? broken?—but he pushed himself harder, fumbling for the keys in his pocket, getting the red key in his hand.

He hit the door, key in hand, just as someone behind him shouted "Hey! You! Stop!"

Something in him wanted to stop. To turn around. Raise his arms, show he was helpless.

They're killers.

In Toby's sweating shaking hand, the tiny key danced off the doorknob.

Another *pow*, this one louder than the last.

Something struck the power room door.

Toby's bowels felt loose as he again stabbed the doorknob with the key.

"I said stop!" the woman shouted.

Then the key slipped into the lock. Toby wrenched the knob and threw himself into the darkened room, yanking the key free as he dashed. He would have sworn he couldn't be that coordinated, but millions of years of not getting eaten by bigger, angrier predators came together enough to let him slam the door shut and spin the doorknob lock, sealing him in stale darkness.

5

In total darkness Toby leaned against the door, trying not to let his overwhelming terror reduce him to a gibbering lump. His heart didn't feel like a hammer any longer, but rather a shuddering beast fighting to break free of his ribcage. The air in the power closet tasted flat and metallic and stale. This room wasn't meant for human habitation—the datacenter crew did everything they could to keep people out of it. The dust on the door stuck to his back, his arms. Combined with the utter darkness, Toby felt entombed alive.

Something big and heavy slammed into the metal door. The door quivered in its frame. An involuntary shriek exploded from Toby's heart.

The impact came again. A shoulder? A gunshot?

The door jerked again, a shorter and sharper impact, accompanied by a muffled *bang*. Too rigid and hollow to scream again, a pained wheeze escaped through Toby's clenched teeth.

The door held.

The next four gunshots were just as loud and shook the door just as fiercely.

Then silence.

The doorknob rattled.

Someone swore.

Toby let out a shuddering breath and sank onto his heels, almost sobbing as relief bled through him. Wiping his hands on his khaki cargo pants, he tried to force his breathing to steady, his heart to slow, the constant shaking everywhere to end. His left foot abruptly throbbed with a stabbing pain, like he'd driven a nail through the base of his big toe, so he stretched that leg out in front of him and hugged himself.

Crimpers on the floor, he thought. *Running in the datacenter. Safety violations everywhere. HR would have his head. And there's gotta be rules about guns, and shooting and, and, and andandand...*

The darkness hid him until he could think again.

Eventually he drew enough air to fill his chest and rubbed his eyes. His gut ached and his mouth tasted like dust and puke. Had he puked? He didn't think so. He'd like to think he would have noticed if he'd been so scared he puked. Unless it was just a little bit, maybe.

Focus, Toby told himself. *Think. You run the equipment that holds this city together. You have a brain. Use it.*

Toby fumbled for the phone at his belt. The screen lit at a touch, searchlight-bright in the total darkness, exposing unread messages from Uncle Dale.

Five minutes ago: *Police are coming.*

Four minutes ago: *You all right?* and *Talk to me kid.*

Two minutes ago: *I'm on my way*

"Shit," Toby said. "No, no, no."

What did Uncle Dale think he was going to do, charge in and save him?

Toby tapped the phone. *In power room. Safe. They can't get me.*

The phone took his words, then added small letters. *Undelivered. Will resend when network available.*

No wireless signal in the power closet.

Toby gritted his teeth.

The darkness didn't seem safe any longer. It felt dusty and cloying. Something about the word "megawatts" made people not want to grab a mop and swill out the place. Toby put one hand on the door and heaved himself to his feet. His sweat had dried in this still stale air, caking him with dust. Keeping his weight off his hurt foot, he fumbled for the light switch.

Under the feeble double fluorescent bulbs dangling from the grungy chains, the power closet seemed smaller than he remembered. Gray panels covered the far wall, each with an oversized swivel handle. A matte metal box the size of a dishwasher sat in one corner, a smaller DC power converter for the air handlers. Another wall held circuit breaker panels for distribution to the upper floors, each carrying a couple thousand amps or so. Heavy coils of spare plastic-clad wiring made an unruly heap in another corner, with handprints on their dusty wire wrappers. A heavy gray toolbox spotted with rust. The only sound was the almost inaudible hum of the power transformer and Toby's own heart.

The killers couldn't get in. The police were on their way. All he had to do was stay locked in this room until he was rescued.

Toby let out a relieved sigh and felt his shocked brain grind towards starting.

What were they doing anyway? Why would someone kill break into the Cage? They couldn't be planting sniffers or loggers—the morning staff would notice the great big hole straight off, and they'd call the Federal Communications Commission.

And the body. The morning crew would notice that poor bastard even before coffee.

Toby clamped down on the giggle that threatened to boil out. He was a network engineer—low man on the totem pole, yeah, but he still knew more about this technology than ninety-nine percent of the human race. All of the really important stuff was redundant.

If this place is still running when the Robinson Building goes down—

Toby's blood ran cold.

One of the senior engineers had talked about visiting the Robinson Building a few months ago. Something about a bad metro fiber ring.

The killers weren't just attacking the Pendleton Building. They had another team in the Robinson Building, across the Mississippi River.

They were attacking someone's main communications, and their backup site.

Cross-river redundancy was expensive. Even life-sustaining services didn't usually spend that kind of cash. The only people who had that kind of money was the Feds—and even then, they'd only do it if lives were at stake.

A whole lot of lives.

Toby grabbed his phone. His last message hadn't been sent, but he added *Bad guys attacking the Robinson Building too. They're cutting comms—* He stopped. Another rule: evidence first, then label your guesses. He erased the last three words and typed *I think they're cutting comms in both buildings. Tell police to find out what runs through both.*

When the signal came back, the alarm would go out.

But the message would only get out when Toby got out the door. Which meant the police would be here.

Which would be too late.

Toby had to warn the police, the Army, someone.

Right now.

Or people would die.

6

Toby had locked himself into a one hundred square foot radio-proof cement box with nothing but dust, wire, and enough electricity to kill a school of whales. He had a big toe that stabbed him with pain every time he took a step and a top-of-the-line-cell phone without signal or Wi-Fi.

And, he realized with abrupt embarrassment, at some point during the evening he'd wet his pants. He couldn't even remember when that had happened. Thankfully the other guys hadn't seen that, or he'd never hear the end of it.

The room had two ways out—the door and the wiring conduits. Toby was not about to open the door to check if the woman with the gun, the second killer, was still there.

That left the conduit.

Toby hobbled to the DC power converter, a vented gray box the size of a dishwasher. Inside his sneaker, his toe felt the size of a football, and flashed with pain at every bump. With a groan he heaved himself on top of the converter, hands grinding in the accumulated years of dirt.

Six foot-wide conduit pipes ran up into the ceiling. Ancient grimy wires in a dozen different styles, an archaeological display of 20th century electrical standards, choked the upward conduits.

Two horizontal conduits sat at the top of the wall, hugging the ceiling as they ran through the concrete out into the datacenter. He'd seen their other end, in the power converter cage, maybe ten feet away. Electrical cables filled one of the conduits, but the other only had a couple of wires. A few months ago, Toby had stood atop a ladder in the power converter cage to feed new power lines as a senior tech used a string to pull them into the power closet.

Toby held his phone up to the almost empty conduit.

No signal.

Wi-Fi didn't flow like water. It needed line of sight, or thin walls at the worst. But maybe some of the signal would bounce partway down the conduit. Clutching his phone tightly, he stuffed his hand down the shaft. By standing on tip-toe, he was able to jam his arm in right up to his shoulder. He held his phone down there as long as he could, teeth gritted against the pain in his toe, but in only a minute he had to pull his arm out and get the weight off his feet.

Message not sent.

Toby swore under his breath. How was he going to get out?

Treat it like an engineering problem. You need to get the message out. That means you need some kind of signal to carry it. This means you need to reach the signal…

Toby slapped his forehead with his palm. Once again, he'd been solving the wrong problem.

Toby didn't need Wi-Fi.

The *phone* needed Wi-Fi.

And the phone would fit just fine down the conduit.

Toby sat on the power converter and slid to the ground, his broken foot forgotten. The heaped coils of wires in the corner yielded a brand-new spool of heavy-gauge Romex, two thick copper strands bundled together in layers of stiff strong plastic. Toby seized a razor knife from the toolbox to slash the layers of shrink-wrap off the coil, then used the heavy-duty clippers to chop off a ten-foot length. The curl of wire didn't want to straighten, but that was the whole point of Romex—once you beat it into shape, it stayed that way. He didn't have gloves, so the fiercely sharp copper tips sliced painful gashes in his hands.

After a moment of sweat, he had a roughly straight chunk of heavy wire. Toby bent the end to form a couple inches of pushing surface, then climbed back onto the power converter.

Toby raised the phone to the conduit, then bit his lip. Sending the phone down the conduit meant losing it. No more messages in or out.

This would be the last thing he'd ever send.

No, Toby told himself. Tomorrow you can go out and buy a new phone. One of those new Nebula things, with the super hi-res screens and three-D sound that came with a keg and a topless model to carry it for you. He'd sleep late tomorrow, once he got out of here. To hell with the ten AM meeting.

Still, his hand shook a little as he typed *Putting phone where it can get signal. Can't get any more messages. Send help. Robinson building too.* His breath felt tight, but he made himself add *This is really bad.*

Was that everything he needed?

I will get out of this, Toby reminded himself. *I will.*

But the animal part of him knew better.

Painstakingly he spelled out *Tell Mom and Dad I love them.* Half a brick in the back of his throat, he read the words twice to be sure autocorrect hadn't ordered louvres.

The phone went in the conduit, lengthwise beside one of the bundled power cables. Fighting to control his breathing, trying to ignore the turmoil of emotion in his guts, he carefully used the Romex to slide the phone towards the circle of light at the far end.

Toby made himself work slowly. He didn't want to push the phone out of the conduit. Falling to the ground, it might break. It might land on a power juncture and fry. But he didn't know exactly how long the conduit was or the length of his Romex prod, and the shadows at the far end of the conduit weren't clear at all. Had he gotten the phone to the edge of the conduit, or was it still two feet away? Was that distant noise the ding of a received message?

Finally he didn't dare push any further. He still had a foot of Romex on his side, but from what he could see he'd come within inches of the far end.

He hoped.

He eased the Romex back out of the tube and peered down. The phone made a shallow dent in the circle of light, not too far from the distant end of the conduit. Toby heaved a sigh and eased himself to the ground, suddenly aware of the swelling pain in his foot and the dirt caking the Romex-inflicted slashes on his right hand.

Someone pounded on the door.

Toby hopped in surprise. Rescue!

"Toby!" someone shouted. "Toby Cook! I know you're in there."

The breath froze in Toby's chest.

That didn't sound like the police.

"Come talk to me!" the muffled voice said. "Talk to me right now! Or people will die, and it'll be your fault."

7

Toby's heart jumped back up his throat. *I'm safe in here*, he reminded himself. Thick concrete walls. Steel door. *Those killers can't get in.*

"You know Jerry King?" the voice shouted.

It sounded like the woman who'd chased him.

Who'd told him to stop, right before she shot at him.

Toby froze. His mouth went as dry as the dust covering everything.

"The night security guy? Works the front desk? My boys have a gun to his head right now, Toby. You don't come talk to me, I tell them to pull the trigger."

Toby thought *Shit. Shitshitshit. Shit.*

"I'm gonna count to five, Toby. Then they shoot. One."

He still clutched the Romex in a bloodless hand.

"Just shout through the door, Toby. Two."

Toby made himself walk to the door. His pulse thundered in his ears. *I'm a network engineer. I'm not a cop, not a soldier. I'm a damn coward. I shouldn't be here.*

"Three, Toby. That's three."

"I'm here!" Toby shouted.

The woman's shout held a hint of satisfaction. "That's good, Toby. We can talk. Everything will be fine if you're sensible. How are you doing?"

"I'm fine thank you!" Toby shouted. His voice warbled, and he cursed himself harder.

"That's good, Toby. I've got a problem I need your help with."

"I'm not coming out!" Toby shouted.

"That's the problem, Toby," the woman shouted. "We have enough crew to watch all of the civilians, if they're all in one place. We've got Jerry, a few housekeepers, a crew of programmers who were working late. But I can't leave you here. Watching you takes up manpower."

Toby's soul plummeted.

"So you need to come out and join the other hostages. Or, if you insist on a private babysitter, you'll force me to kill every last one of them."

Toby leaned against the cool steel door, shuddering. Fresh tears trickled down his dirty face. His hands knotted to fists, filthy from old Romex and older conduit.

Time. He needed time.

Time and a plan.

Time and *something*.

"You killed that other guy!" he shouted.

"He wouldn't help us," the woman called. "He tried to slow us down. Block our mission."

Toby's jaw trembled. "I can't let you in there either. I don't have the codes."

"I know you don't Toby," the woman shouted. "You're not one of the oppressors. You're one of the decent people. Not one of the tyrants who broke the Constitution."

I was right, Toby thought with a mix of surprise and horror. *This is huge.*

"We know you called for help," she called. "We don't blame you. This is scary stuff. But we don't want to hurt you. You're just doing a job. You're one of the people we're fighting for. We're holding the cops off. You can't stop this."

Toby's thoughts shuffled and clattered like a flailing machine.

He couldn't let these bastards kill all those innocent people.

She might kill Toby as soon as he opened the door.

But if he went along, even if she was telling the absolute truth, they'd murder even more people. This was Oklahoma City stuff, Pentagon bombing stuff, 9-11 stuff.

No matter what he decided, people would die.

He couldn't stop it.

The only questions were, who and how many?

8

"I've got to insist on an answer, Toby" the woman shouted. "Right now. Are you coming out? Or are you going to kill Jerry and the cleaning crew and all those computer nerds?"

Time to decide who you are, Toby thought. He glanced around the power closet, the heap of cables, the handful of tools. Charge her with a pair of wire clippers? No, she'd put a bullet in his head before he took a step. You didn't hijack a building, two buildings, unless you knew how to shoot a gun. And not Toby's piddly firing range stuff, either.

He couldn't fight on her terms.

He had to fight like an engineer.

Toby grabbed the wire clippers and his wobbly Romex staff. "Listen," he shouted through the door. *You know how to do this,* he told himself. *Don't think about it, just let your hands do the work.* "How do I know Jerry's still alive?" He needed a minute, just a minute.

Either this would work, or he'd be dead.

Maybe he'd kill himself with this crazy idea. Save Lady Killer the trouble.

No, if Toby killed himself, if he went silent, she'd order her men upstairs to massacre the other prisoners.

"Open the door," the woman said. "I'll hand you the radio."

"Not a chance. You ask him," Toby shouted, desperately clipping the plastic coating on the end of the Romex. "You ask him what I ordered for carryout tonight. He knows. You tell me what I had for dinner, and I'll unlock the door."

How much would that buy him—seconds? Maybe a whole minute?

Toby twisted wire.

"All right, Toby," the woman shouted. "I'll give you that, but then you come along quiet, okay?"

"I promise," Toby shouted.

Toby grabbed a razor knife and attacked the Romex.

Bits of plastic pattered on the dusty barren concrete floor.

Less than a minute later the woman shouted "Pad Thai. With squid. Jerry said it stunk up the whole lobby."

Jerry was alive. Toby's heart felt a tiny bit lighter.

But thinking of what he was about to do dragged that heart further down.

"Okay," Toby said.

He knelt by the door, trying to make himself smaller. Maybe she'd aim for his heart, and the bullet would pass over his head.

"Okay. I'm coming out."

With trembling fingers, he very gently turned the door lock to free the knob. He had his hands at his side when he shouted, "I'm unlocking the door now."

The doorknob yanked.

The door slammed inward, driven by a heavy-booted kick.

9

The woman looming in the doorway was big. Bigger than Toby, especially when he knelt at her feet on the dirty concrete. She wore a heavy black vest and black tactical pants. Equipment dangled from her mesh utility belt. One boot was crashing down from where she'd kicked the door open.

She held an evil-looking weapon in a double grip. Not a pistol—Toby would have recognized a pistol. This thing was boxy, with a handgrip, and a little barrel sticking out one side. Toby had no doubt it was a thousand times more lethal than anything he'd ever touched.

Still on his knees, Toby threw himself towards her.

The gunshot sounded incredibly loud in the tiny space.

Toby didn't have time to think about where the bullet went. Both of his hands plunged forward.

Toby had cut the plastic sheath off the last three inches of the heavy-duty Romex, exposing the stiff and viciously sharp copper wire beneath.

Then he'd pulled along the length of the wire, creating two separate strands.

Toby had one strand in each hand, stabbing forward.

The heavy-duty wires punched through the woman's pants and into the skin of her calves.

The other end of the Romex, also stripped, was jammed into one of the thousand-amp circuit breaker panels.

A sudden chorus of popping noises, like flash-fried bacon.

The woman's back instantly arched. Her hands flailed upwards.

Toby gritted his teeth against the sudden stink of roasting meat and ozone.

The woman's upper body thrashed and convulsed.

Toby shouted again, but not in fear. This was something different. Not even anger, but some sort of alien righteous fury he'd never felt before.

The woman's feet shuffled involuntarily, a high-amperage shuffle.

Toby reflexively leaned forward, keeping the wires jammed into her legs, trying not to shake and let the bare wires slip free or slip into him and kill him, teeth gritted, willing the circuit to hold, to not snap, the wires to not melt in his hands.

Behind Toby, something popped in a cloud of noxious burning plastic.

The woman instantly collapsed backwards, limp.

Gasping for air, Toby pulled himself backwards, yanking his Romex spears free. Gleaming sticky blood covered the copper tips. Shuddering, he carefully laid the wires down a couple feet apart. Even if the circuit breaker panel had blown, he couldn't trust that the wires were truly dead.

The woman twitched once. A leg quivered.

Then she lay still.

The nylon tactical pants had melted, burning a path up one leg and down the other. The textbooks all warned that electricity through the heart would kill, but Toby had hoped that half a dozen households worth of power put anywhere through someone would put them down too.

He hadn't planned to kill her.

He hadn't wanted to kill her.

He'd just wanted to stop her. To not let her kill him.

And there she lay, dead.

Toby's fear hadn't exactly vanished. It still gibbered in one corner of his brain. It didn't make his hands shake any more, though.

Don't stop, Toby told himself. *Don't think about this. You don't have time to think.* The woman's weapon had fallen a few feet away, but she also had a .32 semi-auto much like Uncle Dale's holstered on her belt.

Without looking at the woman's face, Toby torqued the pistol free from the holster and staggered on.

Only an hour ago, the ranked aisles of server cabinets had seemed comfortable and familiar. The mesh doors offered flickers of pinhole vision into hundreds of rack-mounted computers, performing innumerable calculations every second, making the world turn and civilization tick. The cool air had felt cozy, the ozone smelled like home.

The pistol's sweaty plastic grip changed all of that, though. The cabinets could hide enemies, and not enemies like a video game. Enemies with real guns that would really kill him. The only thing Toby could do was move quickly.

Toby stopped at the end of the aisle and peered towards the entrance. The first killer still held the roaring saw, still chopped at the life-sustaining services Cage in a halo of sparks and superheated microscopic steel shards.

Had Toby's life changed so quickly?

Had all this really taken less than twenty minutes?

Not much less than twenty minutes, Toby thought. The saw was almost through.

Behind the killer, a man's body cooled in a drying pool of his own blood.

Toby suddenly shook again.

If this man got into the Cage, he'd cut service. Other perpetrators in the Robinson Building would cut service there too. Something critical would be isolated. And yet a third gang of killers would take the chance to strike at their real target.

If the datacenters in both the Robinson Building and the Pendleton Building went down, today's date would get burned into someone's memory.

The killer with the saw was forty, maybe fifty feet away.

Toby's jaw ached. He burned to shout. Put your hands up! Step away from the saw! Surrender!

He wanted the man to know he was caught, and give up.

This man was a killer, though.

And the dead man lying by the cage couldn't be this killer's first time, either. Toby had to struggle to keep his mind off that body, but the killer didn't even notice the corpse anymore.

If the killer saw Toby—if Toby gave the killer a chance—Toby would die.

And then a whole bunch more people would die.

And someone, another killer from this gang of killers, might appear any second.

Toby braced his stance.

He raised the .32.

Sighted at the man's back.

Slipped his finger inside the trigger guard.

And squeezed.

The gun barked and bucked.

Once the bullets started, Toby couldn't stop.

When Toby noticed the pistol clicking empty, over and over again, he lowered his shaking hands to his sides. Fighting the nausea knotting his stomach, he stumbled forward.

Stepped in the pool of blood spreading from the killer.

Wrenched the semi-auto from the killer's belt.

Made sure the safety was off.

Put his back to the wall.

Then fumbled for the phone on the wall and dialed 911.

10

"You still with me, Toby?" the police officer said in the tinny earpiece.

Toby couldn't help glancing around, the .32 clutched in his right hand, the phone handset in his left. The machine room hummed and blew and roared. Blood oozed under the Cage's bottom rail and onto the cool concrete floor under the life sustaining services equipment.

Something ticked, and Toby whirled towards the back.

Just the air handler.

The gun shook.

"Are you with me, Toby?" the officer repeated.

"Yeah." The cops had kept him on the line for, what, five minutes? A day? Filling time, making small talk.

"Listen carefully, Toby. Do you still have the gun?"

Toby jerked his head in a nod.

"Toby. Do you still have the gun?"

"Yes!" Toby snapped.

"Listen to me, Toby. We have officers right outside the doors. We're ready to come in."

Toby jerked the gun towards a sudden clicking hum. No, not another killer, just the battery conditioning cycle in the DC plant.

Nothing to worry about.

This time.

"We need you to put the gun down, Toby."

"What?" Toby said.

"You need to put the gun down on the ground."

"But they're—"

A pocking noise.

No, just a fan kicking on.

"We got them, Toby. We got them all. Even the ones in the Robinson. You put the gun down."

Toby looked at the door, his brain still spinning at every faint noise.

He studied the quiet, familiar, alien datacenter.

"The hostages upstairs are safe. Thanks to you."

The words seemed malformed. They didn't want to go into Toby's ears.

Then slowly, with a trembling hand and keeping his back to the wall, Toby knelt to set the pistol on the ground.

"Your uncle is up here," the tinny voice said. "He's raising all kinds of hell about you. We need you to calm him down."

"Okay," Toby said.

"You've done it, Toby. It's over. Can you put the gun down?"

"It's down."

"Good, Toby. We're going to open the door now. Two officers are going to get you out so we can finish up."

"Okay."

The door swung an inch open. The sight of the rifle barrel edging through the gap almost made Toby throw himself down for the handgun, but he made himself stand rigid, pressed tightly against the wall.

Then uniformed officers poured into the room.

Toby let the two burly men in military-style body armor take his biceps, not unkindly, and bustle him out of the datacenter, into the hall and the fresh air and the voices of dozens of people, guiding him to the stairwell as quickly as he could stagger.

The fear and paralysis in Toby's mind shattered. In one single second, he felt freer than he ever had before.

And today was going to be a busy day, at the end of an already long day.

The cops would want to talk to him.

A shower. With soap. *All* the soap.

Clean clothes.

Then he had to talk to the boss. He was *not* getting paid enough for this.

And last thing, before he went home, he was going to march over to Accounting. Straight to Kirsten's desk. He was going to say "I'm totally jealous of your Scotty picture. Would you like to get some coffee tomorrow and tell me how you got it?"

What was the worst she could do? Shoot him?

Yesterday's Girl

Reuben kept a special tea for the morning after the inevitable breakup with the latest Annual Girlfriend. A pu'er cake, thick and black and hard. It smelled of the original Silk Road, all dusty black mud and centuries of dried-out camel dung. It fit his mood. The aroma plowed furrows in his sinuses, and its nearly toxic levels of caffeine knocked his sleep-deprived brain into motion.

It had a fancy name. Days like this, Reuben called it Heartbreak Tea.

He lounged in his comfy sweats at the cozy kitchen table he'd inherited from his grandmother, sipping the vile Tea of Enforced Consciousness and doodling in his big notebook. The Annual Girlfriend always took her clothes and left bad dreams. When Alissa had text-ditched Reuben last year, he'd dreamed about the inverted pyramid-sheep that he'd thought might finally let him crack perpetual motion. That's what the world needed to solve the climate crisis, free clean energy. It hadn't worked out, but still.

The old wooden floor under his bare feet was chilly. The sun gleaming through the twin double-hung windows was an autumn lie; he'd need to fire up the boiler soon.

Not yet. Soon.

Tea shouldn't have *fumes*, should it?

His pencil moved deftly, distilling last night's fractured sleep.

Two years ago, after Maggie's rageful flight had left him with the Rocky and Bullwinkle nightmare, he'd detoured into Cherenkov's later neuropharmacological work, agrarian policy, and how both played off that one bit in that 1998 issue of *Astrophysical Review Letters B*. Amazing how you could find the same mathematics in petunias and pulsars. Krissy had given him the dermatropic algae dream—not a nightmare, but a plain weird dream. Turning everyone green would sure cure racism, but he'd discovered a trivial immunizing agent almost accidentally. Even if he'd blown what remained of his dot-com fortune renting enough planes to do the high-level atmospheric dispersal over every major population center, the CDC would cure it before the plague even got really started.

And today, drawing in the notebook kept him from calling Astrid back.

He could probably patch things up with her. Enough to keep her around for another month or two.

He'd dared to think dating might work this time.

But that relationship would end the same way. Just like everyone else, she'd want him to shift out of his comfy life. Invest his money. Give up working, and live a life of leisure. Sell the cozy nine hundred square foot house that he flat-out owned, buy a McMansion, leave Ohio or go to a city, volunteer for charity, or get a real job: priest, prophet, politician. One sort of liar or another. People claimed that they understood how revolution always came from one person working outside the hierarchy, but show them that you intended to *be* that person, prove it to them again and again, and they cut you off.

Maybe he shouldn't even try again.

With a woman, that is. He'd funnel his whole life into changing the world.

No, he was only thirty-eight. He'd try again.

Reuben was brilliant enough to know he was an idiot.

Last night's dreams had been doozies. They always were, when the Annual Girlfriend finally gave up on him. His dreams had been full of shifting angles of curved light, distorted by every thought and the way he'd fallen through them. Numbers that shifted their meaning depending on where you looked at them from.

He tapped the pen, looking at the meager curves and numbers he'd drawn. This really might play off Kampf's work in remote cosmology. Might even be relevant to the arrow of time problem and the antimatter scarcity question.

He raised the big mug of tea, savoring the bitterness as it burned awareness directly into his neurons.

The clock chimed nine AM.

A cyborg clock: half mechanical, half electronic. It took accurate time from the Internet, all geared to an old-fashioned pendulum and chimes and a whole bunch of clockwork to drive the hands and bells.

He'd built it because he could.

Maybe he'd build another clock. No, the house didn't have space for him to build something every time his personal life went to crap.

The kitchen exploded.

One moment he was sitting in his grandmother's wooden chair. The next fraction of a second he was flying sideways, hitting the wall hard enough to crack the plaster and ring his noggin, face both scalded and cooling where he'd spilled tea right over himself.

Reuben hit the floor hard enough to knock his teeth together.

Someone laughed. No—*cackled.* "I did it! Did it did it did it!"

Reuben levered himself up onto one hand, holding his head with the other and trying to focus.

His pristine kitchen, with its uncluttered counters and tidy drawers, looked like a tornado had hit. Cupboards hung open. Water splashed in the sink. Gas explosion? No, that would have taken the whole house.

A stranger stood in the middle of the doorway.

A bald skinny guy, all denim and flannel and boots like a wannabe cowboy. The skin on his face was drawn and tired, but he had a grin like when Reuben's dotcom went IPO and his stock options had bloomed into a sweet hundred million overnight. One hand held a little aluminum box with a blinking LED and a couple of black cables coming out of it, wrapped around the intruder's waist and under his armpits.

Reuben gritted his teeth and drew a breath, just like when he'd gone to yell at one of the bankers. "You! Who the hell are you?"

The stranger interrupted his caper. "My apologies!" He laughed again. "There's no reason you should recognize me. Not yet, at least."

Reuben fumbled for his belt, but he didn't carry his cellphone in his sweatpants. The sweatpants made him feel kind of vulnerable right now. He wore them as PJs, sure, and you didn't wear undies with PJs, and it's not like the guy was threatening to punch him where it'd hurt, but he'd blasted the whole blasted kitchen. "I'm calling the cops now."

"You're an antiauthoritarian, you hate the cops." The stranger peered around. "It's just like I remember."

Reuben ignored the bruises and hauled himself to his feet. The stranger was almost the same height as him, maybe half an inch shorter but he had those stupid boots on. "Get out of here, old man. No—what did you blow up? How did you get in here?"

The stranger laughed. "I look like your dad."

Reuben stopped. The hell of it was, the guy kind of did.

"Tell me you wrote down the arrow of time problem," the stranger said. "Oh, and you've sometimes had this achy-stabby pain in your left nut that you've never told anyone about."

Reuben froze. Telling a doctor about that had always seemed too petty, and he didn't want a doctor up in there for no reason.

The man said, "You don't use drugs cause you're afraid of what you'll do under them. And you had that creepy fantasy about Jess Domathales that you wouldn't dare breathe to anyone."

Reuben swallowed indignation. He opened his mouth to shout something, anything, but his impression of the stranger shifted.

He knew those eyes. He knew that stance.

Arrow of time problem. A weird blend of glee and terror churned in his guts, blended with trepidation. Reuben barely breathed, "You're me.",

"I knew that bit would get you," the not-stranger said. "I've had more time to think about this, and I'm the newcomer, so why don't you call me Sam?"

His middle name. Their middle name. "Sam," he breathed. "What—how? I mean, paradoxes?" Reuben glanced at his notebook, now tented against the wall.

Sam said, "You got down the idea. That's the important thing. So long as you had the dream, wrote it down, and had the inspiration for time travel, my future's a branch from here. Thank God."

Reuben blinked. Those words jarred, coming out of the weirdly familiar face. "When did you start going to church?"

Sam laughed. Was Reuben's laugh that much like a mad cackle? "I don't have to do that anymore." He raised a fist. "It was the courts, you know. The Supreme Court said that religious freedom meant you had to choose a church, then the bit with the Evangelical Pope, and—" He shook his head. "We're going to change all that, you and I." He tugged a phone out of his pocket, much like Reuben's cellphone but even thinner and sleeker. "I got it all here. The stocks we need to buy to get the money, the candidates to block. We might have to blackmail a couple of them, but I have the dirt already. Might be simpler to send them to prison."

"Hang on." Reuben's head was spinning again, and not just from hitting the wall.

"I know, it's a lot to take in. There's no rush." Sam smiled beatifically and stared around the kitchen. "I missed this place after the Relocation." He looked back to Reuben. "We've got a good month until we have to start work. Just know I'll answer anything. I don't have anything to hide from you."

The tea Reuben had spilled on his face was still soaking his shirt, and starting to get a real chill. His feet were downright cold now, and his T-shirt all full of sweat. "Okay," he said. "Fine. We'll save the world. Just... let me get some pants on, we'll talk."

Sam grinned knowingly at him. Damn it, Sam *did* know. This was gonna suck. "I'll pick up in here. Least I can do."

Before Reuben could take a step, the whole house quivered with the groan of metal grinding against metal.

Sam glanced around, obviously alarmed.

Good thing Reuben had better control of his expressions. "What's that? Living room?"

Sam nodded and bolted out the doorway, Reuben right on his heels.

And froze mid-step.

The living room seemed twisted, like someone had grabbed a handful of reality and squeezed. The smell of ozone and roasting ham overwhelmed Reuben. Sam was yelling something, blocking Reuben from trying to retreat back through the doorway—no, not blocking, they were both trying to get out at the same time like a shorthanded Three Stooges. Had Sam been feeding him a line, were the Time Police showing up to—

The room snapped back to normal.

Except for the figure standing there.

Where Sam looked like a wannabe cowboy, this newcomer wore black leather and a biker helmet. The thrill of racing through open air versus the risk of becoming an instant organ donor had never appealed to Reuben, so it couldn't be another future self.

The newcomer wore a broad respirator mask on his face, hooked to a heavy tank on his back. One arm carried a big clockwork machine, all exposed gears and dials and brasswork with tiny cranks along the side.

Reuben froze.

"Oh, no," Sam said.

"You know him?" Reuben said.

"Don't get distracted," Sam said. "We have work to do."

The biker reached up to peel the mask off his face and breathed in, like he was going to pull the whole atmosphere into chest in one breath. "That is so... goood," he exhaled.

"Who are you?" Reuben demanded.

The newcomer peeled the mask the rest of the way off his face. Another face that could be familiar, if Reuben's dad had lived to be eighty. "Call me Sam."

"You can't be Sam," Sam said, "I'm Sam."

The biker peered at Sam through watery eyes. When did he lose those front teeth? "Who are you?"

Sam jerked a thumb at Reuben. "I'm him,"

"Can't be." The biker tugged his helmet off. "I still have my hair."

"I didn't get the transplant," Sam said.

"Stop!" Reuben snapped. "Look." He pointed at his newest, oldest self. "I'm Reuben. He's Sam. You can be Greg."

"I planned to be Sam," Greg snapped.

"I was here first," Sam said.

"Oh?" Greg raised his clockwork device. "We'll see about that."

"Stop it!" Reuben shouted. "Grow up. You're not playing Time Leapfrog. And you've been a Greg before."

Sam and Greg both flushed. "We don't talk about that," Greg said.

Reuben pointed a finger at Greg. "You. Why are you here?"

"Biocrash," Greg said. "Atmosphere's unbreathable. Sky's turning bright yellow."

"We fixed climate change," Sam said. "Sequestration works. Plus reforestation."

"What works?" Greg said.

Reuben shook his head. "Look. Sam. You coming here, you changed things. And Greg, you've changed them again."

Greg drew himself up straight. "Do not use that tone with me, young man."

"Oh, I turn into a cranky bastard?" Sam said.

Reuben said, "I'm already a cranky bastard. All of me, stop it."

"Like you know what's coming," Sam said.

"Listen to your elders," Greg said.

Reuben's stomach cramped tight. The air rushed out of him like he'd been punched in the gut, and the floor skewed beneath him. He didn't feel himself fall, but the rug was pushed up against a cheek and he couldn't feel his feet.

Very far away, Greg said "Some jackass went for superposition."

"I got this!" Sam said.

"Mine is better!" Greg said. "I've been doing this longer."

Strange thoughts oozed through Reuben's turgid brain. Something desperate, shuddery and weak, mental fingers scrabbling to latch on to his soul.

"I've been across the multiverse!" Sam shouted. "Stop interfering with my block!"

"Quit it!" Greg snarled.

The thoughts were strange, but somehow familiar. Like an echo of Reuben's own. He couldn't turn his back on them. Unable to do anything else, he willed them closer.

"Got it!" Greg said.

An impossibly distant plea faded. The room twisted into view. Reuben was sweating like he had just run a marathon through a swamp. His heart pummeled the inside of his ribcage. As Sam and Greg bickered, he needed all his strength to pick himself up off the ground.

He had never realized what an argumentative, boorish jerk he was. How had any Annual Girlfriend stayed around for even a year? He collected himself as Sam and Greg snarled back and forth about the many-worlds interpretation and temporal entanglement and other concepts he almost understood.

"What was that?" he finally managed.

"Some future you tried to merge himself with you," Sam said.

"From way too far in the future," Greg said.

"Didn't have enough humanity left to synch up," Sam said.

"They only do that when they don't have a body anymore," Greg said.

"Probably from a time track where humanity got uploaded," Sam said.

"Could be one of the transcendent ones," Greg said.

"Those are super rare," Sam said.

"But they're valid from this point," Greg said.

"We don't *know* what's valid from here," Sam said.

Reuben said, "Is this happening everywhere?"

Greg and Sam both gave him a look that shrieked *you are an idiot.* Wow. He hadn't believed Astrid, but she'd been right. He did have that look.

"Why would it?" Greg said.

Sam said, "Nobody else invented time travel."

Reuben steeled himself to interrupt when the kitchen doorway flared a brilliant, impossible white that evaporated as quick as it came.

Not again.

Reuben's fewer decades gave him just enough speed to beat Sam and Greg into the kitchen.

A gorgeous broad-shouldered black woman stood in the middle of the kitchen. She wasn't completely naked, but the tinfoil hat didn't cover anything Reuben's eyes wandered towards. In her hands she clutched a pair of potatoes, wired together with copper and a tiny circuit board.

She couldn't possibly be another of him.

She dropped the potatoes. They splat when they hit, skins splitting to expose fresh-baked steam, but before the aroma hit Reuben's nose she threw back her head and cackled.

Reuben had never heard a recording of himself laughing, but after Sam and Greg he knew that annoying sound all too well, as well as the triumphant crowing of "I did it! I did it!"

Reuben raised a finger and opened his mouth.

"Call me Sam," Naked Future Black Woman Reuben said.

"I'm Sam," said Greg.

"No, I'm Sam," Sam said. "You're Greg."

"We don't talk about Greg," Greg and Naked Future Black Reuben said simultaneously.

Reuben glared at Naked Black Reuben. "You can't be any of that. And what happened?"

"What do you mean?" she asked.

"This—" Reuben waved a hand up and down at Naked Future Black Reuben. "I'm not—"

"Oh, right. Can I borrow your bathrobe? Aliens."

"Aliens?" Sam and Greg said together?

"Why not aliens?" Reuben said.

"There aren't any aliens," Sam said.

"The kid's right," Greg said.

Sam said, "I'm not the kid. He's the kid. I'm Middle Reuben. You're the geezer."

"You don't look a day over ninety," Naked Future Black Reuben said.

Greg stiffened. "I'm seventy-four!"

"Wow," Reuben said. "Hard living?"

"I'm three hundred ninety-seven," Naked Black Reuben said.

"No way," Reuben said.

"Call me Grandpa," she said.

"But—" Reuben started.

"Look," Grandpa said, "aliens. They made us all look the same."

"They cured racism?" Reuben said. He was getting really ticked off at Greg and Sam saying things exactly at the same time as him. Okay, they were the same person, but did they have to rub it in like this?

"No," Grandpa said. "And the algae thing wouldn't have worked either. Hey, buddy!" She snapped her fingers towards Greg. "My eyes are up here."

Greg flushed. "I wasn't—"

Grandpa said, "Yeah, you were. I am not available. Bathrobe?"

"Wait a second!" Reuben said. "What is going on?"

Sam rolled his eyes. "I told you. You came up with the idea just now, so this is the furthest back we can go to make changes. These interlopers think they're going to make the future the way they want."

"It's not what I want," Greg snapped. "Breathable air is important."

"Immortal enslavement?" Grandpa snarled. "Hello? It took me two hundred years to get a time machine down to fit in a digital watch and two potatoes."

"Potatoes! Ha!" Greg said. "The air ate all the wiring, so I had to use clockwork!"

"You idiots let things get that bad?" Sam said.

"I had to kill a man to get the second potato," Grandpa said.

Reuben found it really difficult to keep his eyes off his—her—his, well, her... *everything*, so he made up for it in volume. "Hey!"

All three turned to him.

"I'm the local," Reuben said. "I'm damn near ready to call the cops and have *all* of me locked up in the loony bin if I don't quit bickering!"

"I know everything you do," Grandpa said.

"Yeah, you sure look like my driver's license," Reuben said. "All of you. Put the time machines on the kitchen table and go into the living room. Grandpa, you grab the red nightgown and join them."

Grandpa said, "The blue would look better with my eyes."

Reuben swallowed his bile. "Astrid gave me that one. You're not touching it."

"Oh, that was last night?" Sam said. "Maybe if you weren't such a jerk."

"TIME MACHINES!" Reuben bellowed. "On the table."

Outside the double windows, lightning crashed down out of the clear cold sky.

Reuben pointed. "And you can go find out which sort of time traveler that is, and tell him—her—*them* to sit down and shut up too."

"Fine." Greg set his brass and silver clockwork machine on the table with a thud.

Grandpa stripped away the tinfoil hat and the wires, making her body do distracting things. "Potatoes are only good for one hop."

Sam grimaced and unwound the loop of wire from around his waist and set the computer they were attached to into his hand. "We'll get this sorted out. I promise."

"I gotta piss anyway," Greg muttered.

"Put the seat back down," Grandpa commanded.

"Not while I'm the only one living here," Greg and Sam said together.

Not trusting himself to speak, Reuben raised a finger to point out the door.

For a breath, the only sound was water trickling from the broken faucet into the kitchen sink.

A distant groaning began elsewhere in the house. Distantly Sam said, "Hey, one of us built a TARDIS!"

Reuben bent enough to put both his hands on the table's cool laminate, trying to command his juddering heart to steady and slow. His clothes were damp with sweat, and he was going to keep on sweating.

All these different hims, from different but equally horrible futures. Well, maybe the atmosphere turning unbreathable was the worst. Or the aliens.

Just call them bad futures.

He rubbed his hands on his sweatpants, but they were too sweaty to take any more moisture. What kind of shower queue was he going to have, anyway?

A white-and-blue tarpaulin fluttered down outside the window. No, a parachute. A Reuben had parachuted back in time?

Think. He had to think.

The future couldn't be all bad. Sam and Greg had talked about the many-worlds hypothesis like it was a real thing. Most of the Future Reubens hadn't jumped right back here.

But if even a sliver of infinity showed up at his house, his life was basically over. Planet Earth wasn't big enough to hold the tiniest slice of infinity.

He might have only minutes. Seconds.

Only one real choice, then.

Reuben didn't have potatoes, and the clockwork gizmo looked way too complicated to wing. He grabbed Sam's time machine, the little computer with a cable worn like a belt. The four-inch touchscreen on the top had menus designed exactly the way he would have done it.

Target: yesterday evening. 11PM.

Method of travel: physical or superposition?

His finger wavered. Superposition sounded creepy. He'd been on the receiving end of that. But him showing up in his own house last night, surprising him, would just start the whole thing over again. Someone would wind up disposing of a body, and he didn't want that.

"Hey," said a familiar-ish voice that wasn't Sam or Greg or Grandpa, "what are you doing?"

Before he could think, Reuben hit GO.

And he was sitting in the Bachelor Chair, the big comfy leather recliner built for distinctly one, staring out the huge sliding door at the cold dark night outside. He usually pulled the drapes, but Astrid's departure had created a night for staring into the unspeakable void outside rather than the one within. The world doubled up, swimming in and out of focus, and the pendulum clock striking eleven still echoed through the empty, empty house. His lap was crazy cold—he'd spilled the beer. He wasn't a sloppy drunk. He had every reason to be morose, but that wasn't a reason to spill.

His hollow gut grumbled over skipped dinner, but he still wasn't hungry.

Reuben's vision stabilized. Everything that had happened settled in his brain.

Yesterday Reuben didn't doubt it. He knew too much about himself. That sudden rush of knowledge was himself, in a way that the far-distant Reuben hadn't been.

He listened, hardly daring to breathe.

The thuds were just the raccoon crossing the roof. Not Future Reuben Number Ninety-Nine.

The time machine was gone. Was that a good sign? He'd kind of thought it would go back with him. No, never mind, if he had the time machine he'd have to take it apart to see how it worked. He would have said he wasn't going to, but he would have. How could he not? He would have said it was just so he could see future technology, get a jump on the patents, make a second fortune, but he'd know why.

Better not to have the temptation.

And the notebook was gone—no—it wasn't gone, it was still in his study, but he hadn't yet had the dream that led to the sketches and numbers that led to inspiration. They had faded with the dream.

Still, he sat for almost half an hour in beer-soaked sweatpants, waiting for an explosion or buzzing or a flash of light and the smell of potatoes.

Potatoes? Never again.

Finally, he shook his head and staggered over to wash the beer off.

Hours later he was still staring at the bedroom ceiling, letting tomorrow's memories play out against the darkness. The queen-sized bed was far too big. Nobody was stealing the covers, and it was still downright chilly. He tried to convince himself he'd had a stroke, but it was all way too real.

The horrible truth was, he'd interacted with three different versions of himself.

And every one of them had pissed him off. Seriously pissed him off.

But they'd all been him. Sometimes him with great boobs, but him.

He'd always thought of himself as an okay person. He'd believed it, so it hadn't been a lie. It was a lie now, though. And he couldn't tell himself that lie. The arguments he'd always had with Annual Girlfriends weren't about him getting a job. Not really.

They'd been about him.

And even if the dream had faded, he'd remember everything. If he didn't have something else to work on, the question of time travel would niggle at him. He'd think about it five minutes here, half a day there, until inspiration hit again. Knowing it could be done was half the problem, and knowing the general area of science it lay in was the other half.

Reuben had caged himself.

And the bed was cold anyway. No point in staying in.

Cursing the day every one of him was born, he flung the quilt aside and picked up his phone. The number he needed was still programmed in.

Despite the hour, she picked up on the second ring. She sounded like she'd been crying.

"Astrid?" Reuben said. "Whatever it takes, I know I have to make some changes. I'm hoping you'll give me the time for that."

The words felt shockingly good.

Shoot Through the Heart

An *Immortal Clay* tale

Mack had a whole bunch of reasons to feel uncomfortable.

Even in Michigan's muggy summers, he didn't wear jeans or T-shirts. But for this trip, this *expedition*, he'd let his new best friend Larry talk him into a dark green pullover shirt and green-gray camouflage pants. The way his sweat made the clothes cling made him desperately miss his breathable polo shirts and khaki shorts.

If he'd worn those, though, any deer would see him even up the hill and through the trees.

The stupid camo pants were so steamy, they made his underwear cling. And climb. He'd gotten enough wedgies in junior high, thank you *so* very much.

The leaves overhead shifted in a breeze that only occasionally wheezed down to ease the heat. He'd braced one foot in a sort of flat place between two tangled roots, but the slope descending into the Sand River Valley was just steep enough to constantly threaten his balance. He had to keep shifting his weight to keep himself from tumbling downhill and totally humiliating himself in front of his friend.

He was sixteen freaking years old. He should be over all this drama.

But hillside or no, Larry somehow stood still and silent, his rifle braced over a convenient branch.

The clumsy weight of his .30-30 slung over Mack's shoulder didn't help.

Nor did the rising sun's merciless light that occasionally snuck through the greenery and stabbed his eyes.

Mack had spent his whole life avoiding the outdoors. It was either dirty and dusty and hot, or slick and snowy and frozen, and there wasn't a book or a computer anywhere. Just trees and invasive green ivy twining up bark and branch.

Invasive. That was a good word.

And this fake ivy? Doubly invasive.

Those weren't real trees, either.

The shape-changing alien Absolute had eaten the world. Everything that lived was made out of alien. The trees, the ivy, the teeming waist-high drought-browned ferns that filled the air with their heavy musk, all of it: alien.

Including Mack and Larry.

Mack tried not to think about that. He felt as human as he ever had.

The hillside looked exactly like he remembered from last summer, before Absolute, when Dad had marched him out for a "hike."

His chest tightened.

Only a few months ago, Mack had snarled at his friends about how Dad kept screwing everything up. Mack wanted to start his own business, learn more about accounting and incorporation law, maybe run for Frayville High's Student Council. Jobs like President were overrated, but Treasurer? That was real experience, *real* authority.

Instead, in the years since sepsis had killed Mom, every time he'd tried to take a few minutes to do something interesting, Dad had interrupted to drag him out. They'd go target shooting, or fishing, or cut wood for next winter's fires even though the house had perfectly good geothermal heat. An hour or two every other weekend at the firing range. A couple times a year they'd tube a dozen miles down the Sand River, stopping just short of Lake Huron.

For all the times Dad had taken Mack hunting, Mack had never shot a deer. He'd do great on the range, but in the field? Not so good.

Mack had never had the guts to tell Dad that he'd purposely missed every shot.

But here he was, deer hunting. Of his own free will.

Without Dad.

Absolute had duplicated maybe a dozen teenagers, including Mack and Larry. A whole bunch of adults.

But not Dad.

The tension in Mack's lungs threatened to become a shudder.

He pinched his lower lip between his teeth. He wasn't going to cry. Not here. Dad was gone, just like ninety-nine percent of Frayville and every single human being outside of this stupid little backwoods Michigan town.

The whole Earth a smoking cinder, except for one little green dot.

He'd give anything to see Dad again. He'd even climb into a boat and trick fish into impaling themselves on barbed hooks.

Mack bit his lip harder, until pain burned more than the memory.

His right foot slipped an inch downhill, skidding a trail through the dusty black dirt.

"Shhh!" hissed Larry.

Mack didn't dare raise a hand to wipe his shamefully damp eyes. He shifted his stance to steady himself and tried to look away to hide his face. "Sorry," he whispered.

"You're going to scare the deer away," Larry muttered.

What deer? No, Mack didn't want to say that again.

If Mack's clothes were alien, and the trees were literally alien-matter copies of real trees, Larry was the real shock.

Larry always dressed in jeans two threads short of the thrift shop and hand-me-down T-shirts. His folks hadn't had much money. Larry's "hunting clothes," though, looked brand-new. The guy had to be baked half to death inside the heavy cotton and nylon, but he stood straight and didn't pay any attention to the sweat trickling down from his dark brown buzz cut.

Before, when the world had been full of people and Frayville full of Civil Defense preparations, he and Larry never would have talked. Mack hung with the nerds, Larry with the rednecks. Larry was the kind of kid Dad wanted, all steady with a rifle and able to gut a fish with a flick of a knife.

Dad had loved Mack, sure.

But Mack wasn't sure Dad had *liked* him.

Even now, after Absolute had oozed out across the whole planet, Larry almost stank of confidence. If it wasn't for the alien, Mack and Larry never would have been friends.

And somehow Larry wasn't bothered by living on the alien Earth, without his parents or sister or anyone. Mack had no idea how he managed that.

"Chill." Larry adjusted the rifle balanced across the low-hanging branch. "Just wait."

Mack nodded. He couldn't blame Larry for dragging him out.

Not when his own stupid thinking aloud had started it.

Before, ten thousand people lived in Frayville. After Absolute... maybe a few hundred? Call it five hundred.

Each family had food for maybe a week. Say two, once you got in the back of everyone's cupboards and dragged out the coconut milk and the cans of weird soup.

Cut it in half, for spoilage.

Math came up with twenty weeks of food.

Northern Michigan had no real farmland. The only way old Missus Friedland had grown her garden was by shipping dirt in from down South and drenching it with chemical fertilizer. Her cucumbers didn't sprout as much as tried to escape.

Before, Mack had that same kind of talk with his friends all the time. They'd figure out all the things they'd do, all the problems they'd solve, once they were old enough for people to take them seriously.

Larry had taken Mack seriously.

He'd asked questions.

Then Larry had said that Absolute had recreated deer. Old man Deckard had brought fresh venison for dinner one night. And the best way to stretch the food supply was to get more food.

July wasn't deer season, but Absolute hadn't resurrected any game wardens.

"We wait," Larry whispered again.

"You're sure they'll be here?" Mack winced at the insecurity in his words.

"They didn't answer my appointment request," Larry whispered. "I seen them here, lots of mornings. But you gotta *shush*."

Dad always said the same thing. Mack nodded. The motion made his foot slip, again.

Larry rolled his eyes. "Plant your seat."

Mack felt his face flush even brighter red with embarrassment. He eased himself to the ground as quietly as he could manage.

The intermittent wind brought scents of green growing things and ash. His butt started to go numb against the hard dirt. After only a couple minutes Mack wanted to shift his seat, but imagining Larry's disapproval quelled that thought. He tried to keep his attention on the valley, on the sparkle of the broad, deep Sand River wending the final few miles of its journey to Lake Huron, but his stomach kept knotting.

Larry was right. They'd need food. It's not like Absolute was going to serve them pizza and chips all winter.

And it wasn't like Frayville was going to take care of teenagers. There weren't enough people for that.

And if he'd become Student Council treasurer? That wouldn't mean crap today.

A memory bludgeoned Mack: slouching in a tree stand with Dad, surrounded by gold and brown autumn leaves, bundled in a thick coat as the sun started to peek over the valley, waiting for deer in the same silence. He turned away from Larry and wiped his eyes as if the bright morning sun had blurred them.

"Sunglasses next time," Larry whispered.

So Larry could talk, but Mack couldn't? Mack clenched his jaw to hold silent. At least Larry had actually shot a deer before.

What kind of loser fired warning shots for deer?

Larry made a noise closer to a cat's growl than a word.

Mack followed his gaze.

The buck stood by the water perhaps eighty yards away, staring downstream, one foot raised in readiness to flee. Maybe it was a fake deer, created by Absolute's biological alchemy, but peering through the tangled branches and leaves it looked just as real as the trees, just as real as Mack himself.

Mack's pulse thudded in his ears.

Dad had called deer "dinner on the hoof." Mack thought they were handsome, perhaps even delicate.

Larry eased out a breath and raised his rifle.

Through the heart, Mack wanted to whisper. *Just like Deckard told us.*

After Absolute, animals only died when they knew they were dead. A shot through the heart would give a deer time to recognize the injury. Its own brain would tell it that it was dead and shut it down.

Larry had been right there when Deckard told his story. The only thing Mack could do now was ruin his friend's aim.

And if Mack thought he could do better, he should have had his rifle ready. Not hanging uselessly over his shoulder.

Larry moved with total concentration. He carefully braced the rifle over the tree branch. Brought his cheek to the stock. Lined up his shot.

The deer lowered its head to graze at the browning grass at the river's edge.

The crack of the shot made Mack lumber to his feet, struggling for footing on the ragged hillside. His left sneaker skidded on the dusty earth, only a couple inches but enough to make him take a step with the other foot. His rifle swung and tugged him to the side, and suddenly he was scrabbling for balance, his feet taking mincing steps of their own volition, his arms waving wildly. His heart thudded, each beat faster than the last. The valley's steep slope looked like a plunge.

Too fast, one step became two, three, fourfivesix—

Mack's grasping hand closed on a branch. The sudden halt wrenched at his shoulder but gave him the anchor he needed to recapture his balance.

"You okay?" Larry said.

Mack's breath felt hot and hard, like he was inhaling boiling water. "Yeah," he managed.

"Don't worry about it," Larry said. "You'll get used to being a hunter."

Could this be any more embarrassing? Mack unsuccessfully willed his trembling muscles to still themselves and glanced down into the valley.

The deer lay in a crumpled heap.

Whenever Mack had watched Dad shoot a deer, Mack had always felt a little sad. What had been alive and vital only seconds ago was a lump of bloody broken meat. Dad's talk about respecting the deer, making sure it didn't suffer, and not wasting a scrap of it always made Mack feel a little better though.

Larry's disrespectful whoop of "Got it!" knocked Mack from sorrow to desolation.

They had to eat, though.

Mack didn't have much choice but to follow Larry down the hill, skidding and grabbing branches at every step. The trees and slope finally ended together, the last of the hill giving Mack a push to run across the open grassland towards the river.

Larry was already on one knee near the buck's head when Mack staggered up. At least he wasn't gasping like one of the fat guys in gym class.

Even a couple yards away, a deep breath filled Mack's lungs with the rich copper-iron stink of blood. The Sand River's fragile susurrus seemed incredibly loud after the hillside's silence.

Larry leaned over the carcass. "We got it." Pride filled his voice.

The buck's white belly twitched. Dying spasms?

Mack grimaced. "How are we going to get it up the hill?"

"We carry it. Can't be over sixty pounds."

"Did you bring rope for a travois?"

"Nah, we just…" Larry shrugged. "Sling it over our shoulders and carry it. We take turns."

Uncertainty filled Mack. Dad had said you needed to field-dress a deer right away, getting its temperature down quick as you could before decay set in. Dad had always brought a whole backpack with rope, a knife for field dressing, all kinds of tools and lunch and everything.

Larry had said he'd bring everything they needed. Taking turns staggering out of the valley with a carcass over his shoulders didn't strike Mack as prepared. Were they supposed to just—ugh—let the carcass drain out behind them?

More spasms rippled the deer's furry stomach. Mack had seen too many times that death wasn't an on or off state. A deer, and probably a person, was complicated. Dying took time.

Why wouldn't Mack's stomach still itself? "Good shot."

"Thanks," Larry leaned forward to study the buck's back. "My mom taught me to shoot."

Mack wanted to say that his dad had taught him, but choked on the words.

Larry reached for the buck's head.

His fingers came back red.

Mack's stomach tightened further. He took a few steps to the side, crossing behind the buck's tail.

Bright red gore pooled out from the wound in the side of the buck's skull.

Mack's stomach became a single knot and plunged. "Deckard said shoot it in the heart."

"My dad taught me how to hunt," Larry said. "Deckard don't know sh—"

The buck's head crashed forward as its legs thrashed.

Larry shouted and fell onto his seat.

Mack's breath froze.

Step back, he shouted at himself. His feet, his legs, his *everything* refused to obey.

The blood soaking the grass rippled and twitched repulsively, then started flowing back up onto the deer's hide.

"Christ!" Larry shouted. Sprawled in the grass only feet from the carcass, he raised a booted foot and kicked the buck in the head once, twice.

The buck jerked back, legs thrashing in random spasms. One hoof passed half an inch from Mack's shin.

Mack's feet suddenly came unglued and he leapt aside, keeping his feet dancing above the buck's back, only a couple yards from the river.

Larry kicked again, his heavy waffle-stomper crashing into the buck's face.

The buck's head split apart.

Shock poured down Mack's legs, almost knocking him off his feet.

A deer's mouth couldn't open that wide—but the buck's jaw had unhinged like a snake's in those dumb nature documentaries, spreading wide to clamp flat teeth on each side of the boot's thick sole.

Larry screamed and threw himself back.

His foot stayed clamped between the buck's teeth, whiplashing him to a premature halt.

The buck gave an impossible shriek like something out of a demented musician's failed album, a dozen tones at once, full of atonal screeching and an undertone like metal on metal.

Larry's scream joined the buck's, far more human.

Far more fragile.

Mack's pulse hammered in his throat. He staggered to a halt only a yard from the crumbling dirt cliff at the water's edge, paralyzing dread burning in his chest and making his eyes water.

The buck thrashed, raising its head, turning Larry's boot and twisting his friend's leg, wrenching his whole body after it.

Larry clutched at the grass and screamed wordlessly, kicking blindly as he struggled to pull himself away.

Deckard had warned them—but it hadn't sounded real, not real like this.

The water! Mack could leap in. Let the current carry him away—

—but Larry.

You don't really know him. A month ago, he wouldn't have even spoken to you. You were, you still are a total nerd.

The deer's antlers twitched.

Antlers were solid bone, set in bone, but they somehow groaned towards Larry. Mack couldn't help thinking of a triceratops, but with branching horns. Acid vomit burned the back of his throat.

Bitter dread suffused Mack's body, his soul.

It wasn't a buck anymore, not a deer but a creature, a monster, an unspeakable horror like Absolute had used to take the world, something that would devour Larry alive, bones and all.

Would it re-recreate Larry?

Or if Mack came back tomorrow, would there be two identical bucks in the river valley?

If he didn't move, there might be three.

Mack couldn't pretend the valley was normal. Not anymore.

One of the buck's forelegs snagged in the grass.

The whole creature writhed.

Mack took half a step back.

The river's chuckle hinted at safety.

The buck raised its head, pulling Larry's foot up.

Larry's leg and butt came off the ground after it. Larry screamed, thrashing, trying to pull himself away.

No, Mack didn't really know Larry. But he couldn't abandon him.

Mack clumsily tugged the .30-30 off his shoulder. He automatically thumbed the safety as he raised the heavy weapon to his shoulder. The scope—no, he was too close, he'd have to try to sight around it, line up the shot as best he could—

It wasn't the firing range. Not at all.

Except it was.

From the back of his mind, Mack heard Dad's voice. *Brace on your shoulder—good. Exhale. Don't pull, squeeze—like you're getting the juice out of a lemon—yes, that's it.*

The shot startled him—but too late to throw off his aim.

A red blotch blossomed in the buck's chest.

The buck screamed again, a wholly mechanical sound this time.

Mack squeezed again and again. The wooden stock thumped into his shoulder.

The buck's head swung towards Mack. Not the body, just the head. Its neck rose from its shoulder, as if it had rearranged its bones to lift its skull. The legs stuck out at a weird angle to the side. Had they somehow swiveled in their sockets?

Worse, the buck's whole face had rearranged. Both eyes had pushed forward to glare in Mack's direction, but the pupils still pointed in different directions like a lizard. The jaw wasn't just open too far—it was wider, broad enough to seize a whole size eleven. The teeth looked too rough, like they were designed to grind a steel-soled boot into dust and blood.

But the space between those teeth was empty.

Mack didn't dare look away. "Larry!" he screamed. "Larry! Get to the water!"

He reflexively fired two more shots into the creature's chest.

Fresh blood blossomed.

The rifle clicked.

Empty.

The buck spasmed towards Mack.

Mack gave his own shriek.

The buck's legs, still sideways, kicked at the grass to push it forward.

Mack's legs threatened to fold at the knees.

Something big splashed in the river.

The buck was so misshapen, its frenzied legs couldn't launch itself at Mack.

Was that another splash? A gasp for air?

Mack surrendered to instinct, letting his feet launch him backwards until the ground disappeared and he plunged into the disturbingly warm Sand River. Even through his clenched teeth he tasted algae and lime and bitter, bitter dissolved ash. Empty rifle clamped in one hand, he kicked and splashed out into the deepest, fastest part of the water and let the river carry him away.

The monstrous buck's alien screams faded with distance.

Paddling just enough to keep his head above water, Mack struggled to steady his breath. He let himself sink to maneuver the rifle's strap over his shoulder, then spent a desperate minute blinking water away before he glimpsed Larry's brown hair bobbing a dozen yards ahead.

The Sand River should still be icy cold. How was it so warm?

Blame Absolute.

The river carried them half a mile towards the horror of Lake Huron before Mack reached Larry and they struggled up onto the opposite shore. The swim hadn't been that hard, but between shock and fear and stress Mack still gasped for air and his heart struggled to break free of his chest. The river had felt warm, until he collapsed on the pebbly beach.

Larry lay on his side, facing away from Mack, sucking in breaths.

The buzz of flies and bees in the meadow above the beach soothed Mack. The river whispered. The morning sun warmed Mack's sopping clothes, but the bed of water-rounded rocks the size of eggs dug at his sore muscles.

Mack's breath eventually slowed so he could talk without gasping like a loser. He shifted his weight to get the sharpest rocks off his ribs and spine and turned to Larry. "You okay?"

Larry didn't answer.

Fresh fear tightened Mack's spine.

Call Dad. He instantly hated himself for the thought. There weren't any phones, and if there had been there wasn't any Dad either. He'd been afraid of falling down the hillside and hurting himself, but he suddenly realized he'd rather break his own leg than be responsible for someone else's injuries.

They didn't even have rope to make a travois.

The hospital still stood, sure, with all its fancy medical equipment—but Absolute hadn't resurrected one doctor or nurse or even an EMT.

"Larry?" Mack heaved himself up on one hand. Pebbles shifted under his palm, but he steadied himself to reach out for Larry's shoulder.

Larry was quivering.

Had the buck somehow done something to him? Inflicted some kind of nervous system damage? Was Larry about to transform into his own deformed—

No.

Larry was… crying?

The incongruity made Mack freeze.

Larry wasn't the kind of guy who cried. Larry was the kind of guy who told other people not to cry.

He had to be really hurting.

Despite his dripping clothes and sopping hair, Mack's mouth felt parched. His throat seemed to have a lump the size of a fist in it. The rocks beneath him felt harder and sharper than they had a moment ago.

"Hey," Mack said.

Larry shook Mack's hand off his shoulder. "M'fine."

Mack made himself roll to all fours. The rocks brutalized his knees before he could even start to crawl, so he heaved himself to his feet and lurched over in front of Larry.

Larry turned his face further down.

Mack sank back to the ground, trying to arrange his butt around and between the sharpest rocks. "Hey. We'll get you help. If you can't walk, I'll get some of the guys." Bill and Keith were probably playing that old non-networked video game set they'd found. Or Ceren could haul Larry out all by herself—no, Larry'd kill him if he got a girl. Especially a girl two or three years younger than either of them.

Larry twisted a little more, trying to bury his face in the ground.

Should Mack touch Larry again? No, he'd shook that off. "What's going on? What's hurt?" Larry's buck-mauled boot looked torn up, but those flat teeth hadn't ground through it and the sole wasn't at a bad angle, so his foot probably wasn't mangled. Larry's hunting pants, perfect for November, were soaked and muddy, but didn't look torn. His leg wasn't lying at a weird angle, so the buck probably hadn't—

Larry choked out, "I miss my dad."

Pain that had nothing to do with their desperate flight flashed through Mack's chest.

If Mack's dad had gone hunting with them—well, they wouldn't have gone hunting. Not out of season, when the young bucks needed to grow up. Dad would have figured some other way to get food.

And if they'd had to go hunting, Dad would have listened to Deckard.

No, don't say that. Not now.

"He told me all about it," Larry gasped. "How he'd stalk. And wait. How hard it was to lug everything out. How you needed the right blind, the right rifle, the right everything."

"You mean…" Mack paused. "You mean he never—you've never actually been hunting?"

Face pressed against the rocks, Larry shook his head.

"You—" Mack swallowed his shout. "But your clothes."

"Surplus store. Yesterday."

Mack smacked his palm against Larry's bicep. "And you yelled at me for not having hunting clothes?"

Larry coughed. "Yeah, I suck. If he was here… And his rifle."

"His rifle?"

"Lost it. By the deer." Larry rolled onto his back and raised an arm to cover his eyes, like if he didn't see Mack then Mack couldn't see him. "It's gone. He didn't want me to go with him, and I don't even have his hunting piece."

Studying Larry's blotchy cheeks and chin made Mack feel like a trespasser. He leaned back to watch the water, resting both of his hands on the rocks behind him and pretended he didn't hear Larry crying. Sunlight reflecting off the rippling river made Mack narrow his eyes.

Larry had been confident. He'd taken charge.

He had no idea what he was doing.

Mack had never shot a deer, but he'd gone hunting with his dad for the last what… ten Novembers? Eight at least.

Embarrassment flooded Mack—not for Larry, but for himself.

Mack had chafed at every hunting trip.

Larry had gotten to stay home.

Mack had deliberately missed every shot he took.

Larry had never had the chance to take a shot.

Mack's Dad had only sighed and said *that's okay*.

Larry's father hadn't wanted him to even try.

Mack's Dad… *had* wanted him.

Heat flooded Mack's face. Dad had to have known Mack had missed the shots. Dad had to know that Mack hadn't really wanted to go.

Mack's throat tightened. His eyes burned. All those hunting trips he'd begrudged Dad? Dad had left Mack so much better prepared than Larry ever would be.

Those weekends, wasted at the range and on the river? He'd left Mack with so much more than Larry's father had.

Mack needed a moment to strangle his own tears. "Hey," he finally said.

Larry didn't answer.

"That buck—or whatever it is." Mack deliberately relaxed the clench from his jaw. "It's not going to stay there forever. By the time we hike up to the bridge and back around there, it'll probably be gone. I bet your dad's rifle is right where we were."

Larry didn't answer.

"I mean, unless the deer are arming themselves," Mack said. "Then we've got bigger troubles."

Larry huffed. It wasn't quite a laugh, but at least it wasn't a sob.

"Worst case, it's in the water, right there. We clean it, it'll be good as new." Mack kept his eyes on the river, trying to give Larry a hint of privacy.

A beat later, from the corner of his eye, Mack saw Larry nod.

Mack sat, letting his swirling thoughts settle out. He'd wanted to be an accountant, a businessman. He'd wanted to grow up to be in charge of something big, something that mattered. Before Absolute, money ruled the world.

Today? Who knew. But in a few more months, the people who brought in food would be heroes or kings.

Mack had never felt more terror than facing the monster buck. But the thought of how Dad had prepared him to deal with that warmed his heart even as his own tears strayed down his cheek.

Larry lowered his arm to scrub at his eyes.

Mack kept his eyes on the river. "Let's get your rifle. I'll get Dad's hunting gear together this afternoon. Tomorrow morning, we come back with rope and knives and try again."

Larry let out a shaky breath. "Okay."

That meant that the days Mack deliberately missed every shot had to be past. "And this time, like Deckard said. We shoot through the heart."

Perhaps animals had to know they were dead.

But Mack intended to know he was alive. For a very long time.

Forbidden Taste

A Prohibition Orcs tale

1

An orcess placed each footstep with care.

Especially when daring not just beyond her tenement, but beyond her neighborhood.

January's wrath had risen too bitter for fresh snow despite the midmorning Sun. Wind scoured dead snowdrifts, scattering bitter dandelion-seed ice across the pebbly asphalt and sturdy storefronts and Vara's squint, and January's knives had flensed Detroit's trees to the bark. Human shopkeepers scattered sand on the boardwalk so that their human patrons wouldn't slip, but that spray of sand came nowhere near the narrow gap of churned frozen mud that separated the road from the boardwalk. Lumbering canvas-sided trucks and growling gleaming Model Ts further stirred the air into a madness as wild as her two sons in their fourth year.

Unlike her triumphantly unstoppable sons, Vara could offer order to the air one breath at a time. That was an orcess' second greatest duty, offering order to the clan. Each exhaust-tainted inhalation burned down her nose and throat, returning the warmth of her lungs to January. That was the only sacrifice January could claim, thanks to Vara's wonderful new coat. The heavy brown wool hung halfway down her calves, and Vara had used her tiniest stitching on each seam. The cloth in front overlapped by two handspans, and precious smooth bone buttons the size of her thumbnail held it closed from neck to waist. The sleeves were long enough that she could pull her hands up into them, although she had to be careful with the talon she kept unfiled, for slicing while cooking. She'd had enough wool left for a tidy cap that cradled her scalp and ears and even the back of her neck. In a fit of delight she had sewn one of Grandmother's yellowing ribs into the crown as a decoration, declaring that she was an orcess with a long clan. Not a boast. A fact. January set Vara's face to fire and planted an ache in the roots of her Greater Tusks, but her core steamed.

No other orcess owned such rich clothing. Her warrior Uruk-Tai had taken the profits from bootlegging, bought Vara an entire bolt of plush wool from the *tailor*, and demanded she sew herself a coat warmer than his own. Even as she snarled at him for daring to command her, her heart had swelled so hard her eyes threatened to water. She had seen Uruk's fire when they were both young. That bolt of snugly scratchy wool proved that she had not seen deeply enough. Her demands on him had not been fierce enough, something she joyfully righted at that moment and every chance since.

Perhaps there would be a daughter. She loved her boys, but—perhaps.

Vara crushed the thought before January could smell a hint of hope. What happened, would happen. An orc owned only what she could take and hold.

Which made this trip so dangerous. She must not betray even one shred of the foolish childhood hope.

Vara kept her feet on the narrow treacherous track of mud-ice between boardwalk and asphalt where orcs were permitted, huddling her shoulders small as if she thought she could shrink from the sight of the Sun, let alone jealous January. Grandmother's wisdom echoed in Vara's bones. *Is a walk to the grain elevator worth your death? Then don't look at human faces. Dwarves don't care. If you find an elf, or when a human* makes *it worth your death? Meet their gaze with your tusks.*

Vara glanced up every step to stay aware of oncoming Model Ts. After the morning choke, the remaining traffic prowled more angrily. Across the boardwalk, frost and haze gleamed over windows marked by symbols that told humans what the store offered.

In October, those symbols had been wholly unfamiliar. The school thought that her boys could be taught to *read*, however. Oscar and Ivan had brought home flimsy books full of those symbols. Even though Vara labored at cooking and cleaning for the clan, the tenement was small, and she knew her magnificent boys would soon leave to found their own small clans in the greater Tai. Against that day, she stored their every word in the pit of her heart. Their interrogations of each other's knowledge of the un-orcish *letters* and their growls of the Alphabet Chant filled her as she ground corn into meal and scoured the pot with ash. She couldn't help learning to recognize some of them: the half-circle of C, the pregnant-orcess B, the forbidding X.

A tiny part of Vara worried why humans wanted her sons to learn to read. Humans ignored orcs until they demanded service for war. Reading would not make young orcs into better warriors, so why teach them? She had finally decided that humans had strange ideas, but the worry still itched.

Another truck turned the corner ahead. A cat screeched. Vara tensed to leap, but the cat slipped free of the wheels and darted into an alley. Too bad. Found meat was always welcome, even if the clan could afford succulent pork bone with every meal.

But the truck's cargo bulged against the canvas, stealing a precious handspan of space. Vara shifted to step on the boardwalk, but two human women were coming toward her, chattering in their bright coats and feather-topped hats. Vara's fine coat would not protect her from human outrage. Avoiding death by truck was not worth death by human. She pressed her feet against the boardwalk's edge and leaned away from the road.

The truck grumbled past, so close that if she breathed in it would brush her.

Even with her eyes averted, Vara glimpsed the women's faces bleeding scorn. They had only just passed out of view when one muttered, "What is that pig doing here?" as if being out of sight meant Vara couldn't hear.

The insult ached. But Vara had known she would face insult today, and perhaps worse.

An orcess' greatest duty was not to her clan, her warrior, or even her children. An orcess' greatest duty was to choose her wars. The women offered a war she would not accept. They did not even understand that Vara heard them, that she had thoughts and ideas and could labor as hard as her Uruk. If Vara spoke, they would not listen.

There! The storefront where she'd most recently encountered *the* smell, the place where after a lifetime she'd learned its name. A store not meant for orcs, where no orc would dare shop.

For a heartbeat, Vara's legs stilled.

If the humans took offense, Uruk would wake without her. Her boys would return from school to find a dead stove and empty pot. Her clan would never know what happened to her.

She could return to the tenement. Let curiosity gnaw all her days. Her heart thudded against her ribs like an angered sow protecting fresh piglets, making her vision throb.

Or she could choose this war.

Vara took a deep breath and unbuttoned her coat.

January sliced deep, cutting through her canvas pants and both burlap shirts and digging for bone. Vara's sweat burst into steam, instantly ripped away. She held her coat open, offering January her warmth even as the ache settled into her ribs and thighbones. "I choose this war." Shivs scraped up her sleeves. January might not be as rapacious as October, but if Vara denied the Dead Month its due, January would claim it another way. "This war is for blood." She commanded her shivering fingers to still themselves. "This war is for *life*."

Four slow deep breaths and she'd surrendered all to January.

Vara closed her coat and fumbled in one of the pockets. Her questing fingers found the four greenbacks she'd set aside. Paper money! Whoever thought an orc clan would have *paper* money?

Uruk said that their money would change everything.

Vara glanced both ways. The boardwalk was clear.

Not giving herself even time to breathe, she took two steps and used her free hand to gently nudge the door open.

A bewildering storm of scents swallowed her. Human faces turned. Behind his counter, the shopkeeper scowled.

"Man." Vara spoke as quietly as she could, holding out the dollars like a shield. "I seek—" She took a deep breath and forced out the unfamiliar word. "*Cho-co-late.*"

2

Vara had first smelled *chocolate* in her fourth year, when Mother took the children to a human church festival. The booths had closed and the electric lights were dark, leaving the fairground lit only by the Moon's brilliant face. Vara had never before been out of the tenement at night, and every shadow had thrilled her even as the clan searched every knuckle of filthy trampled grass. The human Fair Lord paid a penny for each garbage-stuffed barrel lugged to his wagon, and orcish night-sight could easily pick out every discarded scrap of waxed paper and flimsy greasy cardboard and dog dropping.

Even staying within a dozen yards of Mother, Vara had spotted three pennies gleaming cool against the ground, a scarf of some soft cloth with only a little dirt on it that might fetch another penny, and a tiny pocketknife. Her talons weren't tough enough to slice canvas yet, so she gave Mother the pennies and pocketed the knife in tusk-grinning anticipation of her slightly older brother Kova once again chasing her.

Looking back, Vara was sure that Mother had known about the knife. Vara needed to learn to leave scars, and Kova needed to learn to bleed.

But that night had made Vara understand that humans lived in a world that orcs might only glimpse. The clan emptied every dinner pot Mother brought to the table and the children squabbled for the prize of licking the sides. Humans paid precious pennies for disgusting sweet bread from these wagons and tents, but only ate part of it before flinging it into the trash or straight to the ground. They bought *sausage*, and tossed half to the ground uneaten. Human sausage wasn't bad, once Vara scraped off the nasty yellow and red paste and the bun. Mother said that humans demanded every footprint of the fairgrounds clean and tidy when they arrived in the morning, and that the clan must capture every scrap. If humans wanted clean grounds, Vara wondered why they didn't throw their garbage in one of the many barrels, or at least beside a barrel.

It wasn't until years later that she understood that humans wanted clean ground. They just didn't want to be the ones to clean it.

Kova had lain on his belly with his arm outstretched beneath one of the squat wagons painted with stars and crescent moons, grunting as he tried to cram himself further. Should she use the knife? No, not yet. Stabbing him in the back would spark marrow feud, and Vara wanted only his respect.

Vara dropped to the ground opposite Kova and peered beneath the wagon.

A bizarre scent had slipped through the grass and mud and tickled her nose. Something like fresh-turned earth, but with a bitterness that tantalized even through the sickening sweetness humans coveted. It dug deep into her skull and sparked a shiver in her stomach, like the first time she'd tasted a sliver of pork. She squirmed forward, squeezing herself between the wagon's belly and the grass until her questing fingers found a paper-wrapped lump.

An orcess had only what she could hold. If she dragged out the lump, Kova would take it. The wagon's belly scratched her scalp and she barely had space to breathe, but she ignored Kova's growl and fumbled the paper open.

The earthy scent washed out even more strongly, an alluring richness that not even sugar could bury, all from an ugly brown lump like a wad of wax marked by human teeth. Whatever it was, humans thought it was food, so an orc could eat it. What kind of human would discard this? One without a nose?

Kova snarled a warning, but Vara stuffed the lump into her mouth.

Chewing the lump felt like when Mother had given her draught for a fever and Vara's whole body had melted into warmth. This new thing, it chained that entire sensation within her mouth. The sweetness sickened her, but on her tongue the earthy smell burst into a delicious fruity bitterness. What was it? Where did humans find it? How could she get *more*? She hadn't even swallowed before Kova had leaped to his feet, bolted around the wagon, and seized her ankles.

Vara had just enough time to open her pocketknife before her brother dragged her into the air.

3

Dozens of gallon glass jugs with wire-clamped lids lined the wall behind the shopkeeper's counter, each partially full of ochre and orange and black and yellow powders and grains. A bewildering cloud of unnamed smells tightened Vara's breath, each as distinct as her one son's sweat from the other's.

Rows of shelves held boxes and jars with fancy printed *letters* on their labels. The bottom shelves held familiar burlap sacks that leaked unfamiliar stinks. One trickled white crystals from a badly stitched corner—was that sugar? Why would anybody, even a man, want a whole ten pounds of pure sugar? The aisle was so narrow, Vara wouldn't be able to walk down them without brushing her shoulders on both sides. The shelves were no stronger than needed to support their goods. If she stepped wrong, they would come down.

She needed to trade with the shopkeeper *without* going down the aisle. Stay to the counter.

No, the counter might be worse. It had an oaken frame, but the top and front were polished clear glass. The shopkeeper had a pad of paper the size of Vara's palm on the glass countertop, a tiny metal pen next to it. Glass was fragile. Did humans have special glass that wouldn't shatter at a touch? He had even piled a pyramid of tiny white boxes that stank of lye and ash and flowers at one end of the glass, each turned so their printed labels faced the door. Was he so wealthy that he could afford to replace glass? Vara had seen wealthy humans drive past. This shopkeeper did not look wealthy. He wore a white shirt with a flat cord around the neck, tied in a fancy looping knot over his voicebox. The knot might protect his throat from a slash, but it would do nothing against a stab. His clothes weren't as sturdy as even the youngest orc's, but they would probably protect him from a man's minor burdens. The thin soft jacket had rigid straight lines from folding and looked useless against January. No, the store was warm. The jacket was probably enough, indoors, and she'd seen humans wearing heavier coats on the street. But where was the fire?

The shopkeeper himself looked like someone had seized his lips and pulled, dragging his entire face into a disapproving pout. Metal frames over his eyes supported still more glass. The glass wasn't like a window or the bizarre counter. They stretched his eyes sideways, but Vara still saw their scowl.

She threw her gaze to the ground before the human could take offense.

In the edge of her sight, the two human patrons shifted uneasily.

The outstretched hand clutching the dollars wanted to tremble. Vara commanded it to still. She might fail, but she would not disgrace herself.

The shopkeeper's lips puckered even further, as if he wanted to spit.

Vara said, "You make the best *cho-co-late*."

Without warning, one of the other humans laughed. "You always say you make the best chocolate in town, George. You can't be upset if even pigs hear it." This human wore an unfastened long overcoat and a round-brimmed dome hat with a tiny red feather tucked in the band. Thick black hair filled the space beneath his nose, greased so it could be drawn into points on either side of his lips. Why do that when he could just bite off strands long enough to reach his mouth?

No, Vara couldn't let human strangeness distract her.

One of the other humans gave a high-pitched stuttering laugh. Vara couldn't tell if they were a man or a woman. An orc could speak to a man, but if a man was present they couldn't talk to a human woman. Women were dangerous. Human women wore their hair long and had breasts, but this human wore a shawl and a bulky bright yellow coat that hid everything. Impossible to be sure, though they also wore a long skirt. Skirts meant women, though Vara had heard sagas mention a clan of deadly men who wore them. That made sense, if skirts meant danger. A woman, then. "Go on," the woman said. "Do business with it."

Vara didn't move.

"Chocolate." The shopkeeper huffed. "Fine. Milk?"

Milk? Did human men feed the young? Their breasts were tiny! No, more uselessness. "Not milk. *Cho-co-late.*"

The shopkeeper glanced at his patrons.

The man in the round hat said, "Go on, George. Live up to your boasts."

"Sweet?" The shopkeeper's glare dripped hate. "Or bitter?"

"Bitter!" No, that was too loud! Humans couldn't stand proper orcish voices. The shopkeeper flinched, and the woman retreated a step. But if Vara could get chocolate without the sweetness? Vara fought her surging blood and lowered her voice to a near whisper. "No sugar. Only *cho-co-late.*"

The shopkeeper's eyes flickered between Vara's face and her outstretched dollars.

4

Everything in childhood seemed wizardly only because Vara had never touched or tasted it. That nameless taste lingered in Vara's memory, mingled with the triumph of teaching Kova that she was a proper orc and the fierce scolding Mother had given her for slicing her brother on his bicep instead of his chest. If the Lord Commander President called Vara to serve in war the way Mother had been called, how would Vara survive if she sliced enemies in the *arm*? Vara practiced with that knife every moment she could seize until her arms lengthened and her talons hardened and her mother had nodded unwilling approval. By then, Kova had taken adult labor at the Port of Detroit. Because of Kova, Vara had met her warrior Uruk. A woman fierce enough to scar her own brother on the arm, where others might see, had intrigued him.

All of those memories, churned together with the nameless sweetness-buried earth-roasted bitter delight.

Vara might have thought the brown lump was a childhood dream, except every few years she caught the scent again. At the next year's fair, inside a locked booth. From a bale-laden wagon rolling down the road, skittish horses trapped between the cars on one side and orcs on the other. A taunting vapor of delicious fruity bitterness.

It existed. But without the name, she couldn't seek it out.

Two days before, Vara had been trudging from the orcish tenements of Hamtramck to the grain elevator when a shop door opened and two human women stepped out. Each bore a heavy mug. The scent stopped Vara like she'd walked into a bull. Sweetness, yes, and something nutty, but laced throughout, *the* scent. One of the women hoisted her mug and inhaled the steam. "George says he makes the best chocolate, and I must say I do agree with him."

Already thrilled by a long, deep breath of the scent that had haunted her life, Vara seized the word like a horse snatching an apple. *Show-callit.* She didn't realize she'd said it aloud until one of the women laughed. "See! Even the poor orcs like chocolate!"

The other woman looked away. "Ignore it. I don't know why we let them walk through here anyway."

Vara didn't have enough attention to spare for the insult. Not *show-callit.* "Cho-co-late."

The first woman laughed again, sipped from her mug, and took the other woman's arm.

Mother said that in the Old Country and in war, orcs hunted for their food. Detroit was different. To hunt, you had to know your prey's name.

Chocolate.

The word and the scent echoed in Vara's bones all day. It growled in her dreams.

No orc would dare trade at any human store, let alone a fancy store that was all glass.

But after another day filled with nothing but that echoing bitterness, that morning Vara sent her boys to school and her warrior to bed and armored herself in dollars for a kind of war her mother would not recognize.

5

The shopkeeper dared to judge Vara with his gaze, and she had no shield beyond the flimsy paper dollars. If a man claimed insult from an orc, the orc went to jail. Her weakest strike would crush a man's skull, and the police would kill her. Or, if Vara escaped, some other orc. The police cared only for retribution.

Only humans hid behind weakness.

Bile rose in Vara's throat.

Vara could leave. She could surrender hope of chocolate and go back to the tenement. Back to her fierce warrior and unstoppable boys. None but January and the Sun would know, and they would hold silent.

No. Vara had chosen this war. Victory, defeat, or surrender would account to her. And January accepted surrenders only to return death.

The shopkeeper glanced at the woman. "Very well."

Vara's heart trilled.

The man picked a box the width of his paired hands but thin as his pinky off the shelf behind him. "One bar of dark chocolate."

Vara fought to contain the thrill in her heart.

"One bar?" the man patron laughed. "Don't rip her off like that. Surely a dollar a bar is enough!"

Vara's breath wanted to race. She held it as slow and quiet as she could. Even a snort could scare a man.

The shopkeeper flicked a glare at the man, and choked it back. "Of course you're correct. One must not overcharge anyone. Even an orc."

The woman's laugh was even higher pitched than before. Vara had done nothing to laugh at. What amused her?

The shopkeeper said, "Orc. The money. On the counter."

Vara's bowels tightened. The counter was only two steps away, but one misstep, one slip of her pinky, and the glass would shatter. Police, and jail.

"Quickly, now!" the shopkeeper said. "You want this or not?"

Vara took one step. Another. She lowered her hand to a few inches above the counter and pried her fingers apart, letting the bills flutter to the counter. "Four dollars."

The shopkeeper shoved four thin white boxes marked with printed human letters across the counter. "Four bars."

"Very fair," the man said.

Vara's fingers gave in to the tremble. The boxes were barely thicker than her talons. If she tried to pick up the bottom one, her trimmed talons would scar the glass. Police, again. Could she only take the top three?

"Quickly, I said!"

Vara put one hand behind the bars, letting the pinky hover just above the counter.

"Don't get your dirt on my counter!"

Deftly and gently, she nudged the bars off the counter and into her other hand.

"You've got it," the man said. "Now go."

The woman gave that obnoxious laugh again. "You're a consummate businessman, George."

Heart thrumming, Vara turned.

"You talk with George for a moment, dear," the man said. "I have to take care of something."

Hardly daring breathe, Vara hooked the pinky of her free hand around the door handle. She couldn't break the door. Not now. Not with victory literally clasped to her heart.

The shop would sell her *chocolate*. For too much money, yes, but it was possible. She would eat the chocolate. She would take more money from beneath the floorboards to buy more. Not too much. Not too soon. Maybe next week.

"I'll order a soda," the woman said.

How long could a morsel last if Vara sucked rather than chewed? The way that one bite had come apart in her mouth, was that because of the sugar or did chocolate do that on its own? Even if it dissolved, she could let it coat her tongue and savor it for hours.

If Kova still lived, she might have broken tradition and sent him a bar to celebrate her triumph.

Emerging from the cloud of scents onto the frozen street that stank of exhaust felt like diving into an outhouse. Vara pretended to not notice the man following her out, carefully walking straight to the mud path.

"Hey, pig," the man said.

Vara would not answer a slur. She took a step towards Hamtramck.

"Orc!" the man shouted. "I'm talking to you!"

Vara stopped, throat tight, and turned.

The man said, "Making George sell to you was funny."

Nobody had made a joke. Nobody had even farted. How was that funny?

But the woman had laughed.

"Show up here again," the man said, "and I will call the police on you."

Vara's free hand tensed and flattened, as if to slash the man's face with her talons. No. Police. How many shops did Detroit have, and how many of them sold chocolate? If she dared visit one after another, week after week—

The man held out a hand. "Give me the chocolate."

"No." The word burst from her chest without thought, but when her brain caught up it agreed.

"Orcs do not get chocolate," the man said.

Vara bared all her tusks.

"Don't you *dare!*"

Chocolate in her hand, Vara turned away.

"Come back here!"

The slick frozen mud betrayed her, but every time Vara slipped she scrambled to her feet and ran again, precious chocolate pinned to her heart.

6

The three-room tenement apartment was still the beloved home Vara would kill to defend, but desolation filled her heart.

Her Uruk still slept after a long night's work, so she'd been free to hide the four precious boxes behind the loose board where the pantry shelf met the wall. The smells of decaying wood and long-dead roaches masked the hints of delicious bitterness seeping through the cardboard.

She had *chocolate*. A victory claimed by no other orc.

But she couldn't go back.

Orcs do not get chocolate. Humans valued chocolate more than corn, than oats, than tea or clean water or even money. The shopkeeper had not wanted to sell to her. Only incomprehensible human humor had made him do it. If she stepped back into that shop, police. If she went to another shop, one where the humans did not see the joke? Police. The shopkeeper, the shoppers, all the humans would tell other humans the story of the orc in the human shop. Soon, they would all know.

Those four bars had to last Vara for the rest of her life.

And she felt certain that once she opened the first bar, she would devour it.

Her arms ground corn for mush, but her heart hung like a rotting cow carcass.

When her twin boys Oscar and Ivan returned from school, she fought to take pride in the way they declared the Alphabet Chant. "A, B, C-D-E! F, G, H-I-J!" She knew that the sound roused Uruk, but he would keep his eyes closed and listen, just as she silently chanted along with them.

Their boys. Ten years old, and learning to *read*. To see the words on trucks and buildings and know what lay within. The Tai had a future.

Even if Vara's future would not change.

Feeding the clan and caring for their clothes was worthy labor that more than filled her days. Uruk's success at bootlegging, the way he brought heaps of bills back to the tenement until they had run out of hiding places and heaped them under the bed, did not take away hunger or stains. Vara, Uruk, their magnificent boys, they were all still orcs. No amount of money would make them more than orcs. Nothing Vara bought would change anything.

Out of all the humans her Uruk had met, one listened to an orc. Vara could not spend her days seeking out a human that would listen to her. She had no way to make thousands of humans listen at once.

But if an orc could buy chocolate, why shouldn't she? Orcs were not human, but they fought and lived and felt.

When the mush began to simmer, Vara added the pork bones.

"War," Oscar said. "W! A! R! War."

Their boys tested their knowledge every day after school. Whatever the school's reason for teaching them to read, it meant Oscar and Ivan would be more able to fight a city, a nation, a world that detested orcs.

Ivan grunted. "Dog. D! O! G! Dog."

"Cat," Oscar said. "C! A! T!"

Cat. Vara had almost had fresh cat for dinner. The clan could afford pork every night, but every orc loved fresh found meat. No cat dared haunt a neighborhood of orcs. Only out in the city could a cat be struck down for dinner.

Vara's spoon torqued through the bubbling mush.

The half-circle of C.

Then the upside-down arrow slashed across. A.

The cross, for T.

Not actual cat, but perhaps the nature of catness. You could not hunt unless you knew the name—

Vara stopped. Fire burned through her thoughts.

"Rock," Ivan said. "R! O! K!"

"No!" Oscar snarled. "Would you have Teacher Edwards declare your failure? Again!"

The boys were fixed on each other. Mind whirling, Vara put herself between them and the shelf to sneak out a single bar. Intent on the smell of *chocolate*, she had paid no attention to the cardboard box it came in.

"They go together," Ivan said. "R! O! K! R-o-k! Rock!"

"Teacher Edwards said spelling is stupid," Oscar said. "Remember!"

The box was decorated with the fancy curved lines humans used to say something was just for them. They surrounded two strings of *letters*.

"Stupid enemies are easier to defeat," Ivan said.

The first word was short. It began with a letter Vara did not know.

"Then defeat it!" Oscar snarled.

"R O K!" Ivan growled.

The half circle that opened the second word. Vara had seen her boys practice that over and over on their slates. "C!"

Both boys stopped and looked at her.

"R O K C?" Ivan said in nearly un-orcish quiet.

"What is that *smell*?" Oscar said.

The door to Vara's bedroom opened. The noise might have wakened her Uruk, but the sudden silence would have alarmed him.

The next letter. She had seen it before. An A—no, Oscar and Ivan had talked about this one. An A had a point at top. The two lines on each side of this letter were straight up and down. "H."

"Mother?" Ivan said. "You *read*?"

Oscar sniffed, taking a step closer. "What *is* that?"

In the doorway, Uruk's hands flexed. Vara knew he wanted to move in to stand with her, to take on her enemies. She had chosen this war, and she loved Uruk more for letting her fight it. "O."

Oscar moved to stand next to her. His lips moved. "Yes."

A repeated letter? An orc took every advantage offered. "C!"

Ivan tried to squeeze between Vara and the stove so he could see. A thud and Ivan's hiss told her that he had touched the hot metal. Vara waited a heartbeat so that her son would learn, then took a step sideways to grant him space. "O!"

"Yes." Ivan sniffed deeply. "Put it down, Mother!"

The next letter. A straight line up and down, with a shorter straight line coming out one side of the bottom. Her boys had drawn this letter on their slates. She had watched them draw it. It was part of the Alphabet Chant. Next to the one with the sideways horns.

"Cut it," Oscar hissed. "Cut it deep."

Vara felt her lips pull back to expose her tusks. Not just the Lesser, but the Greater.

Silence filled the tenement.

Next to the horns. The chant rattled through her. A B CDE, F G HIJ, K—"L!" Vara bellowed.

Uruk's snarl of acclaim was louder than her boys'.

"Take it!" Ivan barked.

The smell was an invisible thread through the bubbling mush and pork, but it wove through the air and into Vara's nose. The next one—like an H, but pointed at the top. "A!"

"YES!" Oscar said.

Her Uruk stepped closer. He made no effort to claim a place at her side. The *letters* were incomprehensible to him, so the boys were better judges. But his fierce smile mirrored her own.

She knew the next one. "T!"

"One more, Mother," Oscar hissed. "One more and it *falls*."

A strange one, this. Like the L, but with two more lines coming out the side.

Ivan bit his bottom lip, hard enough to draw blood. He knew this *letter*, but would not steal her victory. She and Uruk had raised him well, and the way he trembled against his need to join her fight made Vara love him even more.

Oscar said, "You can do this." Her love for him was its own creature, also coiled around her liver but as fierce as her love for Ivan.

And Uruk, standing before her? Saying nothing, but pride burning on his face? He could not fight this war, but his trust filled her heart.

The last letter. Only a few weeks ago her boys had talked about this letter, and all the others. Four lines. A W? No, that was up-and-down, the one with the wrong name. Vara's heart throbbed in her neck. All the lines faced her nimble hand. Her hand—the lines, outstretched like three fingers. Three fingers, three talons—the shriek of talons on granite! "Eeeee!"

Oscar and Ivan bellowed her victory, followed in a blink by Uruk. Her whole family seized her, shouting in triumph. Vara let their love and pride carry her even as they squeezed the marrow from her bones.

A sadly short eternity later, they released her, Uruk last. Vara let her fingers trail down his arm, telling him everything he needed to know.

Oscar said, "But what *is* it?"

Uruk's nostrils flared as he sniffed.

"It is *cho-co-late*," Vara said.

She didn't merely know the name. She had taken the letters of its name and nobody could take them from her. She owned the name of her prey.

The hunt would not end today.

Opening the box filled the air with the best smell Vara had ever known. The bar itself had score lines, letting her easily break it into four pieces.

Calling Control

I love my little brother Derek, but this engagement is a mistake. Our dad worked in a shipping plant, repairing the packing robots. Amber's dad is a lawyer. We vacation in state parks, usually in the areas without weather shields. They go on cruises and fly to Paris and Moscow. I've learned the hard way that if you don't have enough in common, a marriage cannot work. At least they're both Fixed.

Maybe I was wrong. Maybe Amber and Derek were a perfect fit. Going to the engagement party would tell me that.

Derek drove me over to the east side of town, next to the river, where all the old money lives and the new money tries to move to. The gasoline engine didn't rattle or smoke, but it still made a muted rumble every time we had to accelerate. Bits of plastic trim and metal joins squeaked and rattled as we went, and the car smelled faintly of uncounted previous owners. Amber didn't live on the big four-lane boulevard, or even on one of the side roads. Her family's street was a cul-de-sac, accessible only through three increasingly thinner streets. Derek parked his battered old gasoline beater next to a shiny new four-seater plug-in. A stiff cardboard sign on the front lawn of a sprawling yellow brick ranch read "Derek and Amber," with two balloons strung above it.

My gut had said I should find an excuse to go to the office today, but I couldn't duck out on my brother. Besides, an office security guard can't choose his own hours.

"You'll like Amber," he said he closed the car door.

"I'm sure I will." The houses here had enough space between them to park three or four cars. The walls of our apartment were thin enough that before Dad died, I heard my parents having sex, every couple of months.

"And our friends are pretty decent, too. I know you're not a college guy, but they're friendly. And you've been a year getting over five months." Derek picked up his pace. "You gotta move on."

I'd moved on. Moved out. Moved back in with our parents, found work. Would I move out? Sure. But I didn't really have any place to move *to*.

Derek led me around the side of the house, up a block walkway to a wooden gate and into the back.

Amber's family had a huge backyard. A deck of big thick bricks, built up high enough so that you could walk straight out through the doorwall in the back of their house. Willow trees with twisting branches and stringy drooping leaves. Aromatic cedar shrubs taller than either of us hedged the property, giving the illusion of a country estate and filling the air with their sweetness. And all the trendy things people have to show they're eco-conscious and have the money to be really snotty about it: pitch-black solar shingles on the south side of the roof, blue and gold carbon sequestration shrubs, a two-foot-tall recreated stegosaurus lumbering around inside the invisible fence, letting out a low rumble like a contented lion, continually munching the grass to keep it a uniform two inches. They did have bug zappers, though. There's ecology, and then there's spending the muggy summer slapping bugs.

"Derek!" The woman on the deck bounced to her feet, and I winced inside. I couldn't stand chipper. She wore a halter top and cut-off jean shorts, letting the June sun soak into winter pale skin.

Derek jogged forward, meeting her halfway, scooping her into his arms and spinning her around in a hug, her body melting into his.

She laughed. He lowered her to the ground and they kissed, three heartbeats of lips pressed tight together.

Derek finally broke the clench. "Amber, this is my brother, Kevin."

"Kevin!" She darted over and flung her arms around me. She released before I could react, before her orange-and-basil perfume hit my nose. "Derek's told me all about you!"

"You too. It's nice to meet you."

She flounced back to Derek, looped her arm in his, and guided him to the deck, leaving me to either follow or talk to the stegosaurus.

I listened to them talk about the wedding for fifteen minutes, nodding and looking interested at the appropriate moments.

Derek's and Amber's friends sifted in over the next hour. You could see the differences if you looked. Derek's high school friends had tattoos. Amber's old friends all had a sparkle of jewelry somewhere on them, a flash of color. The college friends wore everything from T-shirts and shorts to brilliant white neogoth tunics, conservative haircuts and eyebrow piercings to old-fashioned button-down shirts and belted shorts with leather shoes. Two dozen people crammed into a space that would seat half that. Nobody had any real flaws, though. We were all Fixed; the genes for bad eyes, bad teeth, metabolic syndrome, thin hair, all of that turned off. At least Amber didn't know any Ultras, or if she did, she didn't invite them. I made myself inconspicuous in a folding chair, drank my cola, and talked with Derek's friend Keith about the summer's movies. Derek had known Keith since high school, a year behind me. Decent guy.

Then a flash of sunlight on moving glass caught the corner of my eye.

I glanced over reflexively.

A woman stood in front of the barbeque, wooden-handled spatula in hand.

She wore glasses.

I froze.

Not sunglasses. Her round glasses had transparent lenses.

Some people, especially at college, wear glasses to look cool: little Lennons, big geeky Gates, whoever they're trying to copy this year.

The lenses distorted her eyes behind them. Prescription glasses.

A Control. An actual Control.

I'd seen Controls before, of course. I remember staring as a kid, Mom shushing me in the mall. "We don't talk about people's problems," she'd said, her voice hard. I could either stop staring at the Control—he was fat, I think—or get spanked, hard. Mom tried to teach me manners. I've learned to keep my mouth shut.

Keith leaned in towards me. "Hey. If you're gonna ignore me, go talk to her."

I blinked and looked back at him. "Sorry, I zoned out there."

"You did not zone out. You saw a pretty girl." He drained another swallow of lager from his glass. "Either you go talk to her, or I'm going to shout out that you're staring at her."

And he would, too. Dammit. She was pretty, though. A little shorter than me, an inexpensive red flowered dress that came to her knees but left her shoulders and arms bare. Skin the color of pale oak, heavy black hair tied back with a red band and cascading to her shoulder blades. She stared intently at the closed grill, spatula in hand.

With one last glance at Keith, I walked over. "What's cooking?"

She peered at me over the top of her glasses. "Nothing, yet. It's just heating up."

"It's real charcoal?"

"Natural gas." She waved the spatula through the crowd. "Amber's got enough sequestration bushes that they can afford the tax."

"Wow." We'd never had the money to support the neighborhood bush. How much did you need just to run a grill?

"Yeah," she said sympathetically.

"I'm Kevin."

I could see her thoughts through the pale skin of her face. *I know your game, mister.* After what seemed like an eternity, she said, "I'm Fell."

"Fell?" I said.

"Felicity. Fell for short," she said.

"Oh, okay." I glanced around. Derek held a beer in one hand, the other waving wildly as he talked with a classmate, a musician by the looks of him. Amber stood behind him, her arm around his back and her head leaning against his shoulder. A little knot of guys laughed, quietly. "I'm guessing you're a friend of Amber's?"

"And you must be the Kevin that's Derek's brother," Fell said. "The photos don't look like you."

I smirked. "Nobody looks like their picture."

"That one with you and Derek at the pool makes you look taller. Makes your chin look more square." Fell said.

What's wrong with my chin? "I should just be glad it hides my hump."

She chuckled. "I think the grill is hot enough. Can you go in and grab the tray?"

"Sure."

I found my way to the doorwall, through the video room, past a leather couch—real leather, the kind that comes from cows—and to the kitchen, where Amber's overdressed mom directed me to a platter of burgers, sausages, and marinating vegetables. I made it back to the grill without doing thousands of dollars of damage to the couch in passing.

Fell opened the top of the grill as I set the plate down. "Thanks." A wave of heat washed over me at her motion, and I smelled something burning. "I don't think I've ever had soyburger over gas. Looking forward to it."

She glanced at me. "It's not soy," she said quietly. "It's meat."

I leaned my head back. "Wow."

Fell studied my face. "Not vat. Real meat. From cows. And pigs."

My surprise must have shown on my face. That platter had a month of my salary on it.

"Keep your mouth open," Fell said. "That way the flies have somewhere to go, instead of on the meat."

"Sorry, I..." I closed my mouth and took a breath, then said more quietly, "I knew that Amber's family had more than we did. But I didn't know how much more."

"Seems kind of silly, doesn't it?" Fell lifted a patty from the wax paper and set it on the grill. The sizzle carried the smell of roasting meat directly into my brain without passing through my nose. "I mean, my family could do this six nights a week. But we'd rather do something with it, not just eat it."

"I saw cows once," I said.

"Zoo?" said Fell.

"Up north. We went up to the state park in Oscoda, to camp for a week in the forest. There's all kinds of old pasture up there, trees still growing back, but there was this old farm on the river."

Fell fumbled with the second patty, almost dropping it sideways onto the iron grate.

I wanted to help her, but that was expensive meat. What would they do if I broke one apart? Could you get arrested for property damage or something?

"So," I said, "we walked past it one day. You could see the cows out in the pasture, just eating grass. The farmer came by, offered to show us."

She set a third patty on the grill and reached for the fourth. "What's a cow like?"

"Big."

She rolled her eyes, the motion exaggerated by the glasses. "Yeah."

"No, I mean, it's *big*." I started to spread my hands, realized just how juvenile that would look, and dropped them again. "I mean, you get next to this living thing, and it's the size of a car, but muscle and bone and skin. A giant living creature. Their noses move in parts as they chew, and they've got eyes the size of an apple. They look at you, and it's like they can see into your soul. I can see why people argued against eating them, why they shut down the big feed lots, but it seems a shame there aren't so many around anymore. Every time I see one of those Animal Preservation Society donation things around now I stuff some change in, if I've got it."

"Radical, are we?" Fell finished the burgers and started on the sausages. The sound from the patties seemed to change; instead of just the sizzle of meat, I almost thought I heard the faint lowing of cows. The thought made me kind of queasy. I put my hand on the back of a chair and tried to breathe quietly. My stomach knotted.

Fell put the last sausage on the grill and set the spatula aside. Her hands were long and thin, the skin almost translucent. Her fingers seemed almost too long. Was that a Control thing, or just a natural variation? Then something in my face seemed to catch her eye. "Wow. You've really never had cow."

"It's fine," I said. I was *not* going to puke.

She lowered her voice. The sunlight glittered off her teeth as she said, "I'm in culinary arts, but you know what? I don't eat cow. Or pig. I mean, it cooks just like vat, you know, but it's a cow. They've got innards. They eat, they crap." She glanced around. I had to strain to catch her voice. "You know, I've got a bag of soy in the fridge. I brought it for me, was going to make it as part of the second batch. There's extra. You want some?"

I put my hand to my stomach. The roiling didn't stop, but it seemed to lessen. "I'm fine. But you know what? A proper burger would be nice."

Her smile made her cheeks dimple, and I saw a flash in her eyes that didn't come from the glasses. "Sure. You can help me lug stuff around."

My cola was getting warm in my hand. I took a sip. "Do you want something to drink? How do you know Amber?"

"Amber and I went to school together," Fell said. "My dad is Amber's dad's boss."

My surprise must have shown on my face.

Fell said, "Oh, a Control can't be in charge of a Fixed?"

"No! I mean, all this," I waved my hand around, "I just kind of assumed that Amber's dad was the boss. I mean, they must have three thousand square feet of house, a yard bigger than the parking lot at my apartment... I guess I really have no idea how much money buys."

She studied me for a moment. "All right. You should see my dad's place, it makes this look like a backyard shed. Yeah, can you get me a water?"

"Just water?"

She showed those beautiful teeth again. "I'm a Control. Sugar. Teeth. Cavities."

"Oh, that's awful!" I said.

Her face closed.

"I'm sorry," I said. "That sounded terrible. I mean, it's like you didn't even get a chance. You got screwed before you were born."

She sighed. "Look. Amber's my best friend. Amber's with Derek. I like Amber. So I'm trying to get along with Derek. Which means I'm not going to kick you in the balls. Right now, at least. I am who I am. And it's not awful to be me."

"No," I said, "you're not awful at all."

Fell studied my eyes for a moment. "I have to watch the grill. You can get me that water. Or keep standing there. Whatever."

I got her a plastic tumbler with ice and water.

"Thanks," she said, draining it.

"Sure." I gave her a tight smile and turned, intending to kick Keith in the balls for throwing me over here.

"So tell me about camping," she said.

"It's filthy," I said.

Fell laughed.

"Really, there's dirt everywhere. *Everywhere*. It gets in between your teeth if you don't watch out."

We talked about camping, which led to her vacations in Canada and Japan, which took us through twists and turns into school and work and a dozen other topics. Fell had one semester left to get a degree in Culinary Arts at the University of California Santa Clara. She liked mustard, hated ketchup, loved cilantro and garlic, detested prepackaged vegetables but adored fresh apples. "Everything should have apples in it. Well, almost everything. Maybe not garlic." She loved to cook, but didn't want the paperwork of running a restaurant. Her dad might own the company Amber's father worked for, but he'd made it clear that Fell needed to make her own way. The family trust wouldn't be hers until her dad died, probably forty or fifty years from now.

I kept noticing new things about her face. Her teeth were white, but didn't quite line up; one of the canines was slightly out of line. Her ears didn't match. The left sat a little lower than the right, and had a lower arch at the top, but the right was a little wider. Her fingers were long, but not freakishly so. They fit Fell.

As the afternoon went on, as she slipped me a soy burger amidst everyone else's cow, we kept talking. The shape of her ears didn't matter, but every time I noticed they drew me.

Derek became increasingly loud and raucous. I didn't count how many beers he had, but he kept hoisting Amber into the air by her waist and calling her "the best woman ever." Until he started leaning with the booze. When he tried to lift Amber again, and instead dropped her two inches and staggered to the side, I grimaced.

Fell gave a tight-lipped smile. "He's a little loose."

"I better get him home," I said. "Listen, it's been really nice to talk to you."

"Yeah, you had a great time," Fell said. "I was kind of amused, too. A little." She plucked her phone out of her pocket. "Call you sometime?"

I drove Derek's rattling car home, my brother babbling in the passenger seat. My phone felt kind of warm, where Fell had sent me her contact.

All kinds of people live in our complex: mothers on welfare, the mentally ill who get Section 8 support, retirees, police officers and teachers and other people at the low end of the social ladder. The condo our family lives in is at the end of a row, near the back, two stories of aluminum siding and cheap windows concealing three bedrooms and a damp basement spotted with mold.

Mom wasn't surprised to see Derek weaving his way in the door before me. Just as when Dad used to come home that way, she didn't say anything, just took his arm and helped me guide him up the stairs to his room. Mom had piled all sorts of craft stuff in our bedrooms, concealing the faded wallpaper, but left our beds just in case we came home again. Derek came home for school vacations. I'd bounced back a little harder. But not as hard as Derek bounced on the cartoon-character quilt over his bed that night.

My job is in the lobby of one of the old office complexes, a glass-walled chamber with a marble floor worn into shallow trenches by countless feet. Potted palms and ferns lined the edges, the building's effort to keep the D-grade Green Friendly tax deduction. Decades of cheap floor wax hung heavy in the air, and the only sound came from passing cars. From the years I'd spent preparing to be an accountant, I figured that the cost of knocking the building down barely exceeded the cost of paying the taxes on this fuel sink. This wasn't a building for businesses on the way up. I spent most nights in the guard station, watching video screens and reading. Every hour I walked through the darkened corridors of the upper six floors, checking door handles in case someone had scaled the outside of the building, broken into an office, and unlocked the office door. The insurance company said that they had to have a guard. Common sense said that the guard needed basic motor functions and a pulse.

When my phone rang at eleven the next night, I jumped so hard I came down on the edge of my chair, almost tipping over. Had someone died? Had Derek finally driven his car into a tree, or someone? I fumbled for the phone without checking the caller. "Hello?"

"Kevin? It's Fell."

My heart had already been pounding. I tried to sound collected. "Hey, Fell. What brings you here this time of night?"

"You said nothing ever happened at your job. I thought I'd be something."

"You're the best thing that's happened to this place in months," I said. Damn. That sounded so pathetic. Cheesy, even.

But she laughed. "That's pretty sad."

"Well, I'm sitting on a plastic chair with one broken wheel. The monitors are all black-and-white. The last thing that happened down here was when the lawyer on the third floor slipped on the ice out front and broke his wrist. In February."

"Ouch. Really, I'm stuck down at Wayne Airport. My flight back to Santa Clara is delayed. I was sitting down here, thinking 'Who can I call at stupid o'clock, who might amuse me for a while the airline finds their map and their flashlight?' And your name popped into my head."

I felt vaguely disappointed. "I suppose so. One semester left, isn't it? And then you're opening your opening your famous Real Pig and Mooing Cow Bar-B-Que or something?"

"I think I'll get a job at one of the restaurants. One of the high-end ones. Get some real experience."

"I'll give you a real experience."

"Oh?"

"Last year, one of the alarms went off on the fifth floor, right at midnight. That's when the motion detectors turn on. Investigated and found two sixty-year-old guys, a business owner and his assistant."

"What were they doing?"

"Making motion."

She paused for a moment. "You have *got* to be kidding."

"The funny thing was, they insisted that they weren't gay. Like it was a big deal or something."

She chuckled. Fell had a nice voice, a little deeper than most women, with just a little roughness. "Old people."

"Yeah."

We talked until almost one, when her plane finally got ready to leave. I told her to call again, any time.

She did.

Santa Clara is three hours behind us. When it's midnight at work, it's nine PM there. Fell called more nights than not. We'd talk about almost anything, from what had happened in her classes to a screwball missing cat poster I'd seen that night. When she laughed, her voice rose and fell in a syncopated rhythm, like she had an old-fashioned swing orchestra inside her.

She always asked how Derek was, and my mom. "Your dad is dead, isn't he?"

"Yep."

"What happened?"

I shrugged. "He got ill. Congestive heart failure."

"I thought that didn't happen any more? To Fixed, that is?"

I felt a sudden pressure, as if my skin had suddenly become two sizes too tight. "Even Fixed get sick."

Fell paused. "Did he drink?"

My skin shrank another size. "So what?"

"It's not an accusation, Kevin. I just noticed that your brother drinks, and you don't."

"I just choose not to."

"Uh-huh. And you help Derek home when he's had a few."

"I can't let him drive like that."

"Did you let your dad drive like that?"

"What, when I was a kid?"

"No, no, no. But you've had a driver's license for how many years?"

"I used to pick him up sometimes, sure."

"What else could you do, right?"

"Right."

"After all, your dad loved you."

"Sure." I knew he'd loved me. Mom always said so.

"And you can't let something happen to someone you love."

"Right. Look, is there a point to this?"

"Not really," Fell said. "I'm just curious. People ask me about Control stuff all the time, so I feel like sometimes I get to be nosy."

"I haven't asked you about what it's like to be a Control."

"Not since the first time."

"I decided I wanted to keep my kidneys." The tension in me started to bleed away with the sarcasm.

"So go ahead. Ask."

"Your grandparents, however far back, decided to not get their genes fixed. And your parents stuck with it. How come?"

"My grandparents. They thought it was immoral, that it was interfering with some cosmic plan for us. They saved the money they got for having Control children, invested it. Dad actually turned that into a college education, and now he's a big advocate for Control rights."

"Do you ever wish you hadn't been? I mean, that your folks had had you Fixed?"

"Cure my astigmatism? Straighten all my teeth, make them solid, kick up my metabolism so I could eat ice cream and marmalade three meals a day and not have to worry about putting on weight? Does that ever really make anyone happy?"

"I don't know. I think having to get chunks of my teeth chiseled out so they could weld metal in would make me unhappy."

"I avoid that. And besides, what is a defect, anyway? Sure, turn off the genes that trigger the really nasty dementia diseases, or the ones that make you shake and quiver. Go further. Look at the Ultras. Some of them can lift a car, or think faster and better than a computer. Are they happier?"

"I hope so," I said. "I mean, they can lift a car."

"Lifting cars doesn't make you happy. I'm happy when I cook. I'm happy talking to you."

My breath caught in my throat. "I'm happy talking to you, too."

Now and then she'd send a picture: downtown Santa Clara, the view from the streetside cafe where she ate breakfast every morning, a shot of the Pacific Ocean when she got a day off to make a trip, her tiny room near the university. I found myself wishing that she'd take a picture with herself in it. My contract said I couldn't take pictures of the building I worked in, but that was pretty boring anyway. I found myself looking for excuses to head out to work early so I could find something to photograph. A bed of flowers in the easement between road and sidewalk. An old couple walking a ridiculously large dog. An engineered miniature wooly mammoth, two feet tall at the shoulder, obviously escaped from its home and trotting down the street between boarded-up storefronts and bodegas lit in flickering fluorescents, raising its trunk to trumpet its fear as it passed between bottles and abandoned bags of litter and posters advertising beer and cannabis and live shows from bands that had disappeared months ago. When I tried to get close, it fled. We talked for hours about that poor mammoth. All the beauty and hope and even bare interest I could find in the poor part of this crumbling city.

Derek and Amber kept up with their wedding plans. They found an apartment, signed a lease that started in August, the month before they were married. Derek planned to live at home until the wedding. And once a week or so, he came home falling-down drunk.

Just like Dad.

Then one night in July, while I sat behind my monitors and stared at my reflection in the night-mirrored windows, my phone rang. Felicity's number. "Hi, Fell!"

A man's cold voice said, "This isn't Fell. It's not even Felicity."

My heart leaped into my throat.

Cold sweat poured into my armpits.

"Who is this?" I said.

"This is Fenway King," the man said. "Felicity's father."

I blinked in surprise. "Is she okay? She's not hurt?"

"She's fine. I'd never hurt my daughter." His voice was low, but it modulated up and down with some tightly-controlled passion. The tone of his voice tightened my spine. "Actually, I'd never stand by and let my daughter be hurt."

My mouth flapped. "I would never hurt her!"

"You would never pull out a knife and stab her, I agree. I pay all her bills. I see her phone bill, and I wonder: who is behind this number with sixty hours of calls a month? So I ask around. And there's you."

Outrage bubbled in my bowels. "We just talk. She's on the other side of the country."

"A couple hours a month is just talk. No, my daughter has a long-distance relationship. Which I don't care about. With a security guard. Which I don't care about. I don't care that you were married for five months and got divorced after the police called an ambulance for you. From your picture, it looks like they fixed your teeth okay. I don't even care that your brother is a drunk, that your dad drank himself to death, that your mom is living on a pittance of a pension in a section of town that should have been razed to the ground and the earth salted decades ago. No," King said, his voice rising, "what I care about is that my daughter is spending sixty hours a month or more flirting with a Fixed."

I stopped cold.

"I've already told her that she can't talk to you any more if she wants me to pay her bills. I've talked with her about dating Fixed before. She's got a whole bunch of very nice Controls to choose from. She can have her pick. I'd rather have her choose a half-blind leprous Control than one of you shallow-gene-pool Fixed."

I found my voice. "That's her choice. It's up to her."

"That's what you think." His words came fast and hard, so I couldn't squeeze in between them. "And one of these days, something's going to happen and all you Fixed are going to catch something. Your damn genes are all polished flat. They don't have any character left. Do you remember the banana? They domesticated a dozen varieties of banana ten thousand years ago. Then they took it down to two kinds, easy to peel and ready to ship. The perfect banana. Then a virus came along and ate them all. Twenty years from bananas being cheap to being a hothouse exotic. That's you, Kevin. You're a hothouse flower. You'll die out in the cold world. And I'm not letting my daughter fall in with someone like that. And I'm certainly not letting my grandchildren be Fixed."

My mind plucked one word out of that stream of hate and hung on to it. *Grandchildren*? "Look, we're friends—"

"Don't try that line on me, kid. This is how it is. I now own the complex your mom lives in."

I stopped again. "You bastard." The air conditioning felt icy against the sweat drenching my clothes. "I'll get the recording of this conversation from the phone company, you know."

King chuckled. "This conversation isn't being recorded. That's how money works, kid. The rules are for you. Not for me."

My teeth clamped together.

King said, "If you call her again, if you answer the phone when she calls, I will throw your mom into the street. You're doing pretty good there, with your little security job. If you can keep your mouth shut, you might even find yourself with a promotion. I own a lot of businesses around this city. You could do worse than put in for a job at one in a year or so. Hell, finish your accounting degree and send your resume to my attention. Fixed who know to do what they're told make great flunkies, and I pay them well."

Rage turned my vision gray around the edges, and I shook so hard that my free hand rattled against the desktop. If willpower alone had been enough, I would have reached through the phone and ripped King's balls out through his mouth. "I will *never* work for you."

He chuckled. "You already do."

The phone went dead.

I tried to call Fell.

My fingers twitched.

Wrong button. Try again.

Wrong button. Again.

No answer.

Voicemail.

Hang up.

Redial.

No answer.

Redial.

Redial.

"The number you are calling—"

I flung the phone. It skittered across the waxy floor and came to a stop against a potted plant. My head pounded. My fury at King made me shake, but worse than that was my impulse to call Fell, to talk about it, she'd know what to do, she'd help me make some sense of this, there had to be a way, but I couldn't get Mom thrown out on the street, my job made the difference between eating and not some days, and if I had to avoid the companies King owned who knew how many there were left in the city?

I shook. I raged, quietly. I seized my phone to dial again. I'd broken the screen, hurtling it across the room. I didn't even know her actual number, so I couldn't dial from the old desk phone.

Eventually, I calmed down. I wanted to rage all night. The rage was comfortable, compared to the alternative. The truth.

Even if I called her, Fell might not answer. Her dad had power and money.

The truth was, we were friends.

We'd never talked about anything beyond that.

We were friends.

And I could lose one friend.

Or lose my job. And get Mom thrown out of the apartment she'd raised us in. Derek was moving on. Mom was up to me. I didn't have any place to go. Any reason to move anywhere. I'd help her find another place, but it wouldn't be even as nice as the pit she had now.

Or maybe I could go after King. Find a way to break him. One of the richest, most powerful men in the city. Break him to his knees. Make him beg.

I ranted. I raged. I quivered with fury.

The next day, I got a new phone and had the tech restore all my information from the backup. Standing in the parking lot, under a brutal summer sun, I brought up her contact. Her picture, from the day we met. Her phone number.

Deleting it felt like cutting half my heart out.

Fell and I were done.

#

Derek and Amber? Not done.

Amber's father had rented half of the Yacht Club Clubhouse. The walls were thick stucco, cool to the touch and with that irregular texture of lines and curves and soft points. Staff bustled around in jackets that opened at the front and black trousers. The whole place smelled faintly of sandalwood, an effort to cover up the nearby scents of lake water and seaweed. You had to have a city Yacht Club, but it didn't have to *smell* like a Yacht Club. My rented tux tugged at my crotch, and the jacket sleeves were a little bit too long, and the ghastly patent leather shoes sank into the wine-red carpet. I obviously didn't belong here.

After last night's bachelor party, Derek's eyes were red and his breath still smelled faintly of alcohol. I'd poured juice and coffee and aspirin into him this morning, and he eventually rose from the dead and shaved and pulled on his pants and let me take him in.

I was best man, fronting for Keith and two friends he'd made at college that I hadn't met. I'd studied the ceremony. Rehearsed the steps in the upstairs hallway of the apartment. Tried to avoid knocking the dusty pictures of old family trips off the walls as I followed along with the video on my phone. I made sure I had the ring in my pocket, a diamond the size of my pinky nail wrapped in platinum.

But I hadn't rehearsed seeing Fell. She was a bridesmaid.

One of the employees, wearing an extra little flowery smelly thing on his breast pocket that I think meant he was some kind of ultra-staff, directed us down the stairs. The groomsmen had a couple of tiny rooms in the basement, paneled in oak, with a long bar and a refrigerator. Bone dry, but I still felt we were beneath the waterline.

"We're here first," I said.

"We should be," Derek said. "I'm the Man, today." He leaned over the bar. "Empty. Damn."

"You don't want to do this drunk," I said.

"One wouldn't hurt." He sat on the stool and swiveled to face me. "Okay, I gotta ask. Why the hell can't you be happy for me?"

"I *am* happy for you."

"You've been walking around for weeks looking at me like I'd pissed on your dessert. I know your marriage didn't work out, but come on! They're not all like that."

I raised my head, surprised. I thought I'd hidden things pretty well. "It's not you."

"Then what, dammit?"

My mouth worked hopelessly.

Derek studied my face. "It *doesn't* have anything to do with me?"

I shook my head, unable to start.

"Dammit." Derek walked up to me. His hand was hot on my shoulder, even through the jacket and shirt. "Look. We were raised not to talk about things. Everything was fine. Ignore all the problems. But you can't live like that. I've had to learn that. The hard way. You can survive. But you can't *live*."

Derek drank too much. He pissed me off. But he was my brother, and this was his wedding day, and he thought I was pissed at him. I took a deep breath. My sphincter felt loose. "I... I lost a friend."

"Who?"

"Fell."

He looked puzzled. "Fell? Felicity King? *Bridesmaid* Felicity? You haven't seen her since the engagement party."

"No, I haven't. But we talked."

I sagged to a stool.

"We talked a lot. Just about every night."

The whole story came pouring out of me, like I was a broken tanker spilling sludge out into a clean ocean. The phone calls. The laughter. Her pushing me, me pushing her.

And King. Goddamn High-and-Mighty King.

Voices in the hallway. Derek said, "Hold on a moment." He stepped to the door, spoke quietly to Keith, then closed and locked the door.

"Okay," Derek said. "Let me get this straight. You lost a *friend*. If you speak to your *friend* again, her father will throw Mom out of her apartment. He'll get you fired. He will mess up your life in ways you cannot begin to imagine. And not speaking to your... *friend* is killing you."

I couldn't look at him. I couldn't speak. Finally I nodded. Disgorging all of that had left me nauseous, like I'd been the one drinking all night. "It's not that bad. I mean, if I'd gotten to say good-bye or something it would have helped."

Derek grabbed my shoulder. "Come with me. Now."

He pulled me off the stool, dragged me to the door, and seized the handle. His hard jerk almost dislocated his arm. Then he unlocked the door and towed me out. Keith and another groomsman stood there.

"Watch for Joe," Derek said. "We *will* be back before they call us. My big brother needs a slap and a shot."

"I don't drink," I said.

"Not that kind of shot," Derek said. "But I don't have a gun."

He dragged me up a flight of stairs and around to the rear of the club, down white halls, past glass-topped tables and buffets of steaming salty seafood surrounded by another wedding party. "You've got to say something," he said.

"Like what?"

"You didn't get to say good-bye? Fine." He dragged me past an open bar without even glancing at it. "Say good-bye. Tell your *friend* how you feel. If that's how it is, if this King bastard has you over a barrel, you at least deserve the chance to say good-bye. He probably won't even find out. Two minutes, and done."

"She hasn't called me."

"And who knows what he's told her? 'Call that guy again and I'll throw his mom onto the street?'"

"But it's been months."

Derek stopped in front of a door, turned to face me, and said "This is what you say. I'm sorry I haven't called. You've been a good friend. I hope to see you again sometime. That's how you feel, right? Then you listen to what she has to say."

I took a deep breath. "Yeah."

He nodded. "Then you come back downstairs with me. It's closure. Pull out the knife. Say good-bye."

He pushed the door open.

The room was the size of a two-car garage, covered in sparkly white wallpaper, with gauze curtains blocking out the worst of the August sunlight. The furniture was all white and upholstered, fancy curves and gold trim. I smelled lavender and chamomile and a dozen other scents, all mingled together in a fog labeled "bride."

Fell stood behind Amber, helping Amber arrange her hair. Two other bridesmaids sat on a couch in the back of the room, chattering excitedly.

Fell froze, tiara in hand.

I'd heard her voice months ago, but hadn't seen her since months before that. Her black hair, pulled back before, was arranged in great swooping curves, flying buttresses that even a cathedral couldn't compete with. Her face had makeup to shift her color a little closer to Amber's, but I saw the light brown clearness beneath that. The pale blue dress came to her ankle and left her shoulders exposed, with a giant bow on the side of her waist. The dress had some kind of silver sparkle in the fabric, and she'd put a matching sparkle over her bare shoulders and neck. She didn't need the lipstick, or the nail polish.

"Derek!" Amber said. "You can't be here!"

The distant chattering from the couch ceased.

"It's just a minute," Derek said. "Kevin's got a bit of a problem."

Fell's lips parted slightly. I could see the white of her teeth through them. She let out just a tiny whisper of breath. One of her shoulders twitched.

"What's wrong?" Amber asked from somewhere.

I stepped into the room. Derek was right.

"Fell," I said.

She didn't say anything.

I'd never been good with saying how I felt. The only time my dad spoke of his feelings was when he'd had too much to drink and began ranting against everyone who had wronged him.

Derek had given me words. They'd been good words. Good enough.

As good as I deserved.

"I'm..." I started.

What had Derek said, dammit?

"Living without you is like being dead," I said. "It's like being in a box in the ground, with no air and no reason to breathe. I miss your voice. Every minute. Every day. I know we were just friends. We never talked about more. And that's okay. But I had to tell you. It's dragged me down since your dad told me to get out of your life. Since you never called again. I'm sorry. I know that's not what you wanted. That you were just a friend. But I had to tell you. I had to tell you or just die."

A tremble started in Fell's chin, spreading up her face and down her shoulders. I saw her arms quiver.

Someone burst into tears. I don't think it was me.

My legs had turned to rusty metal. My knees creaked.

I tottered in a nonexistent breeze.

Fell's chin quivered. "I'm sorry," she said.

What remained of my soul instantly shriveled.

The ground wavered beneath me.

A black halo circled my vision.

"I'm sorry," Fell said. "I love you too."

Something shattered in me, then I was stumbling forward, arms reaching for my Fell, touching the heat of her hands, then her arms clamped around me so tight I couldn't breathe. Her eyes were huge and brown without the glasses, large enough to drown in, and I lowered my chin and kissed her.

Fell tasted of sweet oranges and life.

Tears filled my eyes. I didn't care.

Fell buried her face in my chest. "I missed you," she whispered.

Someone was bawling, great choking sobs.

Derek said, "My brother is not a complete idiot, Amber. Despite what you might have thought."

I shivered and pulled Fell even closer, so that she gasped.

Then a voice I would never forget said, "This is just lovely."

I turned, my arms still around Fell.

King stood in the doorway. I'd never seen him before. Only imagined a vague figure. Usually with my fists crashing into his nose. He had a great hooked nose. Hair slicked back from a severe widow's peak. For a Control, he had a surprisingly sturdy build, with none of the signs of aging you'd expect from a man in his early forties.

"My conditions still stand," King said. "You don't go anywhere near my daughter. And Felicity, you are to leave this creature alone." Fury had turned his face red.

The tension in my body changed. What had been a desperate, passionate embrace had turned to a readiness to fight. I hadn't taken a swing at anyone since elementary school scrapes, but I was ready to leap across the room and claw King's eyes out.

Fell squeezed me even tighter.

"Or what?" Derek said.

King spoke through gritted teeth. "Or you will wish you had."

Amber looked back at the couch. "Heather?"

The skinny redhead on the couch nodded. "Got it. Uploaded it. Live."

King swiveled his head to stare at Heather, then at Amber.

I felt Fell tremble against me. Then she unclasped her hands and stepped back.

My arms went limp at her motion away.

Fell turned to her father. "You threatened me," she said quietly. "You threatened him. And I'm telling you this. I want to be with Kevin." Her fumbling hand found mine. "I will be with him."

"You've got a good life ahead of you," King said. "And it's not with him."

"You knew I got divorced," I said. "You saw the pictures. Did you read the police report?"

King scowled at me.

I took half a step forward. "Do you know *why* I was in the hospital?"

Another half step. "I told Rebecca that she had to stop drinking."

There.

I'd said her name.

For the first time since signing the divorce decree.

I took a deep breath, more to support the words than to steady myself. "She hit me. I said that hitting me didn't change anything. So she hit me again. I couldn't hit her. I loved her."

My words were getting stronger. Part of me felt a ridiculous elation at finally saying this, at finally finding a use for this pain. "She hit me again, and again. The neighbors called because Rebecca was screaming. By the time the cops got there, she'd knocked out half my teeth. Broken my arm, my leg, ribs. Punctured my spleen. I woke up in the hospital and called a lawyer. I dropped out of school."

I took a breath. "But I never. *Never*. Hit her back."

His furious brown eyes never left mine.

"So it's like this," I said. "I'm going to be with my Fell. The only way you can stop me is to kill me. Nothing less will do it. Are you willing to kill the man your daughter loves?"

Fell moved back to my side. Her arm went around me like a life preserver.

King's eyes moved around the room. "This is a public occasion. Lots of figures here. Otherwise, I'd take the time to explain the error of your ways." He looked at Fell. "You *will* be back."

King stepped back and slammed the door.

Amber threw her arms around Fell and I. "I am so happy," she said. "Fell has been miserable. For *months*."

"He'll be back," Derek said quickly. "That bastard won't waste any time." He looked at Amber.

Amber nodded.

"But don't you worry about Mom," said Derek. "I'll take care of her. I'm going to work with Amber's dad right after the wedding. Start at the bottom, but who knows? It's gotta beat being a security guard."

Amber reached down the front of her dress, fumbling around. "Here." She pulled out a thick sheaf of cash. "I was afraid something would go wrong today. I wanted to be able to buy whatever I needed. But something has gone right." Tears filled her eyes. "Really right." She stuffed the money into my tux pocket. "Go."

"And we've got his threats on video," Heather said. "It won't stop him, but it'll prove motive."

"Yeah," Derek said. "We got your back, brother."

I grabbed his hand, and he pulled me close to pound my back. I was already turning away from him as I stuffed Amber's wedding ring into his hand.

I looked at Felicity. Her eyes gleamed, with more than just light.

"Two things," she whispered.

"Anything," I said.

"If I push you, you push back."

"Yes."

"And I'll cook. If you do the books."

"Done."

"King probably has guys watching around," Amber said. "Maybe you better go out the window."

"Here," Derek said. "Take my car. It's filled up."

Fell and I hugged Derek and Amber. Maybe their marriage isn't a bad idea after all.

Easy, Step-By-Step Preparation

Dear Stefon,

Here's today's Phone Gourmet Meal Kit! Today we have a special treat for you: quick and easy chicken mole! By following our program you won't merely be tonight's cook: you will become a *chef*.

Your preferences indicate you eat dinner at 6 PM on Tuesday nights. Start cooking at 5:15 sharp to have a tasty meal for Jenny exactly on time!

Lay out the ingredient pouches, in numbered order. Get out your large skillet, medium saucepan, immersion blender, and large soup pot. Then click Next.

(click)

Open Pouch 1, All-Natural Organic Chicken Stock, and pour it into the medium saucepan. Be sure to taste just a drop of our savory broth so you understand the flavor underlying your mole. Enjoy the depth of it.

You might notice our stock tastes sharper than any other. That's because the Phone Gourmet makes their chicken stock using only all-natural ingredients and simmers it until it's thick and zesty. Plus, we customized this blend specifically for you and your wife. It's all part of the PG experience!

(click)

Open Pouch 2: guajillo chilies, ancho chiles, pasilla chilies, and chipotle chilies. We usually recommend you taste each pouch as you open it, but you won't want a mouthful of these! Instead, bring it to your nose and take a deep, deep sniff. You might notice an unusually intense burning in your sinuses, but it will quickly pass. Just go with it. Remember our guarantee: you'll enjoy dinner or your money back!

(click)

Yes, those peppers are fierce! Our peppers are especially flavorful, but they won't burn your stomach.

Smell them again.

With your large skillet, over medium heat, toast the peppers. Stir constantly for three minutes. Once they are warm and soft, turn the heat off.

Do *not* eat any peppers. No matter how good they smell.

(click)

When the stock is simmering, add the toasted peppers.

You might notice a faint tingling in your scalp. This is from the natural enzymes of our ultra-fresh ingredients. There is nothing to worry about.

(click)

Open Pouch 3, Bread and Tortilla Pieces. Sample one of the tortilla strips. Isn't it yummy? Your mouth and nose might start to feel numb, but that's only because the tortilla soothes any lingering burn from the peppers.

Do not sample additional tortilla strips. Yes, they're yummy. Don't do it. You'll ruin the recipe.

(click)

Toast the bread chunks and tortilla pieces in your large skillet, stirring constantly, until lightly browned. This will take about three minutes.

Scoop the bread and tortilla pieces into the saucepan. Using a long-handled spoon, fully submerge them into the broth and pepper mixture.

You may now lick the spoon clean. See how the flavors combine? Cooking perfectly delights your soul. Precisely following our directions makes you a perfect chef.

(click)

The bread must soak for a while to absorb the stock and chili mixture. Sit down in a kitchen chair. This will also give time for your dizziness to pass. Everything will be fine.

After ten minutes, the app will ding to tell you to continue.

(click)

Blend the stock, chili, and bread mixture until smooth.

(click)

Open Pouch 4, Tomatoes and Tomatillos. Place them neatly in your skillet, side by side. Cook on medium-high heat until they're soft and starting to turn black, about 4 minutes per side.

Put the tomatoes and tomatillos in the saucepan.

(click)

Open Pouch 5, Lard. Yes, lard isn't very healthy, but it won't matter. Squeeze the pouch into your skillet and melt over medium heat.

Once the lard has melted, open Pouch 6, Spices and Onions. Stir the contents into the melted lard. Stir slowly until the onions become soft and yellow, about 7 minutes.

(click)

 Use the immersion blender to blend the sauce until smooth. Add the onions. Heat on medium-low.

Do not taste.

(click)

Open Pouch 7, Chocolate Sauce. Be sure to taste it—just a fingertip. Isn't it rich and yummy? Pour the chocolate into the large cooking pot. Mix it up with the stock and chili.

From this point on, taste nothing until instructed otherwise.

Stir every minute until the sauce begins to simmer. Reduce the heat to low.

(click)

Open Pouch 8, Chicken Chunks. Add the chicken to the sauce, stirring well until all the pieces are well coated with mole. Leave on low heat until the phone rings.

Load the dishwasher. Leave space for your big pot. Add extra soap, but do not start it yet.

(click)

When your wife's assistant calls to tell you Jenny is dealing with a crisis and she won't be home for dinner, remind the assistant that her doctor forbade Jenny from eating that awful pizza and declare you will bring her a proper meal.

Turn the stove off. Divide the chicken mole between two plastic containers with tight-fitting lids. Use a rubber spatula to get all the mole. Put the large pot and any remaining dishes in the dishwasher. Set the dishwasher to Heavy Duty. Start it.

(click)

Open Pouch 9, Clean-Up. Use the handy cloth to wipe down the kitchen counters, your hands, and your face. If the chemicals irritate your skin, you can wash your face and hands with soap and water afterwards. A good chef is sanitary, even when it's itchy!

Put all of the pouches and the clean-up cloth back in the Phone Gourmet delivery box.

(click)

Take the Phone Gourmet delivery box, your containers of mole, and two forks to your car. Drive to the convenience store at the end of your street. Place the Phone Gourmet delivery box neatly in the dumpster so our staff can retrieve it for recycling.

Take your wife your special hand-crafted dinner. The world is full of complex problems that only she can solve, but even Undersecretaries of Defense must eat.

We promise, nobody will ever forget this meal.

Hero of Fire Life

So I'm walking down Mack Avenue—not the good parts, but down by Grand Boulevard where the old nineteenth-century mansions are either crumbling or braced with twisted two-by-fours and busted breezeblock. The best-looking ones are the mental health group homes. Those places have to take care of their houses, or the State stomps in and shuts em right down. Other houses, folks just make do. There's a lot of busted-out windows with trash bags taped over them. But they swept up the glass, so it's all good.

It's the first fake spring day and the snow's still on the ground, steaming in the sunlight and keeping last fall's leaves frozen so they can't throw up the mold stink, so the air's still winter-fresh. It's warm enough I'm in a T-shirt so the sun can thaw my bones.

Got a warm coat over my shoulder, though. The weather was gonna turn on us real soon. Probably with a blizzard. The warmth lured me outdoors and set me walking, and I'm probably gonna freeze for it, but I couldn't resist.

I'm not the only one. Kids are playing basketball on the court behind the First Baptist, and some idiot's fired their smoker. Pork slow-cooking over seasoned applewood is one of those smells that tells you everything's gonna be just fine. Smoking takes *hours*, though. The chef will finish up tonight huddled in his winter coat tonging ribs while snowflakes spatter the smoker and burn straight to steam.

The idiot's got the right idea.

The neighborhood's starting to poke up little green leaves of life. The storefront COGIC has its doors open for an airing. Someone's even rented the old billboard for an ad for a Wesley Snipes action comeback. Man, that guy can do one hell of a drop-dead crazy glare. Someone walks out of the liquor store a couple blocks up and stretches his arms to catch air that for once is not trying to kill him.

It's that kind of day when you know winter's really gonna get lost and you'll be able to open the door and air the place out. Maybe not now, but some day not too far off.

I've walked so much my feet are starting to hurt. Last summer I'd gone a hell of a lot further, all the way down to Eastern Market, but winter keeps you close to home. Forget the ice, just the slush will do you in. Snow-march cardio ain't distance cardio. I got my boots on, cause the sidewalks are rivers of melt and lots of places the curb's overflowing cause the drains ain't been cleaned since Clinton. My feet are dry, but the instep isn't made for this kind of hike.

Younger me would have gone right on, but I'm just old enough to start to figure out that my feet are gonna blame me tomorrow. I ain't old. Not yet. But I'm at the top of that hill looking down and I can see how the arthritis is gonna get bad.

And the weather was gonna pull a knife any time.

Plus, there's that new history series on Netflix.

So I turn around, and the hero's right there. I damned near jumped out of my skin.

I mean, he had to be a hero, right? Wearing neon blue long underwear, and stupid tight bright-yellow Jockeys over them. And that's the first thing that told me something was wrong, cause those undies were so damn tight his timbits and tonker ought to be poking out—no, I don't go staring at people's junk, but those undies were bright yellow and he was taller'n me, right? I mean, his chest was right at eye level and if I wore undies like that I'd squeak so hard they'd call an ambulance. Made my eyes water.

I ain't never seen a chest so wide—but smooth, you know? The shirt looked tight, but I'm not sure what it was tight *over*. Too flat for muscle.

He got this chin you could plow asphalt with, and bright eyes. No, not like he's interested—they was literally lit up. From inside. Not bright like LEDs, just enough to show you something ain't right.

Anyway, he looks at me and says, "Greetings, Living Fire Person Citizen."

Maybe he's from one of them group homes. "Hey. Howya doing?" I stepped aside into the muddy grass let him pass. You always give crazy the right of way, if you like going home again.

His face was too pink. I thought it was maybe crazy meds that made him that way, that made his skin too smooth. A big chest like that, this time of day, man ought to have a five-o-clock shadow.

He says, "Could you direct me to the nearest bank robbery?"

Now, I've talked to a lot of the crazies. Met a guy once, thought he was Jesus. You shoulda seen the fight he had with the woman cross the street what thought she was Buddha. But I'd never seen no one what thought they were a comic book superhero. And not one of the angsty new ones, but a proper hero. Like I grew up with.

It'd explain the underwear.

"Where you from, mister?" I says.

"I come from the Doomed Planet Cryptic." He sounded like a proper hero, too, like one of those old scratched-up 50s serials they showed on TV when I was a kid. "I'm here to show the Fire Life the meaning of Truth and Justice."

I couldn't help smiling. If you got to be crazy, might as well be one of the good guys, am I right? "I don't know any bank robberies round here, sorry."

He frowned—no, that ain't right. He was smiling, then he was frowning, but his face didn't go from one to the other. It didn't bother to change, it just *was*. Like on a computer, you know? I thought I'd blinked, at first.

"Then perhaps a fire," he says.

A truck grumbled past, right through this pool of melt and throwing up trashy water. Children shouted cheerful smack talk and a basketball thomped wet but regular on soggy blacktop. There's all these folks grabbing all the spring they can steal, and this guy's beginning to worry me. "I don't hear any sirens. Listen, maybe you ought to head home?"

"We have studied the Fire Life People's records," the hero says. "Mastering your language and culture demanded over fifty of your Fire Life Years. I cannot return home from your bizarre and ridiculous world without achieving your respect. You must have a kitten up a tree."

The trees ain't even started to bloom. Winter gales took all the weak branches. "Do you see any kittens?"

"Kidnapping?"

"There you go!" I'm getting tired of the gag. "I'm sure someone's been kidnapped. I bet your caregiver could tell you exactly who."

"My support team is in high orbit. They know nothing of fire-life kidnappers."

I admit it. I kind of get a kick out of some of the crazies, you know? They think their bullshit through. "What is this 'fire life' you keep talking about?"

"Your whole planet!" the hero says. "Every life here. You propel your lives by burning your body in unadulterated oxygen. No other world is so insane as to design their biome such a manner. We needed much research to create probes that would withstand your atmosphere, and until the Fire Suit—" He claps his hand to his chest. "The pinnacle of our technology—none could visit."

It's the way his hand hit his chest that told me something was wrong.

The crazies give a convincing line. Sometimes, part of you kinda believes them.

But no matter how crazy you are, your chest don't clank when you hit it with your bare hand. I swear, it clanked. Not like armor, either. Not hollow. Like when you hit an engine block with an iron bar.

My guts kind of went liquid right then. Lucky I didn't ruin my pants.

I still thought he was a crazy. But a crazy strong enough to carry all that metal—no, it didn't make no sense. He had that smile, that Chin of Doom.

Crazies ain't that pretty.

Heck, movie stars ain't that pretty.

Whatever this guy was, from the Doomed Planet Whatever, he wasn't no normal crazy.

"I thought it best to start small," he says—no, he *proclaims*, like one of those preachers that rip off the poor folks. "Perhaps the Fire Life has solved these lesser problems. Take me to your Hitler."

I looked around for anyone who might help, but the kids are all hooting at their b-ball game and the old ladies chatting around the stoop'll just duck back inside if the trouble starts, and the cars ain't gonna stop nohow. I'm trying to buy some thinking time so I says, "Hitler?"

"Your records show that fighting through an army and punching a Hitler is the standard method of achieving recognition and honor among Fire Life." His chin somehow thrust out even more. "I shall be known among the whole of the pancosmos as the one who first dared to dare the Fire Life!"

Yeah, the way he clanked worried me, but my brain was starting to kick in. The smart part, what insisted he was a crazy, was getting drowned out by the sensible part that said maybe this guy was legit. I mean, he even looked like he was out of a comic book, one of the old ones Dad kept from when he was a kid, where they had big lines and only a few colors of ink. That face was a pink that I ain't seen on *nothing* living. A chest that big ought to have all kinds of muscles showing up through the shirt.

And the undies.

No way any man could wear undies *that* tight.

"Oh, right," I says. "Hitlers." I thought of naming some politicians, you know the ones, but figured that'd just go horrible wrong. "You know we defeated Hitler most of a century ago, right? We're okay. Don't need no heroes no more."

"Fire Life always needs heroes," he says. "Your records say so, over and over again. He almost destroys you, and is defeated. Take me to your Hitler."

"Look." I caught myself licking my lips. Not a good look, and besides, in this weather they'll just chap the hell up. "You said you took many years to translate those records. That ain't what we're like no more. Our heroes are quiet now. Doctors and philanthropizers. Stuff like that."

The way the hero's head turns on his neck isn't right. When a person looks around, their skin moves. His just didn't.

Then his head just… kept turning.

I'm looking at the back of his head. He doesn't have hair, it's like, all plastic.

My guts had gone all soft before, but now they're hard. I've got a brick in my guts and it's gonna need more than a prune to get rid of.

"Aha!" The hero shouts so loud I jump. The steady thomp-thomp-thomp of the b-ball goes all *thompthompthud* and stops, and them kids raise their own shouts.

The hero turns his head back to me, which eases my innards a little but not near enough, and raises his hand. "If you have defeated your Hitlers," he says, "then who does this Fire Life fight?"

He's pointing at the movie billboard, where Wesley Snipes glares all mean and ready to pound someone's face. There's even fire behind him.

I can't help but take half a step back. The hero's frown is bigger now, and his eyebrows have turned way too far down into a scowl. People can't scowl that far, and I should know. My Aunt Rosa was a champion scowler.

"There are Hitlers," he says. "They always come back. Who are you? Are you one of those that saved Hitler's brain?"

I raise my hands up, but keep 'em open. You don't show a fist down here, not less you plan to use it. "It's a story! We tell that story to everyone, over and over again. It's so if a Hitler shows, we know to fight him. That's how you beat them, you stomp them early."

"A story?" He sounds right pissed now. "You lie about your Hitlers?"

I make myself swallow. "It's teaching for the young. For new, new Fire Life. We burn up, right?" Someone's walking up the street behind the hero, but they're still like a block and a half away and I don't know how I could explain this quick enough so they'd help. I mean this hero, whatever he is, showed up ready to punch an army so he could deck Hitler. "We burn ourselves to death, and the new Fire Life need to know of the danger for when Hitlers come again."

The hero eyes me like one of those young men lounging round street corners at three in the morning. "You are among the wholesome citizenry of the Fire Life people."

I nod, quick as I can.

His chest inflates a good six inches, and he gives this sigh that blows my hair back hard. "Then you speak the truth. There is no enemy for me to fight to gain your respect."

I nod. "That's right. We don't need heroes anymore. We done saved ourselves. It's all the Internet and philanthophizers now."

The hero's head does one slow turn, full around. My eyes want to squeeze back into my head just watching.

"Then I cannot do this as I hoped," the hero says.

Between one breath and the next, he's just… gone.

I kind of sag right there. My heart's threatening to run off, and suddenly I'm right cold. The fake spring hasn't gone away, but my shirt's soaked through with sweat and if'n I don't get my coat on I'm gonna catch a chill. I can't miss work no more.

And I'm right tired. Time enough to chew all this over once I'm home.

Or, maybe, someone'll notice that I've lost what brains I had and move me down to one of those group homes permanent-like. That's the kind of things us wacked-out oxygen breathers do, I guess.

I'm barely a hundred feet down the street, just across from the open doors of the COGIC, when a great big voice bellows behind me. "ATTENTION!"

There's a huge black-and-jewel metal spider in the middle of Mack Avenue. Its body fills the turn lane, and all them legs block all the traffic going either way. Trucks skid and the cars are a big tangle of metal straight away, but the spider doesn't even wobble.

I clap my hands over my ears and try to stuff that sickening dread back down.

"Attention!" the spider trumpets. "I am the Mightiest Hitler. Your lives are mine. Your world is mine."

Then—swear to God—it starts growing.

Sore feet or no, tired or no, I start running.

Something gave a big *thomp* behind me, and I feel all this heat at my back.

Something done blew up.

I spare a thought for the kids playing basketball. Hope they're smart enough to run. Then I tuck my elbows into my sides and pound down melt-covered sidewalks.

If I can run far enough, I'll be fine.

See, right when we've lost everything, a hero's coming to save us.

Afterword

Apocalypse gets a bad rap.

An apocalypse is a revelation that destroys your life. Not *ends* your life. Destroys it. Realizing that you're an alcoholic and you can either change or die? Apocalypse. Discovering that the children you devoted your life to don't need you any longer? Apocalypse. The epiphany that you love someone and you'll do anything to fulfill their dream? Total apocalypse.

These days, we use apocalypse as a synonym for doomsday. Saint John the Insane's *Revelations* have a lot to do with that, mostly because people didn't pay enough attention to the "Insane" part of his name, but here we are. Doomsdays sound like fun, at least in fiction, but when I was eleven years old I learned just how limited they are. The local theater showed a double feature of *Laserblast* and *End Of The World*. *Laserblast* became a cult classic of awfulness, but not even the unimpeachable Christopher Lee could make *End Of The World* good enough to be bad. Between them, though, they taught me an essential lesson about doomsday.

Blow up the whole world, and nobody cares.

Blow up one person's world? Pass the popcorn!

A proper apocalypse ends your world, but replaces it with a better one.

This book contains revelations. Some of them destroy the world. In one, the world has already been destroyed and everyone's dead, which presents problems for the things that remember being people. But throughout, life-changing revelation. Apocalypse is not discovering there's a slice of pie left in the fridge. It's discovering that someone loves you enough to leave you that slice. The mildest apocalypse is love, leaping out from behind the curtain and shouting *Hey Boo!* Apocalypse-as-revelation offers wisdom, improves our lives, and suggests paths to a better life and world.

We hunger for that.

Some folks are so desperate for revelation that they declare their bigotries and phobias to be sacred truths that must be shared. Every one of those ideas is built on loathing and selfishness. None of them improve lives. It's best to mourn for infected people, but not so far as to let them have their way.

If you've read my collection *Devotion and Corrosion* you're probably tired of hearing this, but: the difference between revelation and immolation is love. Proper apocalypse is love wearing Groucho Marks mustache-glasses, showing up to spill your fast-food lunch and make sure a damn vegetable makes it into your belly once in a while.

Like in these tales.

Drums with Delusions of Godhood

Blaze Ward asked me for a story about the end of the world for *Boundary Shock Quarterly*. I promptly asked myself *what is the stupidest possible way for the world to end?* Obviously, earworms. Frances makes the hard choices to save her community and her people. There's a doomsday and a revelation, and Frances resists both.

Readers have asked when I'm going to use this as the middle of a novel. I'm not. This is a front row seat of the end. Perhaps a handful of survivors will find each other and humanity will endure, like in Simak's *A Heritage of Stars.*

Or, maybe not.

Live Wired is the definitive Angry Industrial Rock album, by the way.

Waking Up Yesterday

Your brain can't touch a memory without changing it. Yes, edge cases exist for certain people and certain kinds of memories, but for most of us to remember is to change our history. There's no way to consider the facts of your childhood unless you could somehow view them again. I guarantee that if you could view thirty years ago with your current eyes, you would have a revelation.

Just like this poor nameless bastard.

There's apocalypse here, sure. Revelation and doom. It's who he loves that's important.

Forced to Talk, Like, With Your Mouth

One of those predatory ideas is that coddling is bad, and that our civilization coddles us. Anyone who believes that is welcome to sleep in a tree while roaming great cats try to steal your meager supper of uncooked carrion. We built civilization *to* coddle us. The fastest way to appreciate that is when civilization fails: maybe a power outage, maybe murder. Every failure of civilization is revelation.

This nameless detective learns that if civilization is to exist, it'll be because of him. We all know people who need that revelation.

This story was written as an initial study for *$ git commit murder.* I had the revelation that I *could* write about my tech career, but not if I had to spend any more time with this character.

Moonlight's Apples

"There's a beautiful secret world next to ours" is beguiling. We love that story. We want it to be true. But if that world existed and was safe to touch, we'd all know about it.

Dervish gets the revelation. He winds up being someone else's doomsday.

I'm going to offer you a time-limited revelation, though. For the last quarter century the Buccaneer, in Port Stanley Ontario, has served the world's most magnificent perch and chips. Visit the Shaw's ice cream factory on your way out of town and try the Tiger Stripe. Don't ask what's in it, just try it.

Easing Final Fears

Everyone who grew up in the 70s knew that the lucky people would die in the nuclear war. The big city newspaper near my home published a map of where the bombs were expected to hit, surrounded by blast circles arranged like the layers of Dante's Inferno. Anything within the first circle would be instantly destroyed, the next circle would be reduced to rubble, and so on.

The little farm town I grew up in was right on the line between "die of horrid burns" and "you might live," yet silly adults wondered why I wouldn't bother doing my homework. In my defense, if they had offered courses like "Scrounging for Cans in the Rubble" and "Farming Mutant Corn" I would have been all-in.

This tale comes straight out of that.

Wifi and Romex

Toby has the best and worst kind of apocalypse. He sees part of the world he never has before. It destroys his ability to live as he had. I don't know what happens to Toby after this, but I sure wouldn't threaten him.

Yesterday's Girl

Wisdom is knowing yourself. Look in the mirror. Listen to a recording of yourself giving a speech, and cringe. But even more effective than that would be meeting yourself.

I made Reuben something of a jerk—but now, writing this afterword? I wonder how many of us could have withstood this meeting as well as he did, and what changes we would make afterwards.

Shoot Through the Heart

This is a side tale from *Immortal Clay*, also written for a Blaze Ward anthology. One of the things that I enjoy about writing those books is that the doomsday came first, then the revelations. The revelations here are tiny and very personal, but they're the sort we all need.

Forbidden Taste

I wrote this *Prohibition Orcs* tale for this collection, which means it's the only story I wrote deliberately thinking of apocalypse. It's a full-on apocalypse sandwich cookie: a revelation kicks everything off, we get our doom, and the end is another revelation.

Orcs are pretty much doomed anyway. Just ask them.

Calling Control

Some apocalyptic revelations are known ahead of time. A person living with alcoholism or abuse or any exploitative relationship knows they don't have to live like that, but they haven't internalized it. Then one day something happens and they have the apocalypse: *I don't have to live like this*.

One day, this might become a novel.

Easy, Step-by-Step Preparation

With any luck, you're the one who had the revelation. Doomsday is implied.

Hero of Fire Life

When I'm lucky, I giggle while writing something. This is one of those tales. The unnamed hero gets a creeping-crawling revelation, and there's enough doom to go around. Pollution and climate change might threaten us now, but somehow I suspect that our true fate will arrive dressed as a clown bearing an infinite supply of cream pies. Of *dooom*.

And seriously: who the hell designed this biome? Meat suits that run on oxygen? How the heck are we supposed to transcend our limitations while running on goofy hardware that makes planned obsolescence look good?

Wow. Writing these has given me a revelation of my own! "Naming characters is hard, so I don't do it." You learn something every day. Also: I am officially forbidden to name any character Dale ever again.

May you all receive the apocalypse you need.

If you enjoyed this book, please consider leaving a review or rating at your favorite online bookstore or book review site.

Thank you.

About the Author

https://mwl.io

Never miss another new release!
Sign up for MWL's mailing list at
https://mwl.io

Novels and Collections (as Michael Warren Lucas):
Immortal Clay
Kipuka Blues
Butterfly Stomp Waltz
Terrapin Sky Tango
Forever Falls
Hydrogen Sleets
Drinking Heavy Water
$ git commit murder
$ git sync murder
Prohibition Orcs
Frozen Talons
Vicious Redemption
Devotion and Corrosion
Apocalypse Moi

Nonfiction (as Michael W Lucas):
Cash Flow for Creators – Relayd and Httpd Mastery – PAM Mastery
FreeBSD Mastery: Advanced ZFS – FreeBSD Mastery: Specialty Filesystems-
FreeBSD Mastery: ZFS – Tarsnap Mastery – Sudo Mastery – DNSSEC Mastery
Networking for Systems Administrators – FreeBSD Mastery: Storage Essentials
Absolute OpenBSD – SSH Mastery – Network Flow Analysis – Absolute FreeBSD
Cisco Routers for the Desperate – PGP & GPG –FreeBSD Mastery: Jails
Ed Mastery – SNMP Mastery – TLS Mastery – Domesticate Your Badgers
OpenBSD Mastery: Filesystems – Run Your Own Mail Server – Letters to ed(1)
The Networknomicon
Only Footnotes
See your favorite bookstore for more!

www.ingramcontent.com/pod-product-compliance
Lightning Source LLC
Chambersburg PA
CBHW030430120726
47903CB00003B/898